RETURN TO MARIPOSA

ANNE STUART

IMPECCABLY DEMURE PRESS

ACKNOWLEDGMENTS

Jenny Crusie, Lynda Ward, and Pam McCutcheon were invaluable with this book, and they have my slavish devotion.

CHAPTER
ONE

There were boxes everywhere. I hadn't realized I owned so much—my peripatetic existence had hardly been conducive to gathering stuff, but apparently stuff I had in abundance. I couldn't fault the boxes and boxes of books—I was both an academic and a dreamer, and books had always been my lifeline.

I couldn't object to the carton of ancient vinyl LPs, remnants from my mother's own gypsy past and treasures on their own.

But where had all the other shit come from? How had I managed to acquire four wine openers but no wire whisk? It could have said a lot for my priorities, except that I seldom could afford wines with corks. There were clothes I never would wear, shoes that didn't fit, a lifetime of other people's hand-me-downs that were too good to throw out but never felt quite right on me.

And all these things had to find someplace to go to, and no money to get them there.

It was hardly my fault that my deadbeat landlord had defaulted on his mortgage, thereby depriving me of the nice second-floor apartment in the old Victorian house on the edge of Hanover, New Hampshire.

And when you're a graduate student working on clinical trials, it's to be expected that funding occasionally runs out. The problem was I didn't know whether the cruel gods of college loans would countenance any more delays, given that I'd been in school for the last eleven years. Not that I didn't have the degrees to show for it. A BA in English Lit, surely the most useless degree in the history of higher education. Topping that off with a master's in modern Spanish literature, and I'd ensured that I was virtually unemployable. My attempts to remedy that dire situation had resulted in being three quarters of the way toward a PhD in plant eugenics, with an emphasis on olive trees. Why I thought the icy northern climes of New England would be conducive to the study of olives still remained a mystery to me.

I knew why I'd chosen it, of course. A long-distance nod to the happiest time in my life, living in the warm, familial confines of Mariposa, the world-famous olive groves and vineyards owned by the patrician Whitehead family in the south of Spain. My family, once upon a time.

As for my worthless boyfriend, I was well rid of him. The truth was, I had lousy taste in men. I didn't know what I was looking for and so far I hadn't even come close. It was definitely time for another dry spell. I never held with the idea that a lousy boyfriend was better than no boyfriend at all, and I could happily consign Nick, and Simon, and Tony, and Snake (that'll tell you how bad my choices tended to be) to the graveyard of failed relationships.

I had two more days in my denuded apartment, two days to either find a new place, pronto, or the cheapest fleabag motel in the Hanover area, leaving my aging Subaru Forrester filled with as many boxes as I could manage. Or I'd be sleeping with those boxes, and even in the so-called spring, New Hampshire was miserably cold.

I was so busy feeling sorry for myself that I didn't even hear the car drive up our quiet street, the slam of the door, the steps on my stairs. Only the peremptory knock startled me enough to move me from my glum perch on the old sofa with the broken springs.

The knock came again, even more demanding, and I was so not in the mood. "Hold your horses," I snapped, heading to the door. Whoever it was, I knew I didn't want to see him or her. Given my recent run of luck, it was probably trouble.

Trouble that wasn't going to go away on its own. I slammed open the door, about to snarl some off-color demand, when I stopped, struck dumb for one of the first times in my life.

"About time, darling!" My exquisitely beautiful cousin Isabella stood there, and the drizzly gray afternoon suddenly seemed shot with sunlight.

"Izzy!" I screeched, throwing my arms around her. Together we hugged and squealed, jumping up and down as if we were twelve-year-olds spending the summer together after a long winter apart. It had been so damned long.

But then she released me, stepping back and shoving a careless hand through her magnificent mane of golden, pre-Raphaelite curls. "It's Bella now, darling," she said with a throaty laugh, looking me up and down. "God, you haven't changed!"

That wasn't high praise, but I took it in the spirit intended.

"Neither have you," I said. A lie. If anything, my magnificent cousin Isabella was even more of everything. More beautiful, more charming, taller, thinner. Everything about her seemed touched with gold.

All our lives I've been a pale shadow of my enchanting cousin. We'd been born a year and a world apart, but we'd always been thrown together during those long, idyllic summers at Mariposa. Her hair was always blonder, curlier, longer than mine, her eyes a bright green compared to my changeable hazel ones, her porcelain skin an affront to my adolescent breakouts. To make things worse, our features were almost identical.

She was funny and charming, where I suffered from mortifying shyness. And she had cousin Marcus, the most beautiful man I had ever seen in my life, at her delicate feet which were, of course, a full size smaller than mine.

Somehow I ended up inside the apartment, the door closed behind us. Izzy...no, Bella...eyed the tower of boxes cramming the living room. "Going somewhere, Podge?"

I hated that name. It was bad enough that my mother, while giving me the perfectly respectable name of Kathryn, had insisted on calling me "Kitty" after her favorite old black-and-white movie, and the nickname was even worse when you counted the snarky teenage boys who decided to translate it into "pussy," thereby mortifying me for all time. At least it wasn't the cruel, hated nickname from my teenage years.

"Lease ran out," I said briefly, fighting back my instinctive protest.

"Poor baby! I don't suppose you have something to drink in this thoroughly tragic hovel?"

Considering this thoroughly tragic hovel was the nicest place I had lived in in the last ten years, I thought about being offended, then dismissed it. Isabella had more money than God, along with all the Whitehead family—privilege ran in their blood. That is, all the Whiteheads who were still considered part of the dynasty and hadn't been cut off.

"There's a box of wine in the fridge," I said.

"A box?" Isabella said in acute horror. "Darling, what have you come to?"

I managed a cheery smile. "You know I've always been a peasant at heart, Iz...Bella. It might be a little vinegary by now, but it's all I've got. Take it or leave it."

Her beautiful nose wrinkled in distaste. The same nose I saw in the mirror, but for some reason, I never thought of my own as beautiful. "It'll have to do. Do you still have glasses or will I be forced to drink out of the box?"

I laughed. "I can find you a glass. But you'll have to tell me why you suddenly showed up on my doorstep after all these years."

"Not that many years," Bella protested, an enchanting pout on her mouth. Her new name suited her.

4

"Seven since I last saw you. Twelve since we spent any time together," I pointed out with my usual accuracy.

"And whose fault is that? You were the one to walk out on Granda."

"I was sixteen—I didn't have a choice," I said flatly, ignoring the stab of pain her words brought me. No, it hadn't been my choice to leave with my unstable mother. Someone had to take care of her, and I was the only one left.

Granda hadn't seen it that way. I imagine if there'd been such a thing as a family Bible, my name would have been struck from it. As it was, my letters were returned unopened, my phone calls refused, and according to Isabella, my name was never allowed to be mentioned. It wasn't as if I were dead—it was as if I'd never been born.

I'd made peace with it, though it had taken a while. When I was sixteen, I'd had no choice; by the time I was twenty, my sense of responsibility for my erratic mother had taken over, as well as my anger at my autocratic, cold-hearted grandfather. Screw them all, I was just fine on my own.

Until Isabella showed up and reminded me of all I lost. "Let's not argue," she said, pouring herself a generous glass of the merlot, then gave me a significant look until I followed suit. She held the glass up. "To family," she said, tossing back her gorgeous mane of curls.

"To cousins," I amended firmly, and clinked glasses with her.

She grinned, her eyes lighting, and drank deeply. "Bloody Christ!" she said with a shudder. "This stuff is completely ghastly!"

"'Bloody Christ!" I mocked her faintly British tones perfectly. "Completely ghastly or not, it will have to do."

Bella giggled. "You always could mimic my voice perfectly," she said, her own voice a perfect match to my now flattened vowels. "Remember that time when we were fourteen and switched places for a week? We could have carried it off for the entire summer—they had no idea."

I smiled at the memory. Even a taste of being the glamorous Bella had been a treat. "They never did find out, did they? Or did you tell them?"

"Never!" She drained her glass, shuddered, and poured herself another, still maintaining her approximation of my Americanized voice. "We tricked them all."

"Everyone but that wretched little snake Ian," I said, continuing the game. "I swear he suspected something." My hair was in a knot at the back of my head, and I released it, tossing it with a perfect approximation of Bella's signature gesture. I didn't have her curls, or her coloring, but at least it was long. "But then, he always was a devious little wretch."

Bella giggled. "I never could figure out how Marcus could have a brother who was so different from him."

"I'd wonder if Auntie Florence had cheated on her first husband, but that woman was born a saint. You could practically see the arrows of martyrdom piercing her breast." That had been Isabella's line—she'd always had the gift for summing up other people in faintly cruel, concise terms.

Isabella pealed with laughter. "So true!" she said with a sigh. "Tell me, you got anything to eat in this dump?"

"I suppose we can call out for pizza, darling," I drawled.

She frowned. "You'll need to be careful with the 'darlings.' Don't overdo it."

I looked at her in surprise. "Huh?" I said brilliantly, my accent slipping.

She grinned at me. "I'll make a bet with you. I bet I can keep up with your voice longer than you can keep up with mine."

"Don't be ridiculous. I don't want to gamble with you."

I had been speaking in my normal tones, but she shook her head reprovingly. "I don't wish to gamble with you," she corrected in her perfect, throaty drawl. "You need to lower your voice a little."

"And you need to get your head out of your ass. Darling," I added for good measure, back in her voice again. In truth, it came naturally, except for the slightly extravagant way she spoke. We'd come from the same background, spent those long, endless summers together. It was almost second nature.

"So. Food?"

"I can always ring up for pizza."

She tossed me her phone. Latest model iPhone, with all the bells and whistles, complete with a Prada case. "Use mine," she said.

I shrugged, managing to remember the number that was programmed into my humbler phone, and placed the order. To my astonishment, the voice at the other end of Ray and Lucy's Pizza didn't ask for a credit card number, simply said, "Where to, Miss Whitehead?"

I gave them my address, too startled to correct them, and broke the connection. "How did they know whose phone it was?"

"Apps, darling. It's all about apps. Where's your phone?"

Reluctantly, I pulled it from my back pocket and handed it to her. She pushed buttons, then cast an incredulous look up at me. "It doesn't even get internet!"

"It's just for the basics." Belatedly, I remembered our silly game. "Who needs all that stuff on a telephone, for Christ's sake?" I added with a drawl.

Bella grinned at me. "Good answer." She tucked my elderly phone into her own pocket, ignoring my protest, and gestured toward the iPhone. "Keep it. I'm always losing them anyway. I'll just use yours for a while and see if I can survive on something less."

She didn't mean the slight sting. You learned to survive on whatever you had. Lucky Isabella, the one the gods had smiled on, wouldn't even know what deprivation felt like.

"Are you ever going to tell me..." I began, but Bella shushed me, refilling my glass.

"Let's wait till the pizza arrives and I'll tell you everything," she said. "I don't suppose they deliver wine around here?"

"In this benighted country?" I added in her voice. "Only by the caseload."

"Tempting," she said. "Right now, I feel I could put away an entire case, but I suppose it would have to be moved along with everything else."

Her unexpected concern was new too—she usually didn't bother with how her high-flown actions affected everyone else. "You're right. If I was leaving this place to the landlord, he'd probably be thrilled, but the bank is taking it over and I don't think they'd be similarly appreciative."

Bella grinned at me. "Probably not. Though I've known bankers who drink like fish."

"Total sots," I said in her voice. "But then, the bankers you've known are all Spanish. They're used to their wine or sherry followed by a siesta."

She laughed. "You're way out of touch. Siesta has pretty much gone the way of the dinosaur in the cities of Spain. And I haven't been in Spain in more than five years."

This managed to shock me more deeply than anything else about her unexpected appearance. "But why? You love Mariposa. You love Marcus."

"That's old news, sweetie. Marcus and I broke off our engagement ages ago. He's happy staying at Mariposa and charming everyone into buying our olives while I've been following my heart all over the world." She rummaged in the huge designer bag beside her, then tossed her red passport to me. "Take a look."

It was surprisingly thick, and then I realized that official pages had been added to document all her travel. Africa, South America, Australia, the Pacific Rim. She'd come into Boston a number of times over the years, I noticed blankly, and made no effort to get in touch with me. But that was Bella. She always had a clear agenda and anyone who didn't fit in with it was easily discarded. But when she was there she was so sunny and charming that her innate selfishness was easy to forgive. You didn't blame a butterfly for being fragile.

I flipped back, hoping against hope that like everyone else she'd have a lousy passport photo. And then I froze.

The passport photo was lousy indeed. It was a photo of me.

There was no missing the difference. My hair had been photo-shopped into blond, pre-Raphaelite curls, my eyes were now green instead of hazel, but I knew that photograph.

I looked up at Bella, who was watching me without a trace of nervousness, but charm could only get her so far. I cleared my throat, dropping her drawl. "Exactly what the fuck is going on?"

She was saved from having to answer by the sudden sound of the doorbell. "I'll get it," she said, uncurling her long legs before I could protest. I stayed where I was, looking down at the passport in disbelief. From a distance, I could hear her voice, *my* voice, flirting with Al, who ran the deliveries.

"Hey, you clean up nice, Ms. Whitehead."

"Call me Kitty," she replied in my voice, not bothering to correct him. "It's all on my cousin's tab, isn't it?"

"Sure is, tip included," he said with a cheerfulness he hadn't shown in more than a dozen desperate pizza calls over the last year. "You take care, all right? Don't forget us when you find your new place."

"Wouldn't think of it," my voice floated back from the hall, further increasing my sense of unreality. She returned to the living room, setting the box down between us, and dropped into a reasonable approximation of a lotus position with no trouble whatsoever. I looked at her in astonishment.

"I've got a few paper plates..." I offered hesitantly as she exposed the rich, gooey mess. Ray and Lucy's made real New York pizza, to die for.

"Do you use plates when you order pizza?" I shook my head. "Then neither will I," Bella said firmly, helping herself to a slice heaped with olives and prosciutto and peppers.

I had spent the day working hard, packing, and I should have been famished, but a cold knot had formed in the bottom of my stomach, and I wasn't going to touch the stuff unless I could get some answers from Bella.

I poured another half glass of wine. I couldn't begin to keep up with Bella's input, but I was still drinking more than I was used to. The box of wine was, in fact, from a Spanish vineyard, and it had been quite decent when it was first opened. Even now, it didn't taste the slightest bit vinegary. I would have hoped she hadn't noticed what wine I had, but Bella had an impeccable palate. Even if she hadn't read the box, she would have known it was a Spanish vintage.

"So, 'splain this to me, Lucy,'" I said in a fair approximation of Ricky Ricardo's accent. "What's going on? And what does it have to do with me?"

"You better settle back, kiddo," she said, still not deviating from my voice. "It's a long story."

"Can't you condense it a bit? It's been a long day."

"It's a Spanish story," she said. "These things take time to unfold. Didn't you read Spanish literature for your degree? The Spanish can't be rushed. Neither can the ex-pats, who like to think they're more Spanish than the Spaniards."

"And where do you see yourself?" I asked, unconsciously slipping back into her tones.

"As someone up to her neck in a shit storm, and if you don't help me, I might just get buried, literally, which doesn't seem like a pleasant way to go."

My tight muscles were beginning to loosen, just as Bella's tongue was. I reached out for the smallest slice of pizza, brushed off some of the inferior green and black olives, and took a bite. As good as ever. "You might as well get started, my precious," I drawled in her voice, hoping to bring a smile to her pensive face. "For starters, why haven't you been back to Mariposa for five years?"

She took a deep breath, then another swallow of the wine. "A number of reasons. Breaking it off with Marcus didn't please anyone, not Granda who foresaw a dynasty, not Marcus, not our so-delightful cousins, even stick-in-the-mud Ian was pissed at me. Needless to say, decamping with a big chunk of my trust fund didn't further endear me to anyone. In fact, I was planning to keep away for as long as I could, but fate decided to take a hand."

"What hand is that?"

"Granda's, of course. He's dying," Bella said flatly.

"So what else is new?" I was unimpressed. Granda was always dying.

"No, this time it's for real. So real that the forces are gathering. Ian's been off at a seminar in South Africa, Marcus has been schmoozing with clients in the Pacific Rim, and God knows what the cousins are doing, but they've been called home. As have I."

As I have not, I thought ignoring the familiar pain. "So?"

"Kitty, I can't. I simply can't. I've got something to take care of—I don't want to involve you, but you need to take my word for it. It's a matter of life and death. It's not that I need Granda's inheritance; you know I have plenty of money of my own. I just don't want to break the old man's heart."

"Are you sure he has a heart?"

Bella cast me a worried look. "Of course he has a heart. He did what he thought he had to do. You know Granda, he's always been too full of pride. He couldn't admit that he missed you or that he'd made a mistake. Even now, he's afraid to reach out to you. But you should be there. You need to be able to say goodbye. He needs to know his family loves him despite all the bad things he did."

"How many bad things did he do?"

"More than his fair share, I expect. But he's afraid he's going to go to hell."

I laughed heartlessly. "I expect he will, given his hard-core beliefs. As an Anglican, he's more Catholic than the Catholic."

"You're right, of course. You always saw him better than the rest of us. If he could buy his way into heaven he would, but despite all the money he's pumped into the churches of Andalusia, he knows it's not enough. He needs to see me before he dies, and he needs to see you."

"And how is he going to do that when I'm not welcome at Mariposa?" I fought down my grief and longing. It was my world, he was my family, and I'd been banished. I could never go home again.

"Simple," Bella said easily. "You go in my place. He gets the benefit of making his peace with me and saying goodbye, plus, without knowing it, he'll be making his peace with you."

I stared at her. "You must be out of your mind," I said.

"You know you want to go back to Mariposa, at least one more time, and don't deny it. And you'll make an old man who once loved you very happy."

"But what if I'm still holding a grudge?"

"Oh come on, Podge," she said. "You're not the type to hold a grudge. You are the best of all of us, genuinely nice and loving. He needs your forgiveness, whether he can ask for it or not."

"You're insane. I'm not going anywhere," I said flatly, believing it.

"I haven't told you everything,," she said, and for the first time I noticed the faint lines of anxiety in her face, the whiteness around her mouth, the tight muscles on her forehead. Isabella Whitehead was afraid of something, and that fear was more important than her beloved grandfather's deathbed. I hardened my heart.

"You have to go, Bella," I said sensibly. "He always adored you. When I would go to visit, he would talk on and on about his glorious grandchild and how brilliant she was at everything. You are his favorite—you can't abandon him when he's dying and needs you most."

"I don't have any choice in the matter. This business I have to take care of—it won't wait. And no, I can't explain it to you. Suffice it to say I got in with the wrong sort of people and I'm paying the price for it. I've been stupid, Kitty, really, really dumb, and I need to get myself out of a big mess or…" She let the words trail off.

"Too melodramatic by half, cousin," I said in her voice. Except that I suspected she was telling me nothing more than the truth.

And she knew me well enough to know I was being drawn in. She pounced.

"Listen, it would be three days at the most. You fly into Malaga, take a smaller plane to Santa Maria de Fe and then drive to Mariposa to spend the day with Granda. He won't be able to tell the difference once we get your hair fixed. We actually look very much alike—you'd be quite pretty if you bothered to fix yourself up. And remember, he hasn't seen me for five years, and he's nearly blind and deaf. You can say goodbye to him, bid a proper farewell to Mariposa. You were never able to, when your crazy-ass mother dragged you away that summer. This will give you some closure."

Bella knew just what to say, of course. She'd always understood what people really wanted, deep down. "Ian and Marcus aren't half blind and deaf," I said. "You were going to marry Marcus—you slept with him. He'd know the difference."

"We're talking about Marcus, darling. He's not much into questioning the status quo. But he won't even be there, and neither will that snake in the grass Ian. Marcus isn't coming in till next week, and Ian two days later, and who knows if the girls will make it at all. You'll have plenty of time to get in and out before they show up. Not that you couldn't fool them too—you've got my voice and mannerisms down pat, and remember, they haven't seen me in years. But it won't even come up. You fly in, spend a day at Mariposa, and then head back to Malaga. After that, you can go anywhere you want—the flight back is open-ended, and of course I'll give you my charge card and one for the street tills..."

"Street tills?"

"ATMs," she corrected. "You'll need cash. You get a brand new wardrobe—I've been shopping for days. You get a European vacation, cost free, a reunion with your grandfather, no strings, no hassles. You don't even have to spend the night at Mariposa. Just an afternoon with a dying man, and you're free. How can you even consider saying no?"

"Because it's ridiculous," I said, ignoring the surge of longing in my heart. "Not to mention a felony, travelling on a fake passport. This isn't like when we were children and played games on the rest of them, and it sure the hell isn't some stupid Lindsey Lohan movie."

"Lindsey Lohan?" Bella's beautiful brow wrinkled. "What's she got to do with anything?"

"Hayley Mills," I corrected. She still looked blank, and I realized that while I'd been holed up in New Hampshire, devouring old movies, she'd been out in the real world, living. "An old movie called *The Parent Trap*, where two twin sisters take each other's place."

"But why...? Never mind. This will work. Your life is a mess, Podge. You have no home, no job, you're completely at loose ends. And did I happen to mention I'll pay you ten thousand dollars if you do this?"

I'd felt the first tingles of temptation, but her words made me feel sick inside. She was trying to bribe me, pay me, like I was one of the outsiders....

Which I was, I reminded myself, ready to kick her out of my house in affronted pride. And then I saw the fear, real fear in her bright green eyes.

She read my reaction, of course. Bella was always good at that. "I'm sorry, Podge. I know that you'd do it for free, not because I bribed you. But I've got the money, and surely you could find a use for it. I bet you have hellacious college loans," she added with a grin.

Ten thousand dollars wouldn't even put a dent in them. It would, however, tide me over until I found a decent place and a new job. But there were some things I simply couldn't do.

"Tell me about this trouble you're in," I said. "Are you really in danger? Shouldn't you go to the police?"

"The police can't help me. It's complicated, and the less you know, the better off you'll be. Suffice it to say I owe someone something, and I need time to get it to him. Which I can do; I just need to concentrate on that, not on wasting my time with deathbed visits."

I blinked. "Don't you want to say goodbye to Granda? He adores you."

She shrugged. "I don't like death. I'd rather remember him as I last saw him. You'll say goodbye for me and do it far better than I would. Won't you, Podge?"

"No."

A dark look crossed her face for a brief moment, then vanished.

Bella wasn't used to being denied anything, but there was no way I was going through with such a hare-brained idea. These sorts of things might happen in movies, but in real life, it would be impossible.

Bella straightened her back, fixing her steely gaze on me. "Look, Kitty, you're not in a position to say no. You have no apartment, no job, no prospects, and you've been dreaming about Mariposa ever since you left it."

"I have not!" I denied it, but it was a lie.

"I'm offering you a way out of your troubles, time to figure out what you want to do next, and in the meantime you can make your peace with Granda."

"Not if he thinks I'm you. And what makes you think I have troubles?"

"You're sitting in an empty apartment full of boxes and you told me your funding ran out. I call that trouble. And Granda won't think anything. I told you, he's really dying this time—he probably won't recognize anyone anymore. I only need a few days, Kitty. Just to get some people off my back. I've never asked you for anything before, I've always been your biggest supporter with Granda, trying to get him to invite you back, but he's a stubborn old bastard. You owe me this much."

I stared at her. I'd had too much wine, and too many days of uncertainty over the basic necessities of life.

And Lord, how I missed Mariposa, and Granda. I couldn't bear the thought of him leaving without giving me a chance to see him once more.

If I went, was there any chance in the world I could pull it off? Marcus and Ian wouldn't be there—they'd be the most likely ones to see through me. And the cousins, Mary Alice and Valerie, wouldn't know me either, and besides, they weren't anywhere around. It would just be me and Granda, for one short day, and then I'd be free, ready to take on the new chapter to my life in New Hampshire.

I tried one more protest. "I can't do something so crazy..."

"You can. Stop being such a wuss, Podge. I'm offering you every-thing you've ever wanted, and all you have to do is say goodbye to Granda for me. You can't say no."

She had me, and she knew it. As insane as the idea was, I knew I was caving. I was taking her clothes and her passport and going back to Mariposa, one last time, to say goodbye to everything, including the grandfather who'd banished me. I would forgive him, and maybe I could finally let go of the thrall that Mariposa had always held.

"You're absolutely certain no one else will be there?"

She kept the look of triumph from her face, but it was easy to see the relief in her eyes. "Positive. Even if they are, it's been so long since I've seen them, they wouldn't know the difference, but they're way off in the back-end of beyond, and you know the girl cousins. They don't like to bother with us. You'll be in and out before anyone even realizes it." She leaned back against the wall. "I've already made an appointment with a stylist to fix our hair..."

"Our hair?"

"Well, I'm going to have to pass myself off as you, aren't I? I'm worried about your eyes, though. Mine are green. I don't remember yours looking quite so brown," she said doubtfully. "I don't suppose you can wear contacts?"

"I'm wearing them. They're tinted, making my hazel eyes more interesting."

"Excellent!" she crowed. "Clearly, this was meant to be. We can just get new lenses to make your eyes green, and no one will be able to tell the difference."

I looked at her doubtfully. I'd drunk too much wine, and the sight of my denuded apartment was as depressing as the gorgeously dressed butterfly across from me. Tomorrow I'd be wiser, tomorrow I'd see another way out of my current, homeless, impoverished mess.

But tonight the answer seemed clear.

"Yes," I said. "I'll go." And I poured myself another glass of wine.

CHAPTER
TWO

Settling into my first-class space pod on Iberian Airlines, I had plenty of time to wonder what the hell I was doing. Bella had kept me on a dead run, from hairdresser to spa to eye doctor for colored contact lenses. I went through her matched Prada luggage and tried on her brand-new wardrobe. She favored Spanish designers, names I didn't know, but I recognized the quality of the clothes and felt them seduce me.

They fit perfectly, which troubled me. Bella and I had similar bodies, though her boobs were smaller and my hips fuller. Clearly she'd been as aware of our differences as I was, for she had to have had the clothes adjusted for those changes. The thought both embarrassed and annoyed me.

But here I was, Isabella Maria Constanza Littlefield Whitehead, granddaughter of Augustin Whitehead, founder and patriarch of the Whitehead industry and the incomparable olive oil and sherry they produced. I was going to face the man who had broken my heart so long ago, betrayed the trust I'd always counted on. No, not the beautiful almost-cousin Marcus, but my grandfather, the epitome of family, who'd turned his back on me and yet always welcomed my doppelganger into his arms.

Though I suppose if anyone was the doppelganger, it was me. Bella was the real thing, I was the shadow version.

If I was going to carry this off, I would have to channel Bella a little more effectively. And in order to do that, I needed to stop brooding about the stupid choice that had brought me here. For three days, I needed to *be* Bella. Kitty Whitehead had been left behind.

The plane was taxiing down the runway, and I closed my eyes, ready to enjoy the sensation of being coddled for at least the next six hours, when a sudden thought made them fly open again in shock. If Bella's extravagant ways had gotten her into real trouble, wouldn't they come after her? And in looking for her, they'd find me.

I fumbled for my seatbelt, but it was too late—the plane was lifting into the air, and I sat back, trying to breathe. No, I was panicking over nothing. Bella was dealing with things—they would be busy with her, not looking for her imposter. And she had sworn it was all fool-proof and completely safe. Even if she wouldn't tell me what her dire life-and-death problem was, she'd insisted none of it would come anywhere near me, and I believed her. Bella was no saint and never had been—she was perfectly capable of letting someone else take the fall for her mistakes and had when we were young.

But she would never, ever, put me at risk. Childhood games were one thing; life in the grownup world, as hard and difficult as it was, was another. We were sisters under the skin, not just cousins. We were the other side of the mirror, and she would never let me be hurt.

I closed my eyes again, still uneasy. I hadn't had time to think this through—Bella had been a whirlwind of activity after my tentative "yes," and even when I'd gone to bed, as the doubts began to insinuate themselves into my brain, I'd fallen asleep before they could coalesce.

Now I had nothing to do but think, and doubt, and worry. I had never been impulsive, and what I'd agree to was madness. When I landed in Malaga, I should turn around and immediately book a flight back home. In all decency I should pay Bella back for the cost of the ticket. The contact lenses. The soft, tawny curls that drifted past my shoulders and had cost five hundred dollars. Where the hell had Bella found a hairdresser who charged that much?

Not to mention the phony passport, the new clothes and shoes that were clearly made for me. Bella was a size seven and a half, I was close to size nine. And even I recognized the red-soled magnificence of Christian Louboutin.

I had no money. Well, barely enough to rent a new apartment, my Subaru was on its last legs, and there was no job on the horizon. Bella had taken over the Subaru, arranged for my meager belongings to be stored, switched cell phones with me, and seen me to the airport, a slim leather wallet full of euros pressed into my hand.

I was screwed.

Deep breaths, I reminded myself. *Calmar.* The Spanish phrase came back to me. Stay calm.

It was going to be all right. Instead of worrying about Bella, I should concentrate on why I was doing this. I would finally see Granda again, say goodbye. He would hear those words from Bella, but it would be Kitty who said them. I would be the one to hug him one last time, I would be the one to walk through the halls and the olive groves of Mariposa one last time, finding the closure that had always troubled me. I had been snatched from that life, that cocoon of love, without a chance to say goodbye. Now that I could, I would finally be able to move on with my life, no longer in thrall to a place that was no longer mine.

The two glasses of champagne from the flight attendant helped. I wasn't used to drinking, but deep breathing and rationalization did wonders. What was the phrase from the old movie, *The Big Chill?* What was more important, rationalization or sex? The answer? When did you ever go a day without rationalizing?

I was rationalizing like mad, and it was working, thank God. This would be all right, and afterward, I would enjoy a few days in my favorite city before returning to reality. I would be homeless and unemployed with a great wardrobe. Things could be worse.

In just a few hours I would finally be back in Spain. I would smell the juniper trees, the roses that grew in abundance around the big old house, I would see the olive groves and the vineyards that stretched down to the sea. I would be home.

Amazingly, I slept in that strange little pod, like an astronaut on a hyperspace journey to Mars. At one moment, I was sipping champagne and forcing away my second thoughts, in another, I was being tapped on the shoulder by a flight attendant, reminding me to sit up and prepare for landing.

We landed hard, which should have been an omen, bouncing over the tarmac until we came to a halt beside Malaga Airport, aka Picasso Airport. I discovered that first-class passengers were allowed to depart ahead of everyone else, and I fought my instinctive Titanic-induced class sensitivity as I negotiated my almost-stiletto heels out of the plane. I had put my foot down, literally, when it came to the shoes. There was no way I could balance on the six-inch needles Bella tried to talk me into, to make up for the one-inch discrepancy in our heights. People were much more likely to notice me tripping and falling all over the place than a scant inch.

Even so, I was used to my Asics, and I missed them. I'd tried to sneak a pair into the elegant luggage, but Bella had sternly removed them. "It's less than a week," she said. "For a few days, you can survive anything."

Survive. The word gave me an errant chill, and I shook it off as I stepped into the terminal. At least I would only have to face Granda. As sharp as he was, the failings of his sight and hearing would keep me safe from detection. I would spend one last day with him, with Mariposa, and leave.

The small commuter plane would have been nerve-wracking, but I was much too tense about going home to even worry about the glorified flying tin can. We arrived in St. Maria de Fe far too soon.

The first thing I planned to do, I thought as I managed to stride à la Bella through the busy terminal, was to find Granda. After that, I wanted to explore the old house once more, go out into the olive groves, roam the countryside. Pack a lifetime of memories into the short time I would be there.

In four-inch heels.

It was a long walk to the baggage section, and I shoved my soft curls away from my perfectly made-up face, channeling my inner Bella. It seemed to work—I was getting looks from the men as I walked by, glares from the women. I usually walked through airports in complete anonymity. Now I was a goddess.

A driver would be waiting, Bella had assured me. All I had to do was make it to baggage claim and some nice, uniformed man would be holding up a sign. He would take care of everything, delivering me to the villa and returning to fetch me. I didn't have to worry about a thing.

It took me a moment to find the baggage carousel. Bella would have known exactly where it was, but no one was perfect. I'd been so busy sashaying through the terminal, plus using the toilet, checking my makeup, and applying a fresh coat of the cherry-red lipstick she favored, that the carousel had stopped and most of the luggage removed. There was no uniformed man holding a sign with my name on it. Only Bella's expensive Prada luggage piled neatly on a luggage cart.

I glanced around, uneasy. Had I taken too long? But no, I was Bella the Magnificent, I reminded myself, stiffening my shoulders. People waited for me.

And then I saw him, leaning against the wall, watching me. He was a stranger, but there was too much insolence in his posture, too much speculation in his eyes to be a hired driver. I glanced at him, dismissed him, and reached into the Hermès handbag for the iPhone, definitely my favorite part of this entire ruse.

Programming the face recognition had almost been enough to make me change my mind. "If your own phone knows I'm lying, how can I manage to fool people?"

But Bella had once again calmed my doubts, and here I was, about to call for a car when the man moved, coming toward me, and I looked up, letting my eyes drift over him. He was tall, with one of those lean bodies that were deceptively strong. He was wearing rough clothes—faded jeans and a work shirt—and his brown hair was sun-streaked, matching the deep tan of his face.

A good mouth, I thought absently, if it was curled with faint contempt. The same for his eyes, dark, dark eyes, with the kind of ridiculously long thick lashes that proved the universe was unfair. Women had to work for lashes like those; men came by them naturally. He had a nose that would have overwhelmed a weaker, prettier face, but seemed to fit just fine in his, and the kind of high cheekbones that would have made me swoon as a child.

I'd never seen him before in my life. Was he one of the people who was after Bella? Had she miscalculated?

He came up to me, moving with a lazy sort of grace that still managed to convey complete disinterest in my reaction, and stopped right in front of me. I held my ground.

"You don't look particularly happy to see me, Bella," he drawled, and he had a faintly British accent.

I looked at him warily. *And so it begins*, I thought. "I arranged for a driver," I said stiffly, hoping to Christ he wasn't the chauffeur working at Mariposa.

"I cancelled your arrangements. We need to talk."

O-kay, I thought. Hostility from first contact. Not good. "All right," I said in a faintly frosty voice. Bella wouldn't like attitude that wasn't hers.

He nodded his head toward the piled-up luggage. "Where's the rest of your stuff?"

I laughed, though I wasn't feeling particularly cheerful. "I'm only staying one night, and then going on to Paris for a couple of days."

"You usually have three times as much luggage."

I looked at the cart in astonishment. It was piled high with suitcases, three full-size ones, two smaller, and even an old-fashioned makeup case that I secretly found adorable. "I'm working on cutting back," I said vaguely.

Wong thing, I realized, by the way his high forehead wrinkled. "Bella the Goddess cutting back? Surely not! There are only a few things I count on as constants—the ocean, mortality, and Bella's determination to have her own way at all times."

So this was an enemy. But why was he able to speak so rudely? Definitely not a hireling. "Since you know me so well, then you'll realize I said that *I* wanted to cut back, not that anyone was forcing it on me."

"Point taken. I've parked nearby—follow me." We almost collided as we moved to the luggage cart in concert. He grabbed the handle, almost yanking it away, and gave me a speculative look out of those incredibly dark eyes. "Bella managing her own luggage? Say it isn't so!"

"I didn't realize I could count on you," I countered, reasonably certain this was appropriate.

"You can't," he said, turning away. "Push it yourself."

I was about to snap that I had had every intention of doing so when I realized that wasn't Bella. I needed a little elastic bracelet with the initials WWBD—What Would Bella Do? I glanced around me, raised an eyebrow, and immediately three luggage porters fell over themselves to reach me. A moment later, two of them were trundling after me as I sauntered in the unpleasant stranger's wake.

He disappeared a moment later. He was a tall man, and his legs were longer than mine, plus the unaccustomed shoes would have had me sprawling on the sunbaked walkway. When I finally caught up with him, he was leaning against a battered old farm truck, and I stared at it in a delight which I quickly hid. When we were young, one of our favorite treats was to be taken for a ride in the back of one of the noisy old pickups, down through the vineyards, into town on market days, trips to the ocean for picnics and swimming.

If I remembered correctly, Bella had never liked the truck—she always wanted Granda's Bentley. Bringing a farm truck to the airport was a deliberate slight, and I wiped my pleasure from my face, sniffing in disapproval. I was about to reach for the stack of euros Bella had given me when my newfound nemesis forestalled me, giving both the men a healthy tip as they loaded the expensive luggage into the back of the truck. It smelled of hay and manure, two scents I was used to from New Hampshire, ones I remembered from the olive groves. The Prada certainly wasn't used to such undignified treatment, and beneath my feigned hauteur, it amused me. For some reason, the damned luggage even brought out my intermittent inferiority complex, and I'd developed a strong dislike for it. Riding in the back of a farm truck was a fitting comeuppance.

"What's so amusing?" the man said.

I glanced up at him. He was unlocking the truck, and I automatically reached for the passenger side door, then stopped. It was a king cab—wouldn't Bella expect to sit in the back seat, being chauffeured?

"You wouldn't get it," I said, hesitating. He'd probably think I'd gone crazy, imbuing luggage with personality. Then again, everything belonging to Bella seemed to have a certain air.

"Open the damned door, Bella," he said. "Don't think for a minute I'm coming around to do it for you."

I opened the passenger door. Not that I wanted to cozy up to the irascible creature, but climbing into the back seemed needlessly petty.

The front seat was littered with papers, notebooks, tools. I was wearing a gorgeous pale gray suit, and I immediately got a dirt stain on my arm, a grease mark on one thigh, and my pantyhose shredded. The Bella-Barbie I'd become was made for more careful treatment.

"Fasten your seatbelt."

I gave him a cool glance, perfectly calibrated to show my disdain for his behavior. "How long to Mariposa?"

"You act like you've never been there before. You know how long it takes."

I didn't show any reaction. After all, he was right, I had been there before, many times. "I haven't been here for a while, and I usually arrive in more dignified vehicles. I don't imagine this thing goes sixty miles an hour."

Another sidelong glance. "You started measuring things in miles, Bella? When did you start spending time in the States? Last time I heard, you were living it up on the Riviera."

Shit. I cast a worried glance at the truck, then smiled. "This is an American truck. The speedometer is in miles, not kilometers."

He said nothing for a moment, then started the truck. It rumbled beneath me, a pleasant sort of vibration, and then I shut that thought out completely. I wasn't going to be thinking about vibration while I sat next to this man. He slammed it into gear, and we were off, the tires squealing beneath us.

I reached out a hand to steady myself—the ancient seatbelt had seen better days. "You know, I never could manage to peel out like that. I'm impressed that you still remember how at your advanced age. Most boys outgrow their love of burnt rubber."

He laughed, and some of the hostility faded for a moment. "You know perfectly well you had it down to a fine art. Your exits are almost as good as your entrances."

Driving in Spain isn't quite as terrifying as driving through the streets of Paris or Rome, but it was close. My companion clearly knew what he was doing, dodging cars, delivery trucks, carts, and chatting pedestrians with effortless ease, all the while I gripped my seat, a serene smile grimly plastered to my face while I tried not to scream. We were both silent as he left the city, but I didn't relax. This man's arrival at the airport was nothing less than an ambush, and I simply had to wait for him to make the first attack.

He waited until we were out on the high road that led along the coast before speaking. "Why are you here, Bella?" he said in a rough voice. It was an attractive one, low and musical, if it weren't tight with tension.

I kept my gaze fixed on the countryside. "You know why. I'm here to see my grandfather."

"You've kept away for five years. Why now?"

Jesus, why now? Wasn't it obvious? Or had Bella been lying to me? "He's not going to live forever."

"He's not going to make it through the summer," the man said flatly.

"So maybe I wanted to say goodbye."

"And maybe you wanted to make sure you were still in the will. Trust you to keep your eye on the prize."

That was a surprise. "Is there any reason why I shouldn't be?" I countered.

"You tell me."

God, he was making me want to scream. Every time I tried to pump him for information, he simply turned it back on me. I had absolutely no idea who he was, though I expected I ought to know. He certainly bore no resemblance to anyone I remembered from my childhood.

It was time to go All Bella on his ass. "I don't see any reason to discuss this with a farmhand," I said dismissively.

Another quick look, his forehead furrowed. "At least I earn my keep," he said after a moment.

I glanced over at him. He was wearing sunglasses against the brilliance of the midday light, shielding at least part of his face, but the twist to his mouth was expressive enough. He had no use for Isabella Whitehead, and I wondered why.

He was nice-looking, and despite the darkness of his sun-bronzed face, I realized he wasn't an England-educated Spaniard.

Granda never had anyone but locals tend the vineyards and the olives, and I wondered where this man with his Oxford tones had come from.

He had strong, well-shaped hands. Narrow, with long fingers, they looked both strong and capable at anything he chose to do. In another time, another place, I might have found him attractive. Out of my league, but most definitely tasty. He'd rolled his work shirt up to his elbows, and his forearms were just as tanned, the hair on them bronzed by the sun, the scar...

For a moment, I froze, shock rendering everything around me into an odd stillness. And then I took a breath.

"Ian," I said.

THREE

My despised cousin Ian looked at me again. "What?"

"Nothing," I said. There was nothing I could say. He wasn't supposed to be here. Bella had promised that I only had to fool Granda.

And I should have remembered that Bella's promises had never been worth shit. He looked like a different person. As a child, he'd been skinny, his nose too big for his face, his brown hair and hunched shoulders accentuating the difference between him and his older brother Marcus. I never would have guessed he'd grow up to be so...so presentable. I should have recognized the sneer. "I thought you were supposed to be away at some conference," I said.

"I was. Until I heard you were coming. I cancelled, and I told Marcus to get his butt back here as well."

"Marcus is here?" My voice rose in a breathless little shriek, as the sheer stupidity of this masquerade hit me full force. How could I have been such an idiot, to fall for Bella's blandishments? I should have known that disaster would follow me.

"Not yet. I expect him tomorrow."

I didn't let him see the relief that washed over me. "I'll be gone by tomorrow."

"No, you won't. I cancelled your ticket to Paris."

"Why?" I demanded in a frosty voice. But I knew why. Ian Whitehead had been put on this earth to make my life, and Bella's, an eternal misery. All through our teenage years, he'd mocked us, taunted us, teased and tormented us. He was the dark brother, thin and suspicious, always too smart for his own good with a whiplash tongue, as opposed to his brother Marcus. Charming, golden Marcus, with broad shoulders and a smile that could melt the stoniest hearts, and both Bella and I had fallen in love with him the moment we saw him. Marcus was fourteen, Ian was twelve when Granda had the two of them brought to the villa, and we'd both made our choice instantly. After all, they weren't real cousins, but the grandsons of Granda's second wife. But he'd decided they were Whiteheads, and they'd been coopted and even changed their names.

Not that I'd ever had a chance. Bella had captivated Marcus, immediately, and he was besotted in return. They allowed me to tag along most of the time, and with Marcus had come Ian, baiting us. He was the price I had to pay for basking in the glow of Marcus's golden light.

The simple fact was, I'd never gotten over him. I'd spent so many years dreaming of one kiss from those beautiful, perfect lips that I'd paid little attention to the men around me, settling for bad choices.

I didn't want to see him again. Wasn't ready to. Trust Ian to have arranged it.

"I can rebook," I said sweetly.

"No one will drive you to the airport."

"I can hire a car."

He laughed derisively. "You've forgotten what the town is like. Trust me, Santa Maria de Fe hasn't changed. No one's going to go against Granda's word, and I'm his voice. You're staying."

I glared at him, giving free rein to my emotions. "For how long?"

"Depends on how long it takes Granda to die. That, or he gets tired of you, but he's just as fooled by you as everyone else."

"But not you," I said.

"No, not me. You'll stay to make sure Granda has a peaceful passing. I don't want him rewriting wills or cutting people out anymore. Enough is enough."

"Who has he cut out?" Besides me, I thought, but that was old news.

"Damned if I know. Maybe you, maybe me, maybe everyone, and left Mariposa and the business to the Dominican nuns or the preservation of street dogs charity."

"He likes cats better," I said reflexively, remembering Granda's beringed hand stroking the big gray tabby who slept curled up on his lap.

"True enough," Ian said. "But you know as well as I do that he hasn't had a cat in years, not since Salvador Dali died."

For a moment I was startled. The granda I remembered hadn't any use for modern art or Spain's most famous eccentric, and he would hardly go into mourning...and then I remembered that was the name of the cat. "Look, Ian," I said, swiveling around on the bench seat, dislodging more papers. "There's no need for us to fight about things. I can't imagine why you could possibly want me to stay here. You and I have never gotten along and that's not about to change."

He cast a sidelong glance at me. "True enough," he said in a noncommittal voice.

"So why do you want me here? I'll make a fuss of Granda and leave tomorrow and you won't ever have to see me again."

"How big a fool do you think I am? Granda has never been a sentimental man and you know it. He ordered the family to assemble in order to make his final decision about his will. Mary Alice and Valerie are supposed to arrive later today, Marcus tomorrow. If you take off, it would give you the perfect reason to sue everyone for undue influence if Granda decides to cut you out."

It was an interesting thought. Not for Bella—Ian was wrong about that, as he was wrong about so many things. Granda was besotted with Bella—she's always known just how to handle him, flattering him with her rapt attention, and he'd never banish her for disobeying his orders.

As for me, Granda had written me off years ago. Everyone but Bella seemed to have forgotten I had ever existed. To be sure, my father had been Granda's younger son, as much his child as Bella's father, but the old man had never prided himself on being particularly fair. And I didn't want a damned penny of his money.

I just wanted to say goodbye. "I don't suppose you'd believe me if I promised I wasn't interested in any inheritance." Whether it was true or not was beyond me. Bella had been cagey about the subject of money, and I'd been so pathetically eager to talk myself into this ridiculous charade that I hadn't pushed it. How could I have been so stupid?

"You're right," he said. "I don't believe you. Besides, you could hardly leave without seeing your erstwhile fiancé, can you? For years, you and Podge couldn't look at him without dissolving into sighs and giggles."

Podge. That hateful nickname would follow me everywhere. I never found out who had come up with it in the first place, but Ian was the logical choice. However, they'd all used it, and I'd even signed my notes with that wretched phrase. So Ian hadn't forgotten my long-lost existence after all.

"There's a blast from the past," I said lightly. "What made you think of her?"

"Beats me." He shrugged, then shifted down, and I realized with surprise that we were already on the outskirts of Santa Maria de Fe. It had barely changed in the last twelve years. There was a shiny new hotel down by the water, but beyond that, the olive groves and vineyards rose in the hot Iberian sunshine, and I could see Mariposa towering over the fields like Granda lording it over his legacy.

We were through the town in the blink of an eye, then climbing once more, up the narrow roadway to the grand old house. Granda had always refused to widen the road or pave it—it had been good enough for his father before him, it would be good enough for him. Ian gunned the motor, churning up sunbaked dust beneath the tires, and I shut my eyes. I didn't want my first glimpse of Mariposa to be with Ian by my side.

We came to an abrupt stop, and he was out of the truck before I'd even unfastened my seatbelt. I slid down from the high seat, my heels wobbling slightly in the cobblestone yard, brushing ineffectually at the stains on Bella's designer suit. He was watching me, making no effort to retrieve the luggage, but I decided he was the least of my worries. In a few short minutes, I would finally be seeing my grandfather again, and I couldn't wait.

I moved past him, ignoring him, when his hand shot out and clamped around my wrist, hard, yanking me around to face him. "Let go of me," I snapped.

"I want to get one thing clear." That grip hurt. He would leave bruises, damn him. "You're not to upset Granda. He deserves to die in peace, and you have no right to come back here after all this time and disrupt everything."

For a moment, I almost protested that I would have come back long before this if I'd only been wanted, but he wasn't talking to Kitty. He was talking to Bella. "I have no intention of upsetting him," I said stiffly. "Let go of me."

Ian had always had a guarded expression in his dark eyes, the polar opposite of Marcus's warm gaze. I had no idea what he was thinking as his eyes washed over me, but the grip on my wrist loosened slightly, and I realized with sudden shock that he was absently stroking my skin with his thumb. "You've had work done," he said abruptly.

"What?" I yanked myself free. "Don't be ridiculous. I'm only twenty-eight! Of course I haven't had plastic surgery. Assuming that's what you meant when you suggested I had had work done," I added doubtfully.

"You're twenty-nine, Bella," he corrected, and I silently cursed. "And you're so fucking vain you probably would have had a facelift at twenty if Granda had paid for it. Don't bother denying it. I can see the difference in your face. Subtle, I grant you, but unmistakable. Though how in the hell did you find someone who was capable of making you look as if you were possessed of a heart? You found a real artist, no lie."

I growled. Denying it would be useless—at least it would explain any slight anomalies he might notice between Bella's creamy perfection and my own all too human frailties. "It's not vanity, it's maintenance," I said stiffly.

"And just when did you give up smoking?" he added abruptly.

At least we'd been prepared for that one. Bella still smoked, much to my horror, but there was an easy explanation. "Over a year ago. I found it was aging me."

His laugh was contemptuous. "Trust you to have found a shallow reason. Get your luggage. I have better things to do than stand around in the hot sun catering to your vanity."

I glared at him. "I don't think so."

He cursed, low and foul, and a moment later, the luggage was dumped unceremoniously on the cobblestones. He took off, spraying both me and the suitcases with dust, and I watched him go.

Okay, I survived that first, unexpected encounter, but just barely. And Ian the Wretch was one thing; Marcus was another. I really did have to get out of there before Marcus arrived.

I should have made more of an effort to get along with Ian, but he'd always had the ability to rub me the wrong way. Besides, I'd tried to be pleasant, to sweet-talk him into letting me leave, and it had gotten me exactly nowhere.

He'd reckoned without Granda, however, and the way Bella could wind him around her little finger. I wasn't nearly so adept, but expectation would go a long way. The old man would be so happy to see his remaining granddaughter that I could probably talk him into anything.

This was tough enough—I really couldn't stand the thought of the cousins arriving as well, with their knowing eyes. For some reason, Granda's other two granddaughters were always known as "the cousins" even though we were all technically cousins. They were a few years older than we were, and Mary Alice had never wanted much to do with us, or at least, Bella. The two were hardened enemies, and I sighed inwardly. It was bad enough facing Ian the Wretch. Facing the Wicked Witches of the East and West put the icing on the cake.

At this point there was nothing I could do about it, but that didn't mean I was giving up. I could rent my own car, I could fucking hitchhike back to the airport. I would get out of here when and how I wanted, and no inscrutable nemesis like Ian would be able to stop me.

I headed for the wide front door, climbing onto the marble steps for the first time in forever, and I could feel unexpected tears sting my eyes. I scrambled for sunglasses, perched them on my nose, and reached for the knob.

It was locked. That was something new—there had never been any need to lock doors at Mariposa. The entire area depended on the olive groves for income. No one would dare jeopardize his or her livelihood for a little pilfering.

I pushed the doorbell, hearing it chime deep inside the cavernous confines of the house, and felt my momentary tears drying up with irritation. What the hell was going on here?

Maldonado answered the door. Granda's majordomo since the beginning of time, he had always seemed ancient to me, and he looked no different, tall and thin and disapproving as an El Greco, staring down his aristocratic nose. "Miss Bella," he said with a complete lack of enthusiasm. He was blocking the door, and for a moment I wondered if he was going to move out of the way or continue to bar my entrance. The Maldonado I'd known had been austere but friendly to me. What had happened to the old man?

"*Buenas dias*, Maldonado," I greeted him with a cheerful smile that he met stonily. "How have you been?"

I half expected him not to answer, but years of training came into play. "Well, Miss Bella. And you?"

"Quite well, thank you," I said, as he ushered me into the darkened hallway with what seemed like a trace of reluctance. "How's Granda today?"

"Your grandfather is as well as can be expected," he intoned, telling me exactly nothing. "Mister Ian has had you placed in the Queen's Room. If you will follow me, I'll have someone bring your luggage."

Of course Ian had suggested the Queen's Room. It was the farthest from Granda's, the farthest from the bathroom, cold and dark and unwelcoming. The name was, in fact, a joke. No queen had ever visited Mariposa, but Granda had kept an endless series of "friends" in residence, beautiful women who decorated his table and his bed in return for his generosity, and I hadn't realized they were his mistresses until my mother had dragged me away. That had been one of her excuses, citing the immoral example the old man had set.

I never considered how odd the accommodations were until after I had left. Clearly the old man hadn't wanted his women friends to become too accustomed to the delights of Mariposa.

"I can find my way on my own," I said.

"Sorry, Miss Bella. Mister Ian has said you are not to be allowed to roam the house unaccompanied."

I made a disgusted noise. "What does he think I'm going to do, steal the good silver?"

Maldonado said nothing, but there was an odd expression in his dark eyes. Had someone been pilfering things after all? Was that why the doors were locked?

"Very well," I said grudgingly. I gave him a speculative glance. "In the meantime, I'll need to make arrangements to get back to the airport tomorrow. Perhaps you would see to it?"

"What has Mr. Ian said about it?"

I pulled Bella around me like a fur mantle. "Bloody Christ, Maldonado, I don't care what Ian has to say about anything!" I snapped. "I have appointments, responsibilities. I was only able to get away for one night, but then I'm due back in France. I need to make certain I don't miss my plane."

"I believe Mr. Ian has cancelled your flight to Paris, miss," he said, and if I didn't know Maldonado for the basically kind man he was, I might have thought there was a trace of malicious amusement in his eyes. "You'll need to discuss your arrangements with him." He was the best of servants, well-trained, and no one would have seen the dislike and contempt in his flat black eyes if they weren't looking for it. Bella had always been the adored darling here. Of course, Ian had never liked either of us, but there was no explanation for Maldonado's coolness.

I followed him dutifully enough through the cool stone hallways, looking for changes. The paintings still hung on the walls, the furniture was the same, and everything was as well-kept and spotless as ever. For some strange reason I'd been expecting things to have fallen into complete disrepair. Idiot that I was, deep inside, I'd had the belief that Mariposa would fall apart without me.

It was a needed reminder just how unimportant Kitty Whitehead had really been in the scheme of things. A mere blip on the horizon of Mariposa, here and gone in a moment.

The Queen's Room hadn't changed. The double bed was covered with a drab, faded tester, the walls muddy, the brown curtains drawn over shutters that blocked out the powerful sun. I glanced back at Maldonado. "It's exactly the same," I said.

"Nothing changes at Mariposa."

"Granda is dying. Things will change." I kept my voice flippant, as Bella would have.

"Yes." He turned to leave. "Someone will bring your luggage to your room. When do you expect the rest?"

"It's all here," I said, frustrated. "Trust me, there's a shitload." Would Bella have said "shitload"? I'd better watch it.

36

Maldonado frowned but said nothing. "I'll be back to fetch you when your grandfather awakes from his nap."

"Don't you think he'd want to see me right away?" I protested, edgy. After all this time, I needed to see him, to see whether I still loved him or hated him. Or maybe both.

"He's waited five years, Miss Bella. I think his rest is more important." And with those gentle words, he was gone.

I looked around, immediately depressed. The room needed a paint job, new furniture, anything to cheer the place. It did have a wall of closets, enough that the clothes I'd brought with me would be swallowed up quite easily. Maybe Ian had put me in here because he knew Bella's extensive wardrobe—no, Ian would never spare a thought for Bella's comfort. The only people he'd ever seemed to care about were Granda and his brother.

I went over, shoved the ugly curtains aside, and opened the shutters and the windows. And stood there, taking a deep breath as the light and color of Spain washed over me.

The view was magnificent. Mariposa was perched on the top of a hill, the vineyards and olive groves leading down from it, all heavy with fruit. Past that, the town lay in front of me, the terracotta roofs, the bright white buildings so emblematic of southern Spain, the *pueblos blancos*. And beyond that, the sea, a beautiful azure blue. I could smell the ocean, taste the salt on my lips. And then I realized I was crying.

I quickly wiped the tears from my face. I couldn't afford to ruin the extensive makeup job—it took me too long to get it right. Hopefully, I'd get better at it with practice, but in the meantime, it was a follow-the-numbers challenge for someone who had seldom bothered with any makeup at all, much less the complicated high-end ritual Bella favored.

I kicked off my shoes, breathing in a sigh of relief mixed with the tang of the ocean. So I was supposed to sit quietly in my room, waiting to be summoned?

What would Bella do?

37

I headed for the door.

CHAPTER
FOUR

The Queen's Room was at the back end of beyond. Granda's massive suite had always commanded the top floor, giving him three hundred and sixty degree views of the countryside and his possessions. They may have brought him down to a lower floor in deference to his age and illness, but I doubted it. If Granda couldn't walk, he'd make someone carry him, imperious as ever.

I took my time as I wandered through the familiar halls, touching a piece of furniture here, pieces of artwork that I remembered from my childhood. There was the huge copper bowl we'd taken and used as a witch's caldron, the delicate sculpture of the ballet dancer that I now recognized as a real Degas. Everything was the same, even after twelve long years, and it felt unreal.

His door was closed, but I knew he was in there. I could smell the unmistakable odor of medicine and illness even through the door, a hospital-like smell that immediately had my stomach in knots. I had spent too much time in hospitals as my mother had slowly succumbed to cancer, and I could feel the remembered tension running through my body. I tapped on the door lightly, then pushed it open.

At first I thought I'd made a mistake, and the room was deserted. It was dark, the curtains and shutters closed, and the high bed looked empty. And then I saw him lying there.

He was so much smaller than he had been. I remembered Granda as a huge, commanding presence. Tall, overshadowing the adolescents under his wing, he'd been a powerful man with massive shoulders and a leonine head. The man who lay in the bed was only a remnant of that man, a gaunt, still figure barely disturbing the surface of the covers.

The reality of everything hit me then, like a slap in the face. Things were not the same. This was Granda, the man who had meant everything to me, who had turned his back on me, and he was dying. And he still didn't want me.

"Bella? Is that you?" His voice was no more than a faint croak, so unlike the booming strength I was used to, and I moved closer to the bed, giving him a tremulous smile.

"Hello, Granda." I didn't need to affect Bella's husky drawl—my voice was raw with unshed tears.

He looked me up and down in the dim room. "About time you got here," he said finally, his voice a little stronger. "What kept you?"

"I came as soon as I could."

He made a derisive noise, suddenly sounding like Granda again. "I'm sure you had more important things to do than visit your dying grandfather. But that doesn't matter. What matters is you're here now, and you're staying."

"Granda, I can't stay," I said desperately. The charade was already taking its toll, and there was no way in hell I could carry it off for any length of time. "I have things I need to take care of..."

"There's nothing more important than family," he said firmly, and the words sent an unconscious stab through my heart. "You're part of Mariposa, of its past and present and future, and I will have you all here while I decide how I'm going to deal with it."

"Deal with it? I'm not interested in your money, Granda. I came to see you." True enough on my part, and true, I hoped, on Bella's. At least, that was what she'd told me, and I had no choice but to believe her.

He snorted again. "Turn on some lights, will you? I can't see a damned thing."

"You want me to open the shutters?"

"Hell, no. Damned sunshine gives me a headache."

I had passed muster with Ian, who was younger and sharper and more suspicious. I should have no worries about fooling Granda. I moved to the bedside and switched on the lamp. The light bulb was dim, presumably in deference to his sensitive eyes, but I could see him clearly now, as he could see me, and the shock slammed into me, leaving me breathless.

He was old. His waving hair was thin now, white, cut short on his skull. There were liver spots on his cheeks, his eyes were sunken and slightly cloudy, and his body was almost skeletal. I wanted to touch him, to comfort him, to comfort myself, but I stayed where I was. *What would Bella do?*

"You look the same," he said in a grumbly voice, and I relaxed slightly at his familiar, irascible tone. "Shorter, though."

"I'm barefoot. I usually wear heels." Shit. He was more observant than I'd hoped. Still, with those clouded eyes, the differences between Bella and me were almost negligible.

He nodded, accepting. "You saw your cousin Ian."

"Not exactly my cousin," I reminded him. "We have no blood connection."

"Family is more than blood," the old man snapped. "When will you realize that?"

"I realize it," I said quietly. "He wasn't happy to see me."

"I would guess not," Granda said with a rough laugh. "Marcus won't be any happier. You were a fool to break it off with him."

I agreed. Unless he'd changed substantially, I couldn't imagine anyone rejecting Marcus. But clearly Bella had her own thoughts on the matter. "It wouldn't have worked," I said, shoving a careless hand through my hair in a patented Bella gesture. "I did us both a favor."

"You did me no favors!" Granda snapped. "Why do you think I brought those boys into the family?"

"I assumed it had to do with the fact that they were orphaned and the children of your stepson. It was the right thing to do."

"And when have you known me to do the right thing, simply because it was?" he said, sounding more like his old self. He pushed himself up on the pillows, and I wanted to help him, but I knew anything I did would be rejected. He had always been a proud, stubborn man, and that part of him was untouched by illness. "I had no grandsons, and I needed young men to train, to take over Mariposa. But they were supposed to be for you and Kitty, to build the dynasty."

The sound of my own name on his lips was a shock. I'd thought I was forgotten, blotted out of the family Bible if such a thing existed, and knowing Granda, it probably did. I took a deep breath. "You should have known you can't control love."

"Who's talking about love? I'm talking about business, about my empire, about money. You used to have a level head on your shoulders."

"I still do," I said stiffly.

"Well, you're not married yet. Marcus may have gotten over you, but there's always the chance you could make him fall in love with you all over again. He's gullible enough."

"No!" The thought made me ill. How had I let myself get into this mess? It was bad enough that I was getting what I wanted by lies and pretense. To have Marcus, beautiful, unattainable Marcus, touch me, touch Bella-me, would be unbearable. I took a deep breath. "I'm so sorry, Granda, but I can't do what you want me to do. Marcus and I have gone our separate ways."

He made a dismissive noise, and I knew he hadn't given up. "Then what about Ian?"

I couldn't help it, I laughed. "Ian hates me and always has."

"I've never known you to accept defeat. There's not a man who could resist you if you put your mind to it."

He was right. Bella could have anyone she wanted, but the idea of her and Ian was so absurd I laughed again. "Anyone but Ian."

"We have time," he said. "I'm not going to meet my maker for a little while, at least. And if you have any hope of getting your part of your inheritance, you're going to stay put as well. I know your financial situation is far more precarious than you like to pretend—I have my lawyers keep track of you. You can't afford to turn your back on Mariposa, any more than you can turn your back on me."

"I don't want to turn my back on you," I said with sudden intensity. "I love you; don't you know that? I would never leave if I could help it."

For a moment, he said nothing, and I had the odd feeling that I'd manage to startle him. "Well, then," he said in a softer voice, "it's settled. You'll stay."

I stared at him numbly as I felt the walls close in around me. An afternoon, Bella had said. Maybe spend the night and leave the next morning. It would be easy as pie—people believed what they wanted to and no one would ever suspect.

It had been easy enough so far. No one had questioned me, and I'd faced two of the people who would be most likely to notice any discrepancy. I had no particular concerns about the cousins if they showed up before I left, but Marcus was a different matter. He would be the real test, but I somehow knew I could pass that one with flying colors. I was stuck here, in the place I loved most, and the more I struggled, the tighter the bonds were.

I looked down at Granda, and covered his thin, skeletal hand with mine. "I'll stay."

BY THE TIME I made it back to my room, my clothes were already in the vast closets, the expensive suitcases taken away, and I was suddenly unutterably weary. It was early afternoon, and I'd been through a lot in the few hours since I'd arrived in Spain. Bella had said siestas were a thing of the past. Not in my case.

I pushed the shutters closed, leaving enough room for the fresh air to come in, stripped off the ruined suit, and lay down on the bed. I'd been expecting something hard and uncomfortable, but it felt like heaven. All I had to do was close my eyes, and I was gone.

When I awoke, the room was in deep shadow, the light from the cracked shutters murky and dim. I stared at the slim Piaget watch on my wrist. Five-thirty. How could I have slept so long?

I still felt groggy, but I pushed the unfamiliar curls away from my face. In fact the hairstyle had been dead easy, once the color was a match. All I had to do was scrunch my wet hair instead of blowing it dry, and it would become a mass of soft curls. Of course, I was supposed to tighten it up with the judicious use of a curling iron that Bella had paid a hundred and fifty dollars for, ignoring my protest that they could be bought for ten dollars at the local drug store. And I would, at least as long as I was at Mariposa. But once I escaped and got to Paris, I'd throw the damned thing out.

I rolled over on my back, contemplating my situation, trying to still my nervousness. In fact, what did I have to lose? Nothing was waiting for me back in New Hampshire. My belongings were in storage, Bella was looking after my car, there was no place I needed to be until classes started in the fall. Assuming I could find more funding. I could stay here for weeks, even a couple of months, and still have a few days in Paris before I returned, and I could save money while I was doing it. So far, it had been dead easy, and if I was reasonably careful, I could spend time with Granda, at Mariposa, wallow in the joy and feel of the place, storing it all inside for the time I'd leave again, never to return.

I pushed myself out of bed. I felt sticky, dirty, and starving. One thing had changed about the Queen's Room—there was an ensuite bathroom, and I found, to my relief, that it had been renovated so that the shower was a huge marble affair with water spouting from a dozen places with a built-in bench. It was preset for the perfect temperature, which was a heavenly indulgence after years of being frozen, then scalded by cantankerous showers, and I stood beneath the overhead spray and hummed with an almost orgasmic delight. I wanted to stay in there forever, but I was too hungry, and it wasn't until I stepped out, wrapping my body and my hair in thick towels, that I realized I'd washed off all the carefully applied makeup. Shit.

If I were to dress in Full Bella mode, it would take me an hour and a half to get the hair and makeup right, and I'd probably faint from hunger first. I'd already passed muster with Granda and Ian, and there was a strong chance I wouldn't even see them again tonight. I could be relatively safe doing a half-assed job on everything.

I dutifully scrunched my hair, put on the ridiculously flimsy underwear Bella had insisted on, even though the likelihood of anyone seeing my underwear was slim. My makeup was laid out on the dressing table in the bathroom, and I slapped on some foundation and mascara, plus the signature lipstick. That would have to do.

Bella had reluctantly allowed jeans, and the price had been so horrifying that I'd blotted it out of my mind. I couldn't see much difference between my well-worn Levi's and the three figure version she'd okayed, but at least they were denim and comfortable. There was a lavender silk and cotton knit top that clung in all the right places, and a pair of low-heeled short boots that were my best choice for walking. I glanced in the mirror. Yes, it was still Bella looking back, though a more casual, comfortable Bella, and another layer of tension left me.

The vast kitchen was empty. I headed for the refrigerator, pulling out the makings of a chicken sandwich, when I felt someone behind me, and I stiffened before I realized it was only Maldonado.

"May I assist you, Miss Bella?" The question sounded more like an order than an offer, but I turned and smiled at him, and he blinked in surprise.

"I'm fine. I just need something to eat—I'm famished." I set the food down on the wide wooden table. I found a fresh-baked loaf of bread on the counter. "Can I get you something?"

Wrong thing to say. He looked shocked, and I realized that Bella had no trouble thinking of the servants as servants, creatures put on this earth to serve her. After all, they were being well paid for their work, and why should she feel guilty, she'd always said.

But I was half-American, and more sensitive about class issues. I'd never been comfortable with people waiting on me, and the people working at Mariposa had always been my friends, including Maldonado. He'd taught me to play dominoes and told me stories about Spanish fairies when I was younger; he'd been a safe haven when Ian had been a pain and Bella and Marcus had gone off together. I looked at him and realized I'd missed him almost as much as Granda.

"Certainly not, Miss Bella," he said. And then for a moment he unbent, just a bit. "But I thank you for your kind offer."

"No problem," I said, perching on one of the stools. "Sorry I left my room, but I had to see Granda, and then I realized I was starving."

His momentary softening vanished as he stared at me in disapproval. "You visited your grandfather?"

"I did." My throat tightened for a moment, and I put my sandwich down. "He looks awful. He really is going to die this time, isn't he?" I couldn't keep the grief from my voice. I should have been more flippant about it; Bella never liked strong emotions, but I couldn't help it.

"Yes, miss," he said in a marginally kinder voice.

"How long has he been like this?" I was almost afraid to ask.

"He's been going downhill for the last two years. You should have come sooner."

Yes, she should have. "I...I had other obligations."

"He kept asking for you, Miss Bella. And you kept making excuses."

There was no reason why guilt should stab me. It was Bella who had kept away by choice, not me. I felt a faint, seismic shift in my perceptions. Why the hell hadn't Bella come?

"Well, I'm here now, aren't I?" I said breezily, shoving a hand through my hair in her patented gesture. "And I told him I'd stay as long as he wants me here."

I'd managed to surprise Maldonado. "Indeed, Miss Bella?" He sounded skeptical. "Do you need me to make arrangements for the rest of your clothes?"

I'd forgotten that by Bella's standards, my wardrobe was scant indeed. "It'll be fine," I said. "Though I might want to look into renting a car while I'm here."

"There are more than enough vehicles in the garages, Miss Bella, including your Alfa, and needless to say they're all kept in excellent condition. You only need ask your cousin Ian."

Not on my list of top ten favorite things to do. Ian always had and always would be a pain in the butt, a necessary evil, the dark side of Marcus's golden prince. But in the last few hours, things had shifted, our original plan of an afternoon's charade had gone to hell in a handbasket, and I had embraced the new reality without regret. I was staying here as long as I could. If the worst happened, and I was unmasked, what could they do? Only Bella could be damaged by the truth—I was already stripped of my membership in the family, an outcast. If they found out, I would simply leave, enjoy my time in Paris, and return home, at least having had the chance to say goodbye to Granda and Mariposa.

And Marcus.

Maldonado hadn't moved, towering over me disapprovingly. I smiled at him. "Are you going to stand guard while I eat my sandwich? Because I thought I'd take it outside and go for a walk. It's been a long time since I was last here. You can keep me company if you wish..."

In the past, Maldonado would have walked with me, spinning stories of when Granda's father had first come back to Mariposa, after the Spanish Civil War, when everything had been in an uproar and he'd been determined to take the small holding and turn it into one of the world's premier makers of the particularly Spanish form of liquid gold. Olive oil.

But Maldonado had changed. Or maybe, just maybe, it had to do with the woman he thought he spoke to. I couldn't remember whether he had ever liked Bella, but she'd never had any time for him and his stories.

I almost opened my mouth to reassure him, to tell him I'd changed in the years I'd been gone. But that would have accomplished nothing. In the short run, it might make me happier, but in the end Bella would return, and for all her charm, there was no denying she was a cheerfully self-absorbed creature who evinced little interest in other people's stories, particularly those of the people put on earth to serve her.

I immediately felt guilty, disloyal. Throughout my exile, only Bella had remained as part of my family. But loyalty didn't mean being blind to someone's faults and Bella had plenty of them. She just managed to make them seem inconsequential with one of her blinding smiles and sweet words.

"I'm afraid I have work to do," he said in his dour voice. "You should keep to the gardens. Mr. Ian wouldn't want you interfering in the farm."

"Noted," I said breezily, heading back to the massive, restaurant-style steel refrigerator. I observed the lack of Diet Coke with appropriate grief, then grabbed a bottle of limonata. Two months without DC? Impossible! "Could you see if it's possible to get me some Diet Coke? I don't know how hard it is to find around here, but I'd appreciate it."

He stared at me as if I'd grown two heads, and I knew a moment's unease. I quickly scrambled to cover any possible slip-up. "I decided it isn't so bad. But if they don't have any here, then it doesn't matter. Just a thought."

He was still looking at me oddly. "I'll see to it, Miss Bella."

"Cool." I turned, ready to escape, just in time to see Granda's

Bentley glide to a stop by the kitchen door, and my heart sank. Marcus wasn't coming till tomorrow, which mean that it could only be the cousins, Mary Alice and Valerie. I wanted to pound my head against the wooden counter. Mary Alice was the most interfering female I'd ever met, and the momentary peace at Mariposa would be effectively shattered by her presence.

Maldonado moved past me, and a moment later I heard Mary Alice's strident voice issuing orders as I contemplated a hasty retreat to my bedroom.

I waited too long—a moment later, she marched in, coming to a dead stop when she saw me, her patrician face disdainful, and I remembered that she and Bella had always been dire enemies, both of them jockeying to be the lady of the manor.

Mary Alice Ingram was a born aristocrat, from her long, thin body to her silken hair and aquiline nose. She neither listened to nor cared for any opinions but her own, and her sister Valerie was her loyal stooge. They were both older—Mary Alice was probably forty by now, but not a line appeared in her well-preserved face or beneath her slightly protuberant eyes. Her artfully tinted hair was tucked in a perfect knot at the nape of her long, thin neck and her linen suit was both spotless and miraculously unwrinkled.

For her part, Valerie looked like a gym teacher—stolid, no-nonsense, with sturdy legs and stocky body, short-cropped hair, and the predatory look of someone who always knew some better way to do something—and the only person she listened to was her elegant older sister.

Once more, I cursed Bella and her supposedly effortless masquerade. "Mary Alice," I said in Bella's husky drawl. "Long time no see."

Mary Alice looked me up and down and clearly found me wanting. "Don't be ridiculous, Bella. We ran into other last winter at St. Tropez." She eyed me doubtfully. "You look different."

Holy shit. I gave her an easy smile. "I'm still the same, Mary Alice. Hello, Valerie," I greeted the woman behind her.

Valerie, unlike her older sister, had always been victim to Bella's charms, though if she'd ever heard some of the names Bella had called her, that would have stopped. "Podge" was downright flattery compared with Bella's barbs.

She gave me a conflicted smile, and I figured strong-minded Mary Alice would have warned her not to have anything to do with me. At least I hoped so.

"We need our rooms, Maldonado," Mary Alice announced. "Dinner at seven-thirty, not the usually obscene hour you Spaniards prefer. We'll have drinks on the terrace beforehand—you can let the others know."

"Your grandfather prefers to eat at nine."

"Then feed him separately. I assume he's too ill to come to the table. We'll have dinner at a reasonable hour and then visit him."

"Evenings aren't good for him..." he began.

"He'll be fine. Seeing his favorite granddaughter will give him new life."

I rolled my eyes, and Valerie caught me. I immediately came up with an innocent smile. "You might check with Ian about that, Mary Alice," I said. "He's in charge now, and supposedly Marcus will be back tomorrow." I managed not to choke on the words. "I imagine both of them are used to later meals."

"Marcus will be here?" Mary Alice said. "How very interesting for you, Bella. I do hope you'll manage to be civilized."

As Podge, I'd always found Mary Alice extremely irritating. As Bella I wanted to smack her. I gave her a lazy smile. "Being civilized is highly overrated."

Maldonado broke in. "Mrs. Ingram, you will have the pink room. Mrs. Bellamy, you'll be in the nursery."

"Don't be ridiculous, Maldonado. I always sleep in the Queen's Room."

"Miss Bella is in the Queen's Room."

If anything, Mary Alice appeared even more affronted. "I always sleep in the Queen's Room," she said again, spearing me with a meaningful glance.

"Then you'll enjoy the change," I said sweetly. "I'm going for a walk, Maldonado. I'll leave you to get the cousins settled."

And I was gone, out into the early evening light, my food clutched in my hand.

CHAPTER
FIVE

The gardens of Mariposa were magnificent. Granda had always had a slew of gardeners keeping them in perfect shape, full of bright flowers and cool koi ponds and waterfalls to delight the eye. As children we'd loved it, and even now the heady scent of Granda's prize roses hung heavy on the air. Taking in a deep breath immediately transported me back to that time, seemingly so long ago, when I'd been shy and lonely and desperately in love. And Marcus had only had eyes for Bella.

I shook off the memory, looking around me. It wasn't the gardens that I had missed, as gorgeous and colorful as they were. Mariposa was built on the top of a small mountain, and from its lofty perch, everything one could see belonged to the Whitehead family. To the east lay the olive groves, an endless expanse stretching all the way down to the sea. To the west lay the vineyards, the smell of the grapes strong after a day of baking in the hot sun.

In a few more months they would lay down the nets for the olive harvest—blankets stretched beneath the orderly trees to collect the fruit as it fell—but for now I could wander where I pleased.

The vineyards were another matter. When I was younger I would steal grapes, but they probably loaded them with pesticides nowadays. I could still walk along the rows, feeling the good Spanish dirt beneath my feet, the stillness and peace of growing things. Or I could see if I could find my favorite spot, Pinnacle Point, a narrow outcropping of land high above the olive groves, near an ancient elm tree. When I was young it had been my castle. I would sit there and pretend I was a gypsy, living on the land and sleeping beneath the stars. The one time I'd tried it, I'd ended up in my own bed, and I never had discovered who it was who'd carried me there. I'd always liked to pretend it was Marcus, but in truth I knew better. He was too caught up in Bella to notice I was anywhere around, much less missing for the night. It would have been Maldonado or one of the field workers, I supposed. Still, when I'd awoken, I'd been tucked in, and I dreamt a gentle hand had brushed my hair away from my face with surprising tenderness. It was no wonder I had always preferred dreams to reality.

The workers had all retired for the evening, back to their homes on the hillsides, and there was no sign of Ian the Wretch. I started down the hill, nibbling on my sandwich, and by the time I reached the edge of the olive groves, the sun was dipping low in the west. The soft breeze was welcome in the accumulated heat, and I paused, looking up, wondering if I had time to find my old sanctuary. I didn't even hear him approach.

"What are you doing down here?" Ian snapped.

I dropped the rest of my sandwich, startled, then swore. "Damn it, Ian! You scared me! And I wanted that sandwich!"

It was already gone, wolfed down by the disreputable dog by Ian's long legs. He looked as scruffy as his master—some kind of mix that looked vaguely familiar.

"Ollie!" I breathed, squatting down and rubbing his shaggy head. "I've missed you."

I felt Ian's stillness, and I glanced up as the dog happily licked my hand, my arm, and my face. "Ollie's been dead nine years now, Bella. As much as you hate dogs, you still should remember that much."

I had put my arms around the dog, letting him nuzzle me enthusiastically as I laughed, when his words finally penetrated. Hell and damnation. How could someone not love dogs?

I rubbed the dog's head. Kneeling at Ian's feet wasn't a particularly good thing to be doing either, since it brought me eye-level with his belt and the flat stomach covered by a faded black T-shirt.

I rose, shrugging it off. "I finally found a dog I liked, and realized there was nothing to be scared of."

"You were scared of dogs? I thought you just didn't like them."

Maybe I'd been a bit too sanguine about Ian earlier. Then again, he'd always done everything he could to bother Bella and me—I should have expected nothing less.

I shrugged, tossing my hair. That toss was beginning to hurt my neck. "Don't be a pain in the ass," I said, still scratching the blissfully grateful dog behind the ears. "A person can change, you know. And how long has it been since you saw me? Five years? Don't you think I might have grown up a little?"

There was no expression on his face. That had always been the damnable thing about Wretched Ian—you could never tell what he was thinking. "I would have thought that was an outright impossibility. So you've changed your ways, have you? You now like dogs, you travel light, and you've developed an affection for Diet Coke. Will wonders never cease?"

"You've been talking to Maldonado," I said, uneasy. "Then you must know that the cousins are here."

"I know. He also warned me you were off traipsing around the land. Not the smartest thing to do when the sun is setting. Or were you trolling for a farmhand for a quick roll in the hay?"

"A farmhand? Don't be ridiculous!" I said instinctively. Then scrambled to cover my words. "Not that farmhands aren't as worthy as anyone else, but they aren't really the stuff of romantic fantasies. I mean, most of them are middled-aged, with a paunch and dozens of children."

"Getting democratic, are we, Bella-Beast?"

I stiffened. I'd forgotten that little sobriquet. "Why do you do that?"

"Do what?"

"Give people nasty names? Like calling your brother Lunkhead. And poor Podge! That was outright cruel." I shouldn't have brought it up, but that name, which had become a comfortable form of address used by everyone at Mariposa, still burned.

Again that inscrutable expression. "It helps me keep people sorted in my mind. And you know perfectly well you were the one who came up with the name Podge. You're right, it was cruel. Too bad she never realized you were responsible."

I couldn't move, frozen there in the rich soil like an ancient vine. "I..." I began, but my voice felt raw. She couldn't have! Ian was lying.

"You're looking exhausted," he said abruptly, and with anyone else, I might have thought there was a note of kindness in his voice. "You're still jet-lagged. Go back to the house and take it easy. I'm certain Maldonado can forage some food for you."

I wanted to refuse, but too many things were swirling around in my head, and I needed to sit somewhere quiet and pull myself together. At this rate I'd betray myself. I wanted to, desperately, at that moment. I wanted to weep and rail at Bella, my only ally, but I bit it back. Telling Ian the truth wouldn't help anyone.

"Good idea," I said with an approximation of the airy tones I'd perfected. I moved then, my muscles feeling stiff, then glanced back at him. "Are you coming to dinner? Mary Alice has decreed we have it at seven-thirty, but you could overrule her."

"So could you. It doesn't matter to me— I usually eat at my place."

"Your place? You're not living in the house?"

He shook his head. "I have an apartment over the old stables. I like my privacy."

I relaxed, just marginally. "Then I won't be seeing much of you during my stay."

"Don't count on it. When Marcus is here, I spend my evenings at the house, and I visit Granda at least once a day, plus I need to check in with Maldonado to make sure things are running smoothly. You never know when I'm going to turn up, Bella-Beast. You'll need to watch your back."

"Why? Are you going to stab me in it?"

His smile was thin. "You don't know me very well, do you? If I ever decide to stab you, it will be in the heart, looking into your cold green eyes, sweetheart. So watch your step."

His cool words shook me. "Are you threatening me?"

"Yes. It's not the first time. Behave yourself, or I'll make you very sorry you didn't."

Two could play this game. "You like to hurt women, Ian? Why am I not surprised?"

"The only woman I ever wanted to do violence to was you, Bella-Beast. You haven't yet goaded me into it, but sooner or later you will, if you keep on trying."

Bella would too. She would taunt and bait Ian, as she had when we were younger, determined to get his attention. His disdain for her had driven her crazy, and she had always done her best to make him fall at her feet as most other boys did. As far as I knew, he never had.

"Why don't we agree to keep out of each other's way?" I said in my sweetest voice. "You see me coming, you change direction. I'll do the same, and we won't have to annoy each other."

"Go back to the house," he said again. "I don't want to babysit you tonight—I've got better things to do."

I looked at him. He had showered, his sun-streaked hair dark with water, and he'd shaved. "Got a hot date?" I said, irritated.

He grinned. "I do. And I don't want my little cousin interfering like she always did when we were younger. Go back to the house or I'll carry you."

I glared at him. I was so tempted to say "I'd like to see you try" but I was afraid he'd take me up on it. He was strong, and he could do it. And I didn't want Ian's arms around me. "Wretch," I said pleasantly, turning my back on him and sauntering toward the big house.

The big shaggy dog automatically followed, until Ian called him back, and I controlled my regret. I loved dogs. And cats, and birds, and turtles, and hamsters—I had a weakness for small creatures, furry or scaled, but my nomadic life hadn't allowed me to own any.

"I already know about 'Ian the Wretch'," he called after me. "You're going to have to come up with something a little fiercer. How about Ian the Terror?"

I looked back over my shoulder. "You wish."

His laugh followed me back to the house.

The ground floor of Mariposa was filled with large rooms, and I headed straight for my favorite, the ladies' salon, hoping to God Mary Alice hadn't coopted it. Of course it had the same soaring ceilings and dark beams, the stucco walls, but these were painted with a soft warm color, almost a blend of terracotta and peach, and the furniture was overstuffed and slightly shabby. It had always been a neglected room—I had claimed it as my own when we were young, and while Mary Alice and Valerie had objected, Granda had overruled them. They'd never shown interest in the shabby little room before, and they could make do with the vast drawing rooms or the library.

For a moment I was afraid that this had been spruced up like everything else at Mariposa, but when I opened the door I breathed a sigh of relief. It was the same. Spotless, of course—Maldonado would accept nothing less, but the pale, overstuffed furniture was the same, the cabbage roses on the slipcovers slightly more faded. The bookshelves were filled with books written by women, something Granda had always deemed beneath his attention, and there were brand-new glossy fashion magazines on the table in front of the old sofa with the high sides, typical of Maldonado's attention to detail. There was even a small silver tray with a decanter of sherry and a set of glasses waiting.

The room looked out over the lawns, with one wall made up of French doors. I pushed them open, letting the stuffiness out and the deliciously cool night air in. I'd left my e-reader up in my room, but for the moment, all I wanted to do was stretch out on the sofa and look out over the landscape, lit by the reflection of the setting sun.

Granda would be able to see the sunset from his room, since it faced west, and I wondered if someone had bothered to open the shutters for him. I hoped so. A good granddaughter would go and make certain, but I was too tired and confused to do anything but lie there, watching the sky darken. Besides, I didn't think I could handle much more of Mary Alice right then.

I had a lot to think about. About the possibility that Bella had come up with that hateful nickname. Ian had probably lied about that...but then, why would he lie to Bella, who presumably would know the truth? It made no sense. It had to be the truth.

It shouldn't have come as such a surprise. Bella had always had a sharp tongue, though her regret when she let it get away from her was profound. If she had come up with it, she would have been sorry. It would have been Ian who'd taken it and run with it.

Except that I couldn't remember Ian using that name all that much. When we were alone, he'd called me Kitty. In front of the others, he'd called me nothing at all.

And I was starting to wonder who the hell I was. I poured myself a small glass of Mariposa's stunning *fino*, taking a tentative sip and then humming with pleasure. I didn't drink much, but I knew enough to savor the best.

Was I Kitty, impoverished graduate student and exile, here to play a game of charades with people I loved? Was I Kitty, Bella's grown-up cousin, was I Podge, with baby fat and spots, a late bloomer? Was I Bella, the glamorous and charming, or the Bella-Beast that Ian despised? Who the hell was I?

I sank lower into the comfortable sofa. A broad expanse of lawn stretched out in front of me, the gardens and swimming pool off to the left behind a thick row of cedars. They used to have dances on that lawn, the people spilling out from the drawing rooms that led out into the night air. I would dream of dancing with Marcus. I would wear a flowing white dress, my feet would be barefoot in the grass, and for a moment I wondered if that was one more thing I could knock off my personal, Mariposa-ruled bucket list. If I was going to be stuck here, I might as well revel in it. I could live out my fantasies with Marcus, no harm, no foul, and when I returned to real life, it would be something to remember, to treasure.

I closed my eyes, trying to picture it, trying to imagine the feel of Marcus's powerful arms around me, as the music played. His hands were warm, hard, as he pulled me too close, and I smiled as I rested my head against his chest. I looked down at our intertwined hands, the strength in his wrist, the scar showing white beneath the tan, and I broke the fantasy with a cry of horror. Why the hell had Ian hijacked my romantic daydream, damn him?

The scar.

I hadn't thought of that day in years. In fact, not since my mother had dragged me away from Mariposa on that bright summer day, never to return. It was time to revisit that tumultuous afternoon from the perspective of my hoped-for maturity. Hoped-for, because Mariposa was making me feel like an adolescent again, roiling with hormones and emotions I had shut off years ago.

Bella had been bored. We'd spent the last few days lying by the pool, soaking up sun to turn our skin a golden tan. Bella had worn a thong bikini so scandalous I was both embarrassed and in awe. I wore a black one-piece and a voluminous cover-up when I wasn't in the pool, and while sunbathing had always felt like the most boring thing in the world, Bella had made everything interesting.

She rolled over on her back, not bothering to adjust her slipping bikini top, lifted her expensive sunglasses and eyed me. "I'm bored, Podge."

I didn't bother coming up with suggestions—I knew they'd be shot down. Besides, she had a spark in her bright green eyes that always signaled trouble. I sat up, pulled my caftan over my head, and crossed my legs. "What do you have in mind?"

"I think we should go explore the caves."

I took in a quick, shocked breath. "There's a reason we're not supposed to go anywhere near them. They're dangerous."

"Bullshit," seventeen-year-old Bella had said with the easy familiarity with cursing that I envied. "Life is dangerous. Those caves have been here since Roman times and I haven't heard of anyone dying."

"That's because no one's allowed in. They're blocked off."

"I bet we can find our way in."

"Why?" I countered. Silly question. I knew the answer before she said it.

"Because we can."

There was never any question that I would accompany her. Not from slavish devotion, which I knew Bella counted on, but because if she went on her own, she might get hurt. At least if I went with her, I could go for help if she ran into trouble.

I never considered telling Granda, or Maldonado, or any of the adults who watched over us. Ratting on your buddies was strictly forbidden in our loose code of honor, and I knew Marcus and Ian would view me with deep contempt if I did so. All I could do was try to keep Bella from accidentally killing herself in her quest for adventure.

I'd dressed in shorts and a loose T-shirt, meeting her down by the edge of the vineyards. The lands of Mariposa were so vast they encompassed olive groves, vineyards, Roman ruins, Moorish ruins, a stretch of rocky coast, and the dark caves once used to hold smuggled goods, English soldiers, cheese and hams for curing, and occasionally gypsies. Anyone and anything had hidden in its confines, until Granda had irritably declared it off-limits the previous summer, making a place that had never held much interest suddenly irresistible.

Bella was wearing jeans and a halter top, with her hair pulled back and covered with a scarf, and she looked conspiratorial when she met up with me. "Marcus and Ian have gone riding, Mary Alice is sucking up to Granda, and God knows where Valerie is. We don't have to worry about any of them."

"Marcus wouldn't tell," I said, defending my hero.

"Of course he wouldn't. But Ian the Wretch would try to stop me, and you know Marcus listens to him, not to mention that Mary Alice is a tattletale. And I'm not about to let anyone stop me."

Indeed, when Bella had decided something it was almost impossible to change her mind. She was fiercely single-minded when it came to getting what she wanted, and damn the torpedoes. "Then what are we waiting for?" The sooner this was over, the sooner I could go back to my room and finish the thick, juicy romance I had hidden between my mattresses. I'd been mocked once too often by everyone for my choice of reading material.

The caves had never been easy to get to, which had always been part of their appeal. You had to get past the acres of vineyards, through two open fields and into the woods, moving down at an increasingly steep angle toward the sea. If you weren't looking, you could miss them —the narrow path steered clear of the entrance, and if you happened to glance that way, you might think it was simply a pile of huge boulders left by an errant glacier. I'd never been inside, and I somehow had envisioned something along the lines of the cave houses of Granada, but it was a far cry from that rustic charm. There were brambles in the underbrush as we forged our way to the opening, scratching my legs and arms, and I wished I'd had the brains to wear jeans the way Bella had. She paused in front of the entrance, her eyes shining, and turned to me.

"Who's going first?"

I had been regretting this for the last half hour as we'd slogged toward our destination, and I now looked at the narrow passageway with deep distrust. I wasn't troubled by phobias, either fear of the dark or enclosed places, but the vista didn't look promising. "I thought it was boarded up."

"Marcus and I were out this way a couple of days ago, and he helped me move the boards."

Of course he did. Marcus would do anything for Bella. "Maybe we should head back to the house," I said nervously. "I'm not sure I'm up for this."

Bella didn't bother to hide her disgust. "Coward. I'd thought better of you, Podge."

The words stung. I'd always hated to be thought a coward, and Bella knew it. I sighed. "I'll go first. Did you bring a flashlight?"

"A torch? I forgot to. Here. This is almost as good." She pulled out her pilfered pack of cigarettes and handed me the lighter. It was Granda's, from the time he used to smoke, solid gold, dated and engraved, and I took it in awe.

"Granda gave you this?" I breathed.

"Of course not, silly. He wasn't using it any longer, and I doubt he even missed it. And you're not to tell anyone..."

"Who do you think I am, Mary Alice?" I demanded with dignity. "I don't tattle."

She gave me her blazing smile of approval. "Of course not, Podge. I'm sorry I even said anything. You go in and I'll follow. Unless you'd rather me lead the way."

I would have, but I said nothing, mentally girding my loins. I could do this, prove myself worthy. Squaring my shoulders, I stepped into the shadowy confines of the cave, ignoring the sudden squeeze of fear.

It was cold after the heat of the summer afternoon, cold and damp. I held the lighter up, clicking it, and looked around me. It was a small room, with a dark passageway leading off it, but it was big enough to stand up in. "I'm okay," I called back.

The cave darkened as Bella blocked out the light in the doorway. She slipped in beside me, looking around in disgust. "I was expecting something a little more exciting," she said.

"Like what? Pirate treasure? Prehistoric wall paintings? It's just a boring old cave," I said, hoping she'd seen enough.

She hadn't, of course. "Let's go this way," she said, pushing past me and heading into the darkness.

"Wait!" I called after her, rushing to keep up, the meager flame from the light vanishing.

I saw her quite clearly as I felt the earth give way beneath me. She was saying something, a warning, a scream, but I couldn't hear the words as the soft ground crumbled under my feet, and I was falling, falling into a darkness so thick and impenetrable it felt like death. I landed hard, the breath knocked out of me, and I lay there, gasping and choking, certain I was dying. I clawed out, my fingers struggling for something to hold onto, but there was only hard stone all around me.

My breath came back in a painful whoosh, and I could finally hear Bella's voice from far overhead, screeching at me. "Jesus Christ, Podge, why couldn't you watch where you were going? That ground could barely support my weight. You should have stayed toward the middle."

I tried to say something, but only came out with a muffled sob, which surprised me. I never cried in front of anyone at Mariposa—that was kept for the sanctity of the small room I'd been given. Originally Bella and I had shared, just as the cousins and Marcus and Ian had, but as her wardrobe increased, her need for space had increased as well, and she'd been moved out of the nursery into one of the grown-up bedrooms with its own ensuite, something I deeply envied. I hated leaving my room in the middle of the night in my pajamas—it always happened that Marcus or Ian would be wandering around and see me.

Bella's voice softened. "Are you all right, Podge?"

I managed to swallow my next sob. "I don't think so. Everything hurts."

"Can you move? Try to sit up."

I tried, I really did, but it hurt too much to pull myself into a sitting position. "Everything works," I said in a pained voice. "I just don't want to move."

"Light the lighter so I can see how far down you are."

I'd put it in my pocket as I'd hurried after her. I reached for it, and it tumbled out of my hands. Thank God I didn't lunge for it—I would have disappeared into the darkness as well. I could hear it, skittering down against the rock walls, and endless fall that finally ended in a watery plunk. "It's gone," I said miserably.

"Jesus Christ, Podge, Granda is going to kill you!" she snapped from overhead. "He loved that damned thing."

I was feeling too wretched to point out that she was the one who had taken it in the first place. I put my face down against the stone, feeling the grit beneath my forehead, the sting of abraded skin. "Sorry," I managed to mutter with less grace than I could have wished.

Bella's sigh from overhead was long-suffering. "Well, it can't be helped, I suppose. I'll cover for you—don't I always? But in the meantime, we're going to have to figure how to get you out of there without everyone finding out. Try to stand, Podge. I can't see a damned thing and I don't know how far down you are. Maybe you could climb up with the help of a rope or something."

I sincerely doubted I could even manage to stand up at this point, but lying there crying wouldn't do me any good. Gritting my teeth, I pulled myself to a sitting position, ignoring the screaming pain in my side. I'd fallen on something, maybe a rock, and I had probably broken ribs that were about to puncture my heart and lungs and kill me, and then Marcus would realize what he'd lost and...

I stopped my maunderings with disgust, reaching around me gingerly. I seemed to be on some sort of ledge, with unforgiving stone behind me and a steep drop in front of me. Great. I braced myself against the wall and tried to stand up, then collapsed back down with an unwelcome cry of pain.

"What's wrong?" Bella's concern was clearly mixed with annoyance.

"I don't think I can stand up. I think I've broken something." I felt my right leg gingerly, sucking in my breath at the pain.

"People run marathons on broken legs, Podge. It's all a matter of adrenaline and nerve. You can stand if you really want to—I know you can. You can do anything."

That had always been Bella's belief, and it usually made me feel powerful and almost as wonderful as she was. Right then it annoyed me. I sniffed. "Not quite anything."

"Stand up, Bella!" she snapped, harsher now. "Or I'll leave you there."

She wouldn't, of course. But her words were enough to galvanize me. Using the wall as a brace, I rose, slowly, painfully, reaching above me to see how high it extended. Too high. And then my leg gave way and I collapsed, one leg slipping over the edge to pull me downward.

I managed to stop myself, just in time. "It's too high," I said grimly. "You're going to have to go for help."

There was silence from the darkness above me, and for a brief, terrified moment I was afraid she had left. And then her voice came back, a blessed relief. "I'll go find Marcus. He can bring a ladder and we'll get you out in a trice. No one need know anything about it— we'll just say you fell on the rocks by the beach."

"We aren't supposed to go to the beach alone either," I pointed out weakly. There was a dangerous riptide on the rocky coast, making it unsuitable for swimming, and Granda had declared it off limits from the very beginning.

"Trust me," Bella said.

I heard her move away, the sounds of her departure growing fainter and fainter, and I leaned back against the wall to wait. It would take her a while to get back to the house, longer still to track down Marcus and pry him away from Ian. I could expect, at the very least, an hour stuck down here in this dark, dank hole.

I hadn't thought I minded dark, enclosed places, but I'd never experienced such a deep, unforgiving darkness as it was on that hard, narrow ledge. It was like a physical thing, closing down around me, suffocating me, and I felt my breathing quicken, short, shallow pants that were easy to recognize. My fragile mother suffered from panic attacks, and I had nursed her through them any number of times. I was not going to let myself give in to the same wretched problem.

I slowed my breathing. My face was wet and cold, and I pushed my hair away from it, realized with surprise that it was tears, not sweat. I needed to stop, or I'd be all blotchy and miserable when Marcus rescued me. This whole thing was embarrassing enough—I could at least manage to look like a damsel in distress when Marcus came.

He might even have to carry me. The thought filled me with mixed emotions. On the one hand, being scooped up in Marcus's strong arms had been at the base of every daydream I had ever had. On the other, he would notice the very solid weight, still encumbered by baby fat, and probably struggle beneath the burden.

That made me start crying again, which was ridiculous, and I wiped the tears away with the hem of my T-shirt.

I had lost track of time. How long had Bella been gone—an hour? Two? Or maybe only ten minutes? It might take her time to find Marcus, particularly if he and Ian had decided to go for a long ride. Knowing Bella, that wouldn't stop her—she'd simply filch one of the cars. She'd been doing so since she was twelve, and I had complete faith in her.

I don't know if I slept. It seemed to me I might have. It took me a while to realize I was starving—this doomed adventure had started in lieu of lunch, and adding to my misery was the growling of my stomach.

I tried to lie back down on the ledge, but lying on rubble-strewn stone was even worse than sitting up. I leaned my head back against the wall, cried a little, and slept.

When I awoke, I was freezing. I don't know whether the temperature had dropped or it had simply taken that long for the cold to seep in, but the moment I realized it, I started shivering, and once it began I couldn't stop. I tried to clamp down on my quivering muscles, wrapping my arms around my body and hugging tightly, but it did no good. My teeth were chattering, my fingers and toes icy, and I knew beyond a doubt that Bella had been gone too long.

She must have fallen on her way to get help. That, or gotten lost.

Even if she couldn't find Marcus and Ian, she would eventually turn to Mary Alice for help, and she would manage everything with her usual ruthless efficiency. If Granda found out he would be furious, but he never stayed angry at Bella for long, and she would protect me from his wrath. If she hadn't returned, then something had happened to her as well.

For a moment panic swept over me, as I contemplated my imminent demise. And then I calmed down. Granda and everyone who worked at Mariposa, a small army, would move heaven and earth to find Bella, and once they did, they would find me. Unless she'd fallen and hit her head on a rock and was either dead, in a coma, or with a full-flown case of amnesia, in which case I would most definitely die, and considering how cold and how hungry I was, it might be in the next five minutes.

At first, I didn't even hear the noise. The distant scrape of wood against the rock, the merest sense that the stygian darkness was lessening. And then I heard his voice. *His* voice.

"Kitty! Where are you?" Ian's voice was furious.

At that point, I didn't have Bella's facility with cursing, but I uttered a profound "fuck" when I recognized him. As if things weren't bad enough.

"I'm here," I called back. "Be careful or you'll fall..."

"I'm not fool enough to come in here without a torch," he snapped, sounding closer. "How long have you been down here?" The light was growing nearer, a blessed pool of battery-powered electricity.

"I don't know," I snapped, irritated. "I've lost track of time. Where's Marcus?"

His laugh was harsh. "I should have known that would be your first thought. He's back at the house. Apparently he and Bella got distracted on the way to rescue you, and they dispatched me. Sorry for the disappointment."

I fought back the crushing betrayal. "I don't care who rescues me, just get me out of here."

The light came down over me, and I blinked up, blinded. "Shit," he swore under his breath. "You look like holy hell. Move back against the wall if you can. I've brought a ladder."

"Thanks," I muttered, glad the tears and all trace of them were long past as I made myself as narrow as I could. The last thing I wanted was Wretched Ian's pity.

The light was taken away as he worked with the ladder, and I almost cried out at its loss. And then he slid the ladder down till it settled against the narrow ledge, and I heard him curse again.

"What's wrong?" I demanded, unable to keep the fear out of my voice. If I didn't get out of this place soon I was going to turn into a blubbering, frozen baby.

"The ladder's too short. I should be able to pull you up the rest of the way, but you've got to be very careful not to knock it or you and the ladder will go over, and I don't know how far down it is."

"Too far," I said. I wasn't going to be able to stand up, I knew it, any more than I could climb that ladder. But there wasn't really a choice. I shifted onto my knees, gingerly. They hurt like hell, but the main problem was my right leg, which wasn't going to support my weight. That's all right—I had a left leg and two arms that would get me up there, not to mention sheer panic.

I pulled myself up and tried to put weight on my leg. The pain was so intense I almost fainted, and I started to sink down again, then managed to stop myself with sheer force of will. It didn't matter how much it hurt, I had to get up there. I stumbled toward the ladder, and heard Ian curse overhead.

"Are you able to get up the ladder?" he asked in a quieter voice.

"I have to," I said grimly.

"Hold on a moment."

That was the last thing I wanted to do. Standing up had been hard, staying there was just about impossible. I put my hands on the ladder, then resolutely set my left foot and all my weight onto the first rung, leaving my right leg dangling. So far so good, but there was no way I could hop my way up this rickety ladder, especially considering the narrow angle at its base. I put my right foot on the next rung, planning to use it as a tiny bit of leverage, when the pain slashed through again, and I cried out before I could stop myself, starting to fall back, the ladder coming with me.

Something caught it, stopped its descent into darkness, with me clinging to it like a desperate monkey. "Damn it, Kitty, I told you to hold on," he snapped, sounding no more than slightly harassed. "I've got a rope I'm going to toss down to you. I need you to tie it around your waist. That way I can pull you up if the ladder doesn't work."

"Pull me up?" I squeaked. I should have been too far past vanity, but I was fifteen and fragile, and I could just imagine the mockery I'd get from all of them. "I can manage."

"Take the fucking rope."

That was the first time that word had been directed at me in anger, and it shocked me enough that I caught the rope as he dropped it. He'd tied a loop, and I put it up around me, pulling it tight.

"That's right," he said in a calmer voice, soothing me. "Now start up the ladder again. Carefully."

"You don't...need to tell...me that," I gasped, grabbing hold once more, gritting my teeth. I could handle pain. It would only last a few seconds, as I made my way up the ladder, and then I could scream and cry all I wanted, and it didn't matter if Ian mocked me. I'd be safe.

I was past tears—I must have cried them all out earlier in my imprisonment. I gritted my teeth, fighting against the dizziness, and climbed the first rung. Then the second. I even managed the third, when my leg gave way completely, the ladder bucked out from under me and I was hanging by a rope, swinging over whatever lay beyond the edge of the ledge as I heard the wooden ladder splinter below me as it followed Granda's lighter.

I didn't call out. I heard Ian above me, cursing with great inventiveness, and the rope bit into my middle, cutting off my breath, as I felt myself being hauled upward. I was going to die, and I knew it.

Ian didn't have Marcus's splendid muscles, he was only seventeen, not strong enough to haul me up that distance.

"Don't...drop...me," I managed to cry out despite the constriction of the rope, which had now slipped up to my armpits and was choking me even more effectively.

"I'm not fucking going to," he ground out, and I could only hope he was using something for leverage or I wasn't going to be around for much longer. I bounced against the stone wall, slammed my head against the rock, and cried out, feeling the dizziness come over me once again.

"Don't pass out, Kitty," he snarled. "I need your help. I can't handle a dead weight."

I forced myself back. I couldn't climb up the rock, but I could use my hands, my fingers, searching for any kind of handhold, something that could propel me up, taking at least a bit of the strain off Ian. If only he hadn't come alone. Embarrassing as it was, he and Marcus and Bella could have hauled me up with ease, instead of Ian trying desperately to drag me out of the valley of death.

Another yank, and my knees slammed against the rock. I could hear him cursing, a litany of words so foul I didn't know some of them. If I survived, I was going to find out what they meant and use them myself.

And then, wonder of wonders, I felt the edge of the drop, and while some of it crumbled against my desperately grabbing fingers, Ian must have seen me, for he pulled once more, one ferocious yank, and I was lying on the floor of the cave like a landed fish, and Ian had collapsed beside me, muttering "shit shit shit" underneath his breath.

I don't know how long we lay there. I was unable to move, not even to loosen the rope that was biting into my armpits and chest. All I could do was thank God I was still alive. And wish it were Marcus who had rescued me.

Ian sat up first, no longer gasping for breath, and reached for the rope. I tried to slap his hands away, more than capable of untying it myself, but I couldn't even lift my arms. All I could do was lie there and let him deal with it.

Something was wet against my chest, wet and warm, and I recognized the smell of blood. "I'm bleeding," I choked out in horror.

"Not unless you've got your period," he said, and I could feel my face heat. "That's my blood pouring all over you. I gashed my arm against the rock while I was hauling your ass out of there."

Guilt and concern assailed me. "Are you all right? Do you need a bandage?"

"Since neither of us has one, it hardly matters. I'm not going to bleed to death, if that's what you're worried about," he said with his usual lack of charm. "I'll get you back to the house, though I can't promise Granda won't find out. Bella and Marcus were supposed to distract him, but there's never any guarantee that will work, and Mary Alice is always snooping around. So, what the bloody hell did you think you were doing, coming out here? You know it's off-limits."

"Bella...that is, we thought it would be fun."

But he'd caught my slip. "Bella's idea, was it? I should have known. You know, Podge, you're the biggest idiot I have ever seen in my entire life. You think Marcus is a god and you watch him with those sad eyes of yours, hoping he'll notice, and he never will. Marcus isn't the noticing kind of person—you have to hit him over the head to get him to pay attention. And you think Bella is your friend. She's not. She's a snake in the grass."

"Go to hell," I said. For some reason the fact that he called me Podge was almost worse than his warning. "You're just jealous."

"Of whom? Marcus? He's a kind-hearted lunkhead, and you're smart enough to know better, but you're too blinded by his pretty face."

"Of Bella," I snapped. "You're in love with her, and she only has eyes for Marcus, and you're not half the man he is."

It was the one thing I never should have said. Bella had confided in me, last summer. How Ian had tried to kiss her, and she'd rebuffed him. That it wasn't the first time it happened, and it explained all his hostility.

I couldn't see his face in the darkness. He was still fiddling with the rope, but for a moment his hands stilled. "When I fall in love with someone, Kitty, you'll be the first to know." I could feel him rise, towering over me as he pulled the rope free, and I didn't have to see him to know he was winding the rope up in neat, mechanical movements. "Give me your hands."

I had managed to sit up, coughing a bit, and I glared up at his shadowy figure, secure in the fact that it was too dark to see expressions. "I can take it from here. Why don't you head back to the house and I'll follow on my own."

"Don't bother giving me dirty looks," he said. "I'm not leaving you until you're safe inside the house. I don't trust you not to wander over another cliff."

"The cave floor gave way beneath me!" I protested, incensed. "It was hardly my fault."

"You're right about that," he said grimly. He reached down, caught my arms, and hauled me up to stand in front of him. Or he tried. My leg immediately gave way, and he caught me, pulling me against him.

I had never felt a boy's body against mine, a boy's arms around me, and I almost cried. I'd wanted it to be Marcus, I wanted my first kiss to be from Marcus.

Not that Ian had any intention of kissing me. Instead, he simply picked me up into his arms, holding me high as he carried me out of the cave.

And into darkness. Night had fallen—I had been trapped in that cave for hours, and it was little wonder I was still shaking from the cold.

The moon was high, and we could see each other more clearly. He set me down on the ground, more carefully than I would have expected from bad-tempered Ian, and I could see his arm beneath the rolled-up shirt sleeve was dark with blood.

"You should bandage th...that cut," I said through my shivers. The night was cool, the heat from the blistering sun had vanished.

"When we get back to the house. In the meantime, you're going to freeze to death and probably go into shock, which will make things even more of a clusterfuck than they already are."

"I don't like your l...language," I said primly.

"And I don't give a fuck." He was stripping off his loose cotton shirt, and for a moment I thought he was going to bandage his arm after all. Instead, to my shock, he wrapped it around me.

It still held his body heat. It smelled like him, and I wanted to close my eyes and pretend it was Marcus's, but that was stupid. I tried to shrug it off. "You need it more than I do," I protested.

"I haven't been freezing my ass off in a cave for six hours."

"Six?" I echoed. "What took you so long?"

"That's not the right question."

Ian wasn't as broad as his brother. He had a narrow body, wiry, with slightly bony shoulders. But he was stronger than he looked, and he scooped me up effortlessly before I could protest. "Let's get the hell out of here."

Being held by a shirtless boy was...confusing. His skin was warm, smooth, a furnace against my chilled flesh, and the muscles beneath it moved easily as he carried me up the steep embankment. I kept expecting him to make some snide comment about how much I weighed, to call me Podge again, but he said nothing, moving through the woods at a steady pace. I closed my eyes and was silent too, letting my head rest against his warm shoulder, simply because I was too wrung out to keep it upright any longer. Everything hurt. Everything but where Ian's warm skin touched mine.

CHAPTER
SIX

The fallout from that misadventure had been surprisingly slight. Once we returned to the safety of the big house, the doctor had been called, and my cracked ribs and broken tibia had been dealt with quickly and efficiently, as well as the scrapes and bruises that covered my body. Granda was fortunately out that night, and he had no idea what time of day I'd been injured. He was told I'd fallen near the rocks at the edge of the vineyard, and apart from vast annoyance and the surprising appearance of a plate of my favorite cinnamon buns, no mention was made apart from a few dozen stern warnings. Even Mary Alice couldn't find out the truth about my injuries, or she would have immediately told Granda, so I managed to recover with just the right amount of pampering.

For some reason, I'd been too embarrassed to meet Ian's disapproving gaze in the next few days. I avoided him, as I avoided Bella and Marcus. For once, her sweet excuses didn't penetrate the deep hurt I felt, and I stayed in the women's salon, my splinted leg straight out in front of me, reading romances and not giving a damn who saw me. I didn't realize until later that Ian had been fool enough to ignore the gash in his arm, when a few stitches and disinfectant would have taken care of everything. Instead, it got infected, and while I had healed very quickly, he still bore the scar of our misadventure to this day.

My misadventure. My stupidity. And it suddenly struck me that I had never, ever thanked him. He had rescued me, saved my life, and I had been too self-conscious to say a word to him.

"Shit," I muttered beneath my breath, suddenly filled with the need to say something. But I couldn't. I was Bella-Beast—I could hardly tell him I was sorry I had never thanked him.

Or could I? It was after nine, early for a Spanish evening, and given the jet lag and my long nap, I still had plenty of energy. I needed to go find something to eat, but first I needed to take care of business. After all, that was why I was here, wasn't it? To right any wrongs I may have done, to finally let go of my obsession with this place and my lost family.

Now was as good a time as any. Tomorrow, Marcus would be here, bringing his own set of issues, and I would need all my wits, all my energy to deal with him. I could dispense with any lingering issues with Ian tonight and move on.

I passed no one as I moved through the tiled halls with their towering ceilings. Mariposa, in its current incarnation, was a bit over two hundred years old. Beneath the maze of cellars were Roman ruins, with Moorish ones laid on top of them, and the Moorish influence could be seen throughout the house. The tiles were cool beneath my bare feet, and I considered heading upstairs to grab a pair of sandals with their teetery heels, then thought better of it. I headed for the kitchens and the door to the side courtyard, the stretch of drive that lay between the old stables and the big house.

As I expected, there were a number of pairs of mud boots, work shoes, and even clogs. I slipped the clogs on and headed out into the warm night.

It was easy enough to see where he lived. The original stables had been vast, large enough to hold the army of horses, both for riding and working the land Mariposa had required before the advent of tractors. Now most of the stables had been converted, leaving only a small section that still held half a dozen horses.

The first floor was ablaze with light, and I could hear music on the night air. I recognized Juanes, and smiled. I loved Juanes, the warmth of his voice, the passion in his heart. I would never have thought Ian the Wretch would share my taste in music.

I glanced around. He'd said he had plans for the evening, but I could see no sign of a car near the building. He'd probably been lying, trying to annoy me. As if I cared what he was doing.

The stairs were the same, worn, narrow stone. We had played up there occasionally, but back then the dusty space, once lived in by the stablemaster, was simply filled with storage. Typical of Ian that he'd choose to live in a hovel rather than enjoy the comforts of Mariposa.

My stomach was in a knot, but I knew this had to be done or I wouldn't be able to sleep. I wish I didn't remember it all so clearly, but there was nothing I could do except face it and get it over with.

I knocked on the door, loudly. A moment later the music was muted, and I heard Ian walking toward the door. What if someone had come here some other way, I thought suddenly. What if I've interrupted some idyllic sexual encounter?

No, sex would never be idyllic with Ian. He was too big, hard, unrelenting. And I felt heat flame my face at the thought.

The door was flung open, and he stood there, all six feet two of him, looking thoroughly annoyed. "What do you want now, Bella-Beast?"

I wasn't going to let him intimidate me. He was only Ian the Wretch, not some big, scary monster. "I wanted to talk to you. If you're busy I can go away..."

"I wish you would," he muttered beneath his breath, so low I could barely hear him. "I've got a minute," he said in a louder voice.

Belatedly he stepped back. "Come into my parlor, said the spider to the fly."

I gave him a withering glance as I stepped inside, then stopped. The place had been transformed. The wood floors had been varnished, the walls painted a soft white, the carpets rich and color-ful. I recognized some of the furniture from the big house—a carved wooden chest, a beat-up old sofa that had once been in the so-called nursery, a wooden chair fit for a legendary Spanish monarch. On the wall hung the small, dark El Greco that had once adorned the west salon, and I drew in my breath.

"Does Granda know you have that?" I demanded sharply. If he was stealing from Granda, I'd have to do something about it, even if it meant exposing my masquerade.

"You know as well as I do that Granda gave it to me for my eigh-teenth birthday. He said the disapproving face reminded him of me." His voice was casual.

What Would Bella Do? I surveyed him slowly. "Maybe at eigh-teen," I said judiciously. "Not anymore."

"Are you suggesting I may have improved in my old age? I'm flat-tered, Bella."

"Don't be. The bar was set low."

He laughed, unperturbed by my snappishness. "So to what do I owe the honor of your visit? I told you I had plans."

I glanced around me. "I don't see anyone. Or are you going out?" Indeed, by Spanish standards, the evening had barely begun. The restaurants and bars in town would be open late, filled with throngs of people.

"I'm expecting a visitor. Not you." He crossed his arms, waiting.

It took me a moment to remember why I came there. "I needed to tell you something about...Podge." It took an effort to come up with the hated name.

For a moment he looked surprised, then he nodded. "Go ahead."

He was wearing a white shirt, sleeves rolled up, and I could see the scar. It strengthened my determination. "I saw her recently, you know."

"No, I didn't know. Where?"

"In the States. She lives in New Hampshire. That's up north..."

"I know where New Hampshire is. Continue."

He didn't ask how his long-lost cousin was, I noticed. He'd dismissed me as thoroughly as Granda had, and for some stupid reason it hurt.

I stiffened my spine. "She asked me to give you a message."

"Did she indeed?" He started moving then, through the apartment, around me, slowly, lazily. It was unnerving, and I wanted to tell him to stand still, but Ian had always been restless and prowling.

"She said she never thanked you for saving her life. Back in the caves. You remember..."

I expected him to glance at his arm, but he didn't. He simply nodded, saying nothing, forcing me to continue babbling.

"Anyway, she said she never told you how much she appreciated what you did, and she needed to make amends."

"Is she an alcoholic?" he asked mildly.

"No!" I said, startled. "Why would you think that? She barely drinks."

"Because it's usually recovering alcoholics or dying people who feel the need to make amends. I assume she's not dying." It wasn't even a question, damn him.

"No, she's healthy and happy and doesn't miss this place or any of you in the slightest," I snapped, goaded.

"Glad to hear it. When you see her again, you can tell her that her conscience is now clear. At least as far as I'm concerned." He let his dark eyes run over me, an enigmatic expression on his face. "Is that all? Or did you have other old times you wanted to discuss? Perhaps your own amends that you need to make?"

She probably did, I thought darkly. Then again, apologies came easily to Bella, so easily it was hard to stay mad at her. I'd forgiven her for abandoning me in the caves within a week, and we'd been best friends again, with Bella waiting on me and plying me with little treats and presents to cheer me up and entertain me as I convalesced.

"Hardly," I said. "I'll leave you to your plans."

In his prowling, he'd managed to box me in, so that I had to move around him or bump into furniture to leave. And he had stopped moving, deliberately blocking the way. "Will you really?" His voice was low, unnerving, and I felt a sudden uneasiness. Bella had said she was in danger. Was Ian part of that danger?

I would be a fool to underestimate him, and apart from agreeing to this stupid game, I was no fool. I took an involuntary step back. "I wouldn't want to interfere with your evening."

"Bella, you don't have the ability to interfere with anything in my life. Show me your hands."

He'd managed to surprise me even further. "What?"

"Show me your hands. I want to make sure you didn't lift anything. You've always had such sticky fingers."

Immediately I shot my hands out, defiant. I was wearing Bella's rings: a fat Canary diamond that had once belonged to Granda's wife, an ornate sapphire beside it, the world's most expensive manicure on my nails. Unfortunately, my hands trembled slightly, and I quickly stuffed them back in my pockets again. "You are such a bastard," I said.

I had only one physical advantage over Bella. I had better hands. Her fingers were short, squarish, and her original nails equally short. My fingers were long, graceful, the palms narrow and delicate. They were my only vanity, and I'd decided on my own to keep them out of sight. I didn't think they would give me away, but I couldn't afford to risk it.

Fortunately, he didn't appear to have taken any notice. "Fair enough," he said, stepping out of my way. "You can go. For now."

"Oh, may I?" I mocked him. "At least I've done what I promised. We don't need to repeat this, do we?"

I was almost past him, reaching for the door, when his hand shot out, capturing my wrist and swinging me around to face him. His eyes were dark, unreadable in his tanned face, and for a moment I was afraid he'd look at my hands again, then loudly declare me an imposter.

What he did was even worse. "I just want to check something," he murmured in an offhand voice. And in the next moment he'd pulled me hard against him, his mouth covering mine.

I was shocked. Horrified. I fought, pushing at him, trying to dislodge him and the hard pressure of his mouth. He caught my flailing hands with one of his as the other held me firmly against him, and I was going to stomp on his foot with the heavy leather clogs when something stopped me. Something changed.

He was warm, all hard muscle and bone, big against me. I stilled in his arms, not fighting anymore, trembling slightly. In a moment of complete insanity, I wanted to see what would happen, what he would taste like, how it would feel to be held, to be kissed by a man whose strong body came from hard work and not a gym. I wanted the reality of his kiss, the dream of it. His grip loosened around my wrists, then released me, coming up to cup my chin, and he slowly, carefully pushed my mouth open with his, deepening the kiss.

The touch of his tongue surprised me. The men I had known didn't use their tongues when they kissed, but Ian did, pushing into my mouth, tasting me, and my trembling grew stronger, until I felt his hand on my back, gently stroking me, up and down, soothing me as his kiss shattered me, and I wanted to kiss him back, to tell him I was sorry I was lying, to tell him I wanted him.

Because I did. Trapped in the confusing shelter of his arms, I could feel my breasts growing tight and hot, could feel the unexpected clenching low between my legs. Desire. Lust. Feelings I had thought weren't part of me.

But they were. Ian was arousing them, as his hand slid up and down my back, calming me, seducing me, and oh, God, I wanted to be seduced.

And then, unexpectedly, he set me away from him, and I blinked, confused, swaying slightly. "Don't tell me my kisses make you faint, Bella-Beast?" his sarcastic voice came to my ears, and my knees straightened, my eyes shot open, and all that erotic lassitude vanished.

I rubbed my hand across my mouth to wipe away the taste of him, giving him my most powerful glower. "What was that for?" My voice came out very husky and Bella-like without even trying.

His face was absolutely blank. I would have expected mockery, amusement, triumph, but instead, he had the same inscrutable expression he always did. "I just thought I'd see what you tasted like. Turns out it's nothing special."

If I'd been a wild animal I would have curled my lip in a snarl. As it was, I kept my face as neutral as his. "Well, now that you're satisfied, I don't see any need to do it again. One kiss is one too many."

This time the smile was so faint it was almost a mirage, but it lingered in his dark eyes. "Oh, I'm far from satisfied. But we'll talk about that later. In the meantime, I'm expecting someone, and I don't think she'd like running into you."

"And who is she?" I said haughtily.

"None of your damned business, Bella. Go back to the house."

"When I'm good and ready," I shot back.

He took a step closer, when he was already too close, and his body was vibrating with menacing grace. "Are you sure you want to tempt me?"

"I'm ready," I said hastily, hating myself for my cowardice. But he made no attempt to stop me, and I was across the courtyard, opening the kitchen door when I saw the car drive up.

I didn't know cars, but I recognized hers as something sleek and obscenely expensive. She climbed out, and I watched her from the shadows, honestly curious, I told myself. What kind of woman would waste her time with someone like Ian?

She was gorgeous. Voluptuous, sensual, with flowing black hair and a generous mouth, and she moved into the stables with a fluid grace I could never hope to master. So she was a paragon. With lousy taste in men. It meant nothing to me.

No, I had more important things to concentrate on. Saying goodnight to my dying grandfather. Getting the hell out of Dodge as soon as I could.

And facing the long-lost love of my life, Marcus Whitehead, when he walked back in.

God help me.

CHAPTER
SEVEN

I didn't sleep well. I blamed it on jet lag, on the long nap I'd taken, on the stuffiness of the room, on the distraction of the soft night breeze after I opened the shutters. I blamed it on Bella and the unexpected hurt of her betrayal. She was the one who'd come up with Podge. Of course, she'd never known how much it would hurt, or how it would stick. But still.

I blamed it on worry about Granda. For all his rallying, I could see he was barely clinging to life. I blamed it on the charade, the lies I was spouting every time I opened my mouth, the lie I was living. And most of all, I blamed it on the fact that in the morning I was going to have to face the only man I had ever loved, Marcus Whitehead, and it was going to be devastating.

But even though I was living a lie, it was another thing to lie to myself. As I lay on the comfortable bed, looking out at the inky black sky, I went over each worry and dismissed or explained them away in a futile effort to soothe myself. And each time, I came back to the one thing that I couldn't explain.

Ian's unexpected kiss. Ian the Wretch, the nasty bane of my existence, had kissed me. And it had started out like the kind of kiss Ian would give—hard and insulting and totally devoid of emotion.

But it had changed. The feel of his hand, soothing me, running down my back, the softening of his mouth against mine, the taste of him, dark and foreign and bewitching. And the way I had kissed him back.

Was I out of my mind? I had to have been. Because that kiss had been different than anything I had ever felt before. He could have had me on the floor beneath him in seconds if he'd wanted, and I'd spent my twenty-eight years carefully avoiding most sexual encounters. And yet, if he'd pushed it, he could have had it. Had me.

That would have shaken the very pillars of heaven, I thought grimly, rolling over in the bed. Marcus would have returned to find Bella in his brother's bed—who would have guessed? And no one would ever know that it was the exiled Kitty who'd let herself be ravished.

Except it wouldn't be like that with Ian, I knew that instinctively. He'd have no interest in a pliant partner, which was exactly what I was. And Ian would know immediately that I wasn't Bella, who would be voracious, demanding what she wanted, taking it.

Sex with Ian was the last thing I was interested in. If he hadn't kissed me, if I couldn't still feel his mouth, the hard warmth of his body, the strength in his hands, then I wouldn't even be thinking about it. Him. Damn him.

It was dawn before I finally drifted off to sleep, and then I only managed a few short hours before I was wide awake again, this time concentrating on the one thing I should be worrying about.

Marcus was coming. And I needed to be ready to face him.

It was another perfect day, the sky bright blue, and I wanted to laugh. Rainy days were few and far between in my memories of Mariposa, but I'd always assumed that had been revisionist history. Two perfect days in a row hardly made up a halcyon existence, but I somehow knew I was only going to get bright, sunny weather as long as I was here. I just wished I could relax and enjoy it.

Today I managed the full Bella on my face and hair, so that I looked perfect, from my skillfully arched brows to my pedicured toes in the high-heeled sandals. I dressed in silk slacks and a loose silk top —just the look for a life of leisure. I knew I was going to get dirty in a matter of hours, I thought gloomily, but first impressions were paramount. I'd made a few false steps yesterday, tiny ones, and I couldn't afford to falter in front of Marcus.

I headed straight for the kitchens and coffee, only to find a cheerful-looking woman at the stove. I stumbled my way toward the dining room in a caffeine-deprived haze, only to halt in the doorway as a momentary panic sliced through me.

Marcus. Golden, beautiful Marcus was there, and for a moment I was a podgy, awkward sixteen-year-old, desperately in love.

"God, Bella-Beast, it's not as if you haven't seen him in a decade," Ian drawled from the sideboard where he was pouring himself a cup of coffee. There was no sign of Mary Alice and her faithful shadow, for which I had to be grateful.

"Bella!" Marcus said, his rich voice full of warmth as he rose from the table. "Just ignore Ian—he's jealous."

"I always do," I managed, quite proud of myself, only to falter a moment later when I realized Marcus meant to kiss me. I didn't have time to duck, to prepare myself, before he pulled me into his arms and kissed me smack on the lips as he gave me an enthusiastic hug.

I was then held at arm's length as he surveyed me, and I might almost have thought there was surprise in his eyes as they swept over me. "Beautiful as ever," he said.

"Would you expect anything less?" Ian drawled. "You want coffee, Bella?"

"Yes, please," I managed, wishing Marcus would stop looking at me. I wasn't unaware of the irony of this—all my life I'd wish he'd really look at me. "Black," I added, pulling out of Marcus's hold with a shaky little laugh. And then my inner demon made me add, "You're as beautiful as ever yourself, Marcus."

Ian made a disgusted sound as Marcus beamed. But it was

nothing but the truth. He was a shade shorter than Ian's lean length, but he was much wider, with broad shoulders and chest, blond hair swept back, beautiful blue eyes and a granite jaw. He was Prince Charming or a Greek God, take your pick, and I waited for my heart to quicken.

It didn't. I looked at him, surveying him as he'd surveyed me, and waited for the old attraction to sweep over me. How could it not, when a man looked like that, and he was staring at me as if I were a T-bone steak?

Whose idea had the break-up been? Who was I kidding—of course it had been Bella's idea. No one ever said no to Bella, at least no man in his right mind.

But I was prepared now, grateful for an impartial providence that made me momentarily resistant to Marcus's golden glory. It would probably wash over me once I had coffee, but for now, too much was crowding my mind with not enough caffeine.

The sideboard was piled high with food and I was famished. By the time I filled my plate with eggs and tostadas, jambon, and crispy churros, I was ready to start drooling, and I sat down where Ian had placed my coffee, only to find he was between me and Marcus. Just as well, I thought, though proximity to Ian wasn't much safer.

Ian surveyed my plate with amusement. "Where's the dry toast you usually favor?" he said. "Have to keep that girlish figure, don't you?"

They'd all teased my appetite when we'd been teenagers, and I could feel a tell-tale flush starting. Defiantly I speared a sausage and took a healthy bite. "I decided I was too skinny," I replied in a silken voice.

"And you used to be a firm believer that one can't be too tanned, too skinny, or too rich. As a matter of fact, you're looking a little less leathery today. I imagine you'll be spending the day at the pool trying to turn yourself bronze." It was the trace of a question, but I didn't answer it.

"Remember you haven't seen me in five years," I said blithely. "A woman can change."

"And that's the first time I've heard you refer to yourself as a woman, not a girl," Ian continued. "Has my Bella-Beast grown up?"

"Leave her alone, Ian," Marcus said gallantly. "Let Bella do what she wants, okay?"

"Not okay," he snapped, no longer teasing. "No one sees her for years, and then the moment the estate is on the line, she comes rushing back, the prodigal daughter."

"Prodigal granddaughter," I said flippantly. "And I came because Granda is dying, not because I care about the money."

"Granda's been dying for the last year—it might have been nice if you'd come to see him while he could still enjoy it. And the day you don't care about money is the day I become one of your euro-trash lovers."

"You'd like that, wouldn't you!" I snapped back, infuriated, only to see the sudden heat in his eyes, a heat that effectively silenced me.

A moment later it was gone. "No, I don't think I would. You're not my type, Bella, and you never have been."

Marcus cleared his throat. "Don't be such a prick, Ian. We're delighted to have Bella back, and it's made Granda very happy. Can't you be pleasant for once in your life?"

I could feel Ian's now-wintry eyes brush over me, and I stared back, uncowed. Ian had never frightened me in the past, and I wasn't going to let him get to me now. There was a lot of conflicting emotions assailing me at Mariposa, and I needed to sift through them if I was going to make it through the next few days.

"I need something to be pleasant about," Ian said, rising from the table and taking his coffee with him as he strolled toward the windows looking out over the hillside. He was dressed as he'd been yesterday: worn jeans, a black T-shirt, boots. Even if he didn't have Marcus's magnificent physique, he filled the T-shirt out nicely, and it looked like he was ready for a day of hard work.

Marcus, on the other hand, was in white pants and a white linen shirt, a match for my pricy outfit. He'd probably be spotless by the end of the day whereas I'd be reduced to a ragamuffin.

I glanced at Marcus shyly. He hadn't changed, not really. He was still perfect, from his dazzling white teeth to his swimmer's build. I was the one who had changed.

It only made sense: what shy, sensitive teenage girl wouldn't be dazzled by a golden god? But it had been twelve years, and I'd grown up. It was a good thing I was no longer besotted, but a small, contrary part of me missed that desperate, innocent passion.

"Granda's waiting for us," Ian said abruptly. "Are you going to finish that churro?"

Despite the undercurrent of tension in the room I'd managed to go through all the food I'd piled on my plate, and I scooped up my remaining churro as I rose. "I can take it with me."

I was expecting a snort of disgust from both of them—after all, as a plump teenager they had teased me unmercifully about my appetite, but neither of them said a word, and it took me a moment to remember this was Bella they were seeing, Bella the glorious, not sad little Podge.

We headed upstairs in silence, the tension growing thicker as we reached the third floor. There was a nurse on duty this time, and she viewed us with disfavor.

"I'll check if he's ready to see you," she said in her soft Andalusian accent, running a contemptuous eye over Marcus and me. Her disapproval didn't seem to extend to Ian, and I could understand why. Marcus and I were butterflies, uselessly flittering. Ian was cut from a different cloth.

A moment later we were ushered into the sickroom, and I felt a small surge of relief. Granda was sitting up against a pile of pillows, freshly shaved, his thinning white hair combed over his pink skull, a trace more life in his sunken eyes. "What took you so long?" he demanded in a shadow of his cantankerous voice. "I've been waiting hours, and this scheming bully won't let me have coffee. I had to endure Mary Alice reading Dickens to me, and I hate Dickens!"

The nurse, seemingly used to being called names, simply held out a glass with a straw, and he sucked at it for a moment, giving us a chance to react.

Marcus reached the bedside first, all handsome deference and charm. "Granda, you know you're glad to see us. Sorry it took me so long to get here, but the flights were horrendous. But look, Bella is here!" he added enthusiastically, pushing me forward.

"I know she's here," Granda snapped. "She came in yesterday, along with the other girls, probably wanting to know if I kicked the bucket yet."

WWBD, I reminded myself. "Nothing could kill you, Granda," I said cheerfully, wishing it were true. "The devil's not ready for you yet."

"Hmph," he said, sounding pleased, and I knew I'd hit the right note. "It's good to see the three of you together again. Mind you, Ian's worth more than you two wastrels, but you're family, and that's what counts. Even Mary Alice and Valerie belong here, much as I wish they hadn't come. I just have one question to ask." He fixed his faded gaze on me, staring through my Bella-tinted green contacts. "Where's Kitty?"

The name was like a bomb dropping in the room—dead silence from the three of us, as if he'd said something unmentionable. Oddly enough, Marcus was the first to recover.

"Granda, you know you sent Podge away. You didn't want her to come back."

It was all I could do to keep silent. Granda hadn't sent me away —my mother had dragged me, and I'd had no choice. He was the one who'd cut off all communication, effectively exiling me from the family, but he hadn't been the one who'd banished me in the first place.

Granda didn't correct him. "I told you to bring her too," he snapped. "Where is she?" And once again his eyes moved over me.

"She told you long ago she didn't want to have anything to do with you," Ian said. "I don't think that's going to change."

It was another shock to my system, another lie, but not one I could refute. Ian was enough of a snake to have made it up on his own, in order to secure more of his inheritance, and I finally said something. "Are you sure? Podge never struck me as one who held grudges."

Ian's smile was nothing short of cruel. "Am I sure? You're the one who told us she never wanted to hear from Granda again. Changing your story at this late date?"

I couldn't let this pass. "She was hurt," I said. "She's probably changed her mind."

"Not according to you. According to you, Podge said Granda could go to hell and take all of us with him."

Granda wheezed with laughter. "She always did have more spunk than the rest of you gave her credit for. I don't blame her if she doesn't want to see me. But just so you know, that doesn't mean she's out of the running for a piece of the pie."

"Don't be ridiculous—you haven't seen her in fourteen years," Marcus said irritably.

"Twelve," Granda corrected, clearly not as feeble as he appeared. "And here or not, she's family, just as much as the rest of you vultures."

Shit, I could feel a tightening in my throat, tears starting in the back of my eyes. How many times had I wanted to hear those words? Only to find out they were waiting for me if I'd come back as myself.

"I'll tell you what, Granda," Marcus said grandly. "I'll get in touch with her myself, see if she's changed her mind. "And none of us are worried about the estate—there's more than enough for all of us. It's you we care about."

"Bullshit," Granda said. It would have been a perfect exit line, but he began to cough then, his frail body shaking from the force, and a moment later we found ourselves bundled into the hallway by the officious nurse.

"That was pleasant," Ian announced when the door closed behind us. "Maybe we'd better keep it to one at a time—we don't want him too agitated." I could feel his curious gaze on me. "You all right, Bella? You looked a bit shocked back then."

"I was thinking about Podge," I said foolishly. I should have dropped the subject. "I think she might have liked to return."

"Don't be silly, darling," Marcus said heartily. "You told us she had no interest in any of us, that she'd moved on with her life, don't you remember?"

"Besides, we treated her like shit," Ian said, watching me.

"That's not fair," Marcus protested. "I was nice to her. She had this huge crush on me, and I tried to be kind."

"When Bella would let you," Ian reminded him.

I needed to get away from them. The sense of betrayal ran deep, and I had a lot to sort out. I didn't need to listen to them hash out my past. "I'm going to my room," I said abruptly, pulling away from them. "I don't think I can face running into the cousins right now."

"Bella, are those tears in your eyes?" came Ian's teasing drawl.

Damn. I would have to be very careful with Ian—he was far too observant. "You may view your grandfather's upcoming death with equanimity, but I find it upsetting," I said stiffly.

"Bella, your heart is harder than a stone," Ian said. "The only thing that would make you cry would be a torn fingernail."

Instinctively I glanced down at my long, slender hands, so different from Bella's short ones, and I immediately put them behind my back. "Go to hell," I said, turning my back on them and starting down the stairs. I needed time on my own, time to think, time to make sense of things. That wouldn't happen with Marcus flirting and Ian jibing at me, and I moved quickly, the high heels as unsteady beneath my feet as my masquerade felt on my skin. I needed some-place to hide, to think, to make sense of all this, and when I reached the second floor landing, I slipped off the heels and ran.

CHAPTER
EIGHT

I wanted to cry, but instead I was dry-eyed with frustration and anger. None of this was making any sense—Bella had visited me off and on during my time of exile and never once had she ever suggested that my banishment might be over. Of course, I'd kept insisting it didn't matter, that I never wanted to see Mariposa or Granda again, but she had to have known it was deep hurt causing me to say such things. She hadn't even so much as hinted there was a softening in Granda's attitude, or the possibility that I could have returned to Spain as myself.

I'd learned long ago that with Bella you had to take the good with the bad, and there was no question that she wasn't powerfully self-motivated. She made up for that with her charm and generosity, just as she had after the debacle in the caves, and you either accepted her or lost her. And I didn't know what to do with this sense of betrayal running so deep.

She'd been frightened when she came to me, there'd been no denying that, and I would have done anything to help her. She could have simply told me the truth and I would have come to Mariposa as her if she truly needed me to.

But Bella had always had an elastic arrangement with the truth, one of those things you simply had to accept about her. I'd always known it, and it did me no good to get angry, but her recent prevarications were taking some getting used to.

The very last thing I wanted to do was spend more time with Ian and Marcus, but the Queen's Room was getting stuffy in the midday heat. Glancing at my discarded sandals, I groaned at the thought of putting them on again. The silk slacks were now hopelessly crumpled, there was a splash of spilled coffee on the top that I couldn't remember getting, and everything in my closet was too fancy, too precious. I needed to find something comfortable, just for quiet times, and something to walk in. If I had to be Bella twenty-four/seven I would go insane.

The brilliant idea was there a moment later—I would take one of the cars and drive down into the village. Santa Maria de Fe was not a cosmopolitan place, but it had street vendors and tourist shops. I would be able to find a pair of flat shoes and some plain sundresses to hide out in, to remind me that Kitty Whitehead still existed. Not Bella, not Podge, but Kitty. It was the only way I could survive.

I found Maldonado in the kitchen, sharing a cup of coffee with the cook, but he rose abruptly, all starched butler behavior. "Would you like Selene to make you something for lunch, Miss Bella? Mr. Ian usually eats in the field and Mr. Marcus and the cousins have gone out."

Normally the thought of Marcus going off with Mary Alice would have left me feeling abandoned, but all I could feel now was relief and a quiet amusement at the thought of Marcus stuck with Mary Alice. "I'm fine. In fact, I thought I might go out myself. You mentioned there were several cars available."

"Yes, miss. Your Alfa Romeo was recently tuned."

Shit, I'd forgotten about Bella's Alfa. "I'm not sure if I'm in the mood for a sports car," I said. I was a relatively timid driver with a strong dislike of heavy traffic and aggressive drivers, and an Alfa was probably a very aggressive car. Even more important, I'd never learned to drive a stick, and Bella's car hadn't been an automatic. I didn't even know if they made automatic Alfas.

"I'm afraid that's all that's available, miss. Mr. Marcus took the Bentley and the Mercedes is having an oil change."

A Mercedes and a Bentley probably wouldn't provide an easier driving experience, and I was about to change my mind when Ian strode into the room. He looked tired, a little dusty, and not particularly happy to see me. The feeling was mutual.

"Have you seen my brother, Maldonado?"

The old butler shook his head. "He's taken the cousins out for the day—Mrs. Ingram said she had errands to run. So does Miss Bella."

Ian finally looked at me. "So what's keeping you?"

"Nothing. I just wasn't in the mood for a sports car. Though it's probably tame enough..."

Ian snorted with laughter. "Not after all the money you put into it, souping it up. Don't tell me you've turned chicken shit in your old age."

"I'm only twenty-eight!" I shot back.

"Twenty-nine," he corrected me, and I cursed inwardly. "And I've got to go to town myself. I'll drive you. That is, if you'll let me."

The idea was tempting, yet I couldn't like the idea of racing around the countryside with him at the wheel. "Can you handle an Alfa?"

"Bella-Beast, I can handle anything, including you," he said. "Give me half an hour and we'll go."

"I don't think..."

"Did you want to go to town or not?" Ian was his usual, impatient self.

I wanted to stick my tongue out at him. "I'll be ready."

I cursed myself for the next thirty minutes. I ought to keep as far away from Ian's sharp gaze as I could. Marcus was a different matter —he'd accepted me as Bella without a second thought, but I wasn't so sure about Ian. He'd caught me on too many little slips, and every now and then I would catch him looking at me with the intensity that had always made me edgy.

Though there was no real reason he would suspect, no obvious reason for Podge to be there in Bella's place, particularly since apparently I'd been invited on my own, something Bella had forgotten to tell me. In the end it wasn't surprising. Bella always said and did exactly as she wanted, and the rest of us, with the exception of Ian, had gone along with it all, dazzled by her.

In fact, Ian's suspicious attitude probably had nothing to do with his long-lost cousin Kitty and more to do with his life-long irritation with Bella. He just wanted to shake the unshakeable cousin.

Their antipathy had been so strong that I'd always wondered whether he secretly liked her. If he had, those feelings were long gone.

What Would Bella Do? Not let Ian the Wretch demoralize her, that's for sure. If I could deal with Ian, I could deal with anyone, and a ride down to town would give me the chance to hone my skills, wipe away any possible doubts. I was ready to be Bella in all her glory, at least for the afternoon.

The bright red Alfa was waiting for me at the kitchen door, just where Ian had dropped me off the day before, and I took in its beautiful lines with just a trace of trepidation. Bella liked speed—she'd cursed my aging Subaru as we'd driven down to Boston for my makeover, and I knew this thing could probably make a showing at the Grand Prix.

Ian strolled out of the stables across the way, greeting me with mock amazement. "Bella-Beast on time? Will wonders never cease? I assumed I'd be waiting for you for at least an hour."

Don't let him get to you, I reminded myself. "I can always go alone if you're busy with something."

"My afternoon is yours, my queen," he said extravagantly, and memory came flooding back. He used to call her Queen Isabella in that mocking voice, something that had annoyed Bella no end.

"I think I prefer Bella-Beast," I said as I climbed into the passenger's seat, wrapping a Hermès scarf around my hair.

"I think I don't give a rat's ass what you prefer," he replied, still standing by the driver's side door. "You're really going to let me drive 'my precious'?"

I managed a luxuriant stretch. "I feel like having a chauffeur."

A moment later we were off.

He drove very, very fast. The main road down from Mariposa was wide and winding, and he took it at breathtaking speeds, the wind whipping past our heads and thankfully making conversation impossible. I did my best to keep my expression sanguine, all the while I was digging my nails into the leather cushion beneath me and surreptitiously pressing on my nonexistent brake pedals. I had no idea whether he was deliberately trying to terrorize me or loved speed as much as Bella did, but by the time we arrived in the small town, I was ready to throw up in his lap.

"I didn't make you nervous, did I?" he asked in a dulcet voice.

"Me? Don't be absurd!" I replied, a little weaker than I could have hoped. "Where shall I meet you?"

"Nowhere, Bella-Beast. I'm coming with you."

"You said you had business in town."

"I did. Business getting reacquainted with my long-lost cousin."

That didn't help my nerves. "Five years isn't that long a time, Ian," I managed.

"No, it isn't. And yet sometimes it can seem like you're an entirely different person."

I really wanted to puke. Instead, I forced a smile. "I'm looking for flat sandals and a couple of loose sundresses. Then I have to stop at the Pharmacia and buy tampons and condoms. Are you going to help with that?"

He didn't even blink. "I can lend you the condoms."

I didn't blink either. "But I doubt you have tampons."

"Someone might have left some behind."

"I only use a certain brand."

"Oh, really? Are you built strangely down there?"

God, I wanted to slap him. "I'll meet you at the Pelican in an hour," I said, naming our favorite meeting place in an effort to shut him up.

"The Pelican's been closed for ten years now and you know it. The hotel bar will do." And he strode off without a backward glance.

There was no doubt—Ian was winning the battle of wills. I was going to need to keep away from him if I wanted any kind of peace of mind. I still didn't believe he suspected—he was just trying to rattle his detested cousin. Unfortunately, he was doing too good a job.

Not that he'd detested me, but he would once he found out what I had done. We'd always had a wary truce, thrown together by Marcus and Bella's mutual infatuation, and beneath his sharp tongue had been, if not kindness, at least no enmity.

The return of Bella Whitehead was greeted with joy and affection by the merchants, and it had been a simple matter to find a pair of plain, flat leather sandals and a couple of loose cotton dresses. At the last minute, I splurged on a pair of running shoes, cursing myself for not demanding them earlier. Even a style icon could use sneakers, though Bella's probably cost hundreds of dollars.

Which made me ten minutes early to the darkened confines of the old hotel bar, where Ian sat drinking a cup of coffee.

He eyed the small bags I carried, but made no comment, when I'd braced herself for snark. "You want something to drink or shall we head back?"

"Marcus is probably back by now, don't you think?" I don't know why I said it, but the sudden tightening of Ian's jaw almost made me regret it.

"Since I don't know where he's gone, I could hardly guess when he'd return. Are you hoping to rekindle your grand passion?"

"Why not?" I said recklessly. "Maybe we were meant to be together after all." I wasn't quite sure why I said it, I only know I wanted to annoy him, and it worked better than I would have expected.

"He's not your type," he growled.

"Tall, blond, and gorgeous?" I said. "Maybe you think I'd be better off with someone dark and dangerous, like you?"

He'd risen from his barstool, and he stood there for a moment. "At least you recognize I'm dangerous," he said in a dulcet tone that did just what it was supposed to do. Send a shiver down my spine.

The fact that it sent a betraying heat as well only made it worse. "Is that a threat?" I demanded.

He took the packages from my hands. "Now why would I be a threat to you, Bella-Beast?" he said reasonably enough. "Looks like you forgot something?"

"What?" I demanded as we stepped back out in the blinding sunlight.

"Your condoms. If you find yourself overcome with need, you know where to find me."

"I expect Marcus has his own."

He drove even faster on the way back. "This isn't the way back to Mariposa," I pointed out with gritted teeth as we roared up a narrow road.

"I'm taking you the scenic way. You always preferred it."

No, I did not. The road ran along the cliffs overlooking the sea, approaching the house from behind, and it curved and swooped like a roller coaster ride. All three of my cousins had liked nothing better than to drive like hell, and all I could do was hold on and plaster a grim smile to my face. Things hadn't changed.

We'd reached the peak of the hill behind Mariposa, where I half expected Ian to do his patented bat-turn with the help of the emergency brake, but nothing happened. We kept going, higher and higher, and sooner or later we were going to run out of road and I was going to scream.

With a screech of tires, he managed to pull a one-eighty, and I glared at him. My hair was whipping into my eyes, despite the expensive scarf, and enough was enough.

"Could you slow the fuck down," I said tightly as he careened up the narrow road, away from the cliffs.

"No," he said, an odd note in his voice, and I realized his hands were white-knuckled on the steering wheel. "The accelerator is stuck and the brakes aren't working."

I didn't scream, I just stared at the deep trees on either side of the narrow road and knew I was going to die. I ought to tell Ian who I was, I thought in an almost dazed state of mind. It would be very awkward for Bella to come home to find herself dead and buried.

I clutched the seat tighter and shut my eyes. Maybe if I couldn't see it, it wouldn't happen.

"We're not going to die." Ian's rough voice was ruthless, "so don't start looking all tragic."

"Don't look at me!" I screeched. "Watch the road!"

"That's the last place we're going!" he snapped back. "Put your head down between your knees."

"Why?"

"Because we're going to crash, you idiot, and I'm trying to save your life." He put one hand on my neck and shoved me down, then yanked the steering wheel with tremendous force.

I'd never liked thrill rides, and roller coasters terrified me. The only thing that made them bearable was watching, and with my head crammed down beneath the dashboard, I couldn't see a damn thing as we seemed to take flight. I did the only thing I could think of —I prayed, as I felt Ian's hand at the back of my neck, holding me down.

We slammed into something, my head bashed against the dashboard, but we still hadn't stopped moving, though we'd slowed down. I tried to look up, but Ian kept me down as we plowed through what I could only guess was forest, the whip of the branches against the car, the jerkiness beneath the tires as we finally, finally ground to a thunderous stop.

CHAPTER

NINE

I didn't move. There was something warm and wet on my face, but I didn't care, I just wanted to crawl beneath the dashboard and hide.

Ian was swearing. My God, he was swearing with such obscene invention that I was awed, even as his fingers massaged the back of my neck.

"Are you all right?" he asked finally, as I struggled to sit up.

I was right—he'd driven straight into the woods, and the crumpled hood of the Alfa was pressed around a decent-sized tree. The windscreen was gone, the engine was hissing, but we were alive.

"Oh, God!" I cried and would have flung my arms around Ian the Wretch if he hadn't jerked out of the way.

"You're bleeding," he said tersely. "Lie back."

"I bet you say that to all the girls," I mumbled, realizing what the warm, wet stuff was. He didn't wait for me to move, simply pushed me back against the seat, and I would have protested if I'd had the energy.

"Shut up," he snapped.

I opened one eye to look at him. He was unbuttoning the crisp white shirt he'd worn into town, and if my face hadn't been bashed, I would have raised an eyebrow. "You're stripping?" I managed to say, struggling to sit up.

He shrugged out of the shirt and pushed me back again. A moment later the soft cotton was held against the side of my face, and I felt some of the tension leave me. "Am I going to die?"

"No such luck, Bella-Beast." He sounded shaken, something I wouldn't have imagined. "You've got a cut on your forehead that's going to bleed like a son of a bitch, but it's not going to mar your gorgeousness. Maybe it'll even give you character."

I sank back, reaching for the makeshift bandage, only to encounter his hand. He pushed me away. "Just stay still. Someone will be here to get us before long, and in the meantime, I don't want you jarring anything, at least not until we can get you checked out."

"Checked out where? The nearest hospital is forty-five miles away."

"Still talking about miles and not kilometers?"

Shit. I let out an effective moan. I felt as if I'd been put in a blender—my brain and my body were all jumbled, and I was in no shape to carry off an elaborate masquerade with Ian watching me.

Fortunately, he didn't wait for an answer. "There's a clinic in Santa Maria that can take a look at you." I could feel him move, and suddenly he was looming over me, blocking out the light. "Let me see your eyes."

"Leave me alone," I began, but of course, Ian paid no attention, checking one eye and then wiping enough blood away to check the other.

"You look okay—your pupils are the same size," he said.

"And when did you become a doctor?" I grumbled.

"I have my uses." He pressed the shirt against my head again. "Are you feeling sleepy? Nauseous?"

"No," I said grumpily. "I'm fine. I just got a knock on the head, and that'll be fine if I get some ice for it. I'm fine."

"You're fine," he echoed, his voice mocking. "At least you aren't crying."

I'd been very much on the edge of tears but that brought me up short. Not that I should care one way or another about Ian's contempt for me—nothing would change that.

"I hear the truck. Just lay still and try not to bleed anymore, okay?" Was there a tender note in his gruff voice? Of course not—there couldn't be. Not from Ian the Wretch.

Even I could hear the rumble of the truck, and I wondered if it was the same one he'd used when he picked me up at the airport. Was I going to be lying in the back among the manure as they carted me off? Ian had already scrambled out of the front seat, and while I could hear the authoritative sound of his voice I couldn't translate his rapid Spanish. My brain felt too scrambled. I reached for my own door, determined to be self-sufficient, but it wouldn't open, and I realized it was jammed up against a sapling.

And then I heard him. Marcus's rich voice, sounding appalled. "Jesus, Ian! Jesus! What the hell happened?"

"Alfa malfunctioned," he said shortly.

I turned, and out of my one clear eye I could see that Marcus's perfect golden tan had faded and he was white with shock.

"But Bella should have been driving. Since when does she allow anyone else to drive her beloved Alfa?"

Shit, I'd forgotten that. Bella'd been a new driver when I left Mariposa—I'd assumed she'd grown out of that possessiveness. Then again, Bella had always been the possessive type, whether something or someone was really hers or not.

Two men had helped me out of the car, and at least I was standing on my own, not wavering, Ian's shirt pressed to my head. "I didn't feel like driving," I said.

Marcus finally remembered I was there, and his bright smile should have dazzled me. It didn't. "Bella, my angel!" he cried. "I was so frightened for you and Ian! What in the world happened?"

"I told you—car trouble," Ian said impatiently. "We need to get her down to the clinic..."

"No need," Marcus said, taking one of my arms and leaning over me in what was supposed to be a comforting gesture. It made me claustrophobic. "I had them send Dr. Madhur up to the big house—he can check her there and that way she doesn't have to go racketing all over the place. You'd rather just go home, wouldn't you, Bella?"

I made the mistake of nodding my head, the pain increasing at the gesture, and Marcus put his beefy arm around me, leading me to a passenger van that looked marginally cleaner than the farm truck. It wasn't until I was tucked into the passenger's seat that I realized we'd left Ian behind.

"Shouldn't Ian be checked as well?"

Marcus gave me his magnificent smile. "You know Ian—unless a limb's been severed, he doesn't take it seriously. He'll be fine. I still don't understand what happened to the car, though. It's been serviced and checked on a regular basis—there's no reason it should break down."

For some reason, I didn't feel like elaborating. My head was throbbing in time with my heartbeat, and I just wanted to curl up and sleep. I roused myself. "It's not good to let cars just sit around. Things can freeze up, malfunction."

"Is that what happened?"

"Ask Ian." I leaned back, a little light-headed as Mariposa came into view. It was early evening, the sun gilding the white stucco walls and blanketing the surrounding olive groves, and I was very tired.

Dr. Madhur was young, efficient, and concerned as he poked and prodded me. Marcus had ushered me up to my room, holding my hand in his big, beefy one while the doctor stitched me up, all the while murmuring comforting words that I didn't want to hear.

"Is Ian all right?" I asked once he was finished with his handiwork and I was bandaged. My clothes were stiff with dried blood, and I felt sticky and just the slightest bit dizzy.

"Nothing bothers Ian," Marcus said heartily, and I wished he'd lower his voice.

"You're going to need to watch her," Dr. Madhur said as he packed up his instruments of torture. "She might have a slight concussion—she really needs to be in hospital for observation."

"She's better off here," Marcus said firmly. "We can look after her as well as anyone. We'll take turns."

Dr. Madhur grumbled under his breath like an old man. "You'll need to wake her every hour to make sure she's still alert, and keep the wound iced. Call me if she has any nausea, if her pupils are of a different size, call me if anything seems wrong."

"Ian's a trained EMT," Marcus said. "I'll call him if there's trouble. She'll be fine. She's very dear to us all—we won't let anything happen to her."

Bella was very dear to them all, not me. For one horrified moment, I wondered whether I'd said that aloud, but no one even glanced at me, so I assumed I'd just thought it.

"See that she stays quiet and comfortable. No alcohol, small meals, and make sure she's alert. That's the best I can offer."

"She'll be fine," Marcus said with his usual good-humored charm, ushering the doctor from the room, leaving me alone.

I sat up, very carefully, and set the ice pack on the table. I was a mess—my clothes were sticking to my skin, and while he'd cleaned the wound, he hadn't done anything with my neck and shoulder. The silk outfit was ruined, not that I cared, and I wanted nothing more than one of the loose cotton shifts I'd bought. They were probably still in the smashed Alfa, but I was damned if I was going to lie around in the heat like this. No one had even opened the casement windows to let the evening breeze in, and I was hot and miserable.

Reaching for the pearl buttons, I began to undo them, one by one, and I'd just finished when the door opened again, without warning, and of course it just had to be Ian.

I quickly yanked the blouse back around me. "You could knock," I said in a cranky voice.

"And you could wait for help," he replied, shutting the door behind him and moving into the room. He looked completely unruffled after our harrowing afternoon, and I wanted to kick him. For some reason, I always wanted to kick Ian the Wretch.

"Go away," I grumbled, glaring at him.

"No." Fortunately he went straight to the shuttered windows and opened them, and the resulting breeze blew over my overheated body like a blessing. "Lie back down."

"Go away," I said again.

"Lie back down or I'll make you." He disappeared into my bathroom and I could hear the water running. I lay back on the bed, not because he told me to but because my head ached.

A moment later he was back with a pile of towels. "Move over," he said. "I need to clean you up."

"Absolutely not! I can take care of myself," I protested.

"Not right now, you can't, and there's no female around to preserve your modesty. Valerie has gone for a hike, and Mary Alice says she faints at the sight of blood, which I find hard to believe. Besides, your modesty doesn't exist and never has. I've lost count of the number of times you've stripped down in front of me to swim nude, not to mention the many views I've had of your ridiculous tattoo."

Ice sliced through my veins. "My tattoo?" Bella had never mentioned that she'd acquired a tattoo.

He sat down beside me, so close his hip touched mine, and I quickly scuttled out of the way. "The bird in the bush. The hummingbird in your pubic hair, though come to think of it, last time you stripped down, you'd shaved everything. Sort of ruined the effect."

I just stared at him with glazed eyes. How could Bella have forgotten to tell me? Why had she insisted on buying me string bikinis that I would never have worn in the first place? What if I'd been braver than she thought?

Coming here had been far more adventurous than I would have

thought myself capable, and Ian was right. Bella had always been an exhibitionist, and off the top of my head I could think of no reason why she might have changed.

"Maybe I just don't want you ogling me," I said stiffly.

"You want everyone to ogle you, Bella-Beast. Especially me." Before I could ask him what he meant, he'd reached for the ruined blouse and slowly pulled it away from my skin. It stuck for a moment, then came loose, and I let out a little gasp.

"Did I hurt you?" Oddly enough, he sounded as though he actually cared one way or the other.

"No. Look, can't you just let me...?"

He pushed the blouse off my shoulder, and my head hurt too much to fight him. I let him divest me of the blouse and then I lay back against the pillows, clad only in my lavender lace bra. He wasn't getting my pants off me, but I could still be glad I hadn't worn the matching thong—butt floss was not my idea of comfort.

The warm, wet towel felt like heaven against my skin, and I let out a sigh of pure pleasure, closing my eyes in appreciation. In the long run, Ian was going to do what he wanted, and it was a waste of time to fight him. I simply stayed still and let him wash the blood from my body with the lavender-scented soap that had always reminded me of Mariposa.

I lay back against the pillows again once he'd done, only to feel his hand beneath my bra strap. I slapped it. "We can leave the bra on."

"There's blood on it."

"I'll survive."

Dead silence, and I cautiously opened my eyes. He was still sitting beside me, a dry towel in his hands. "So you got a boob job?" he said.

I wished I could remember some of the curses he'd come out with when we'd hit that tree. "Of course not!" I shot back, incensed.

"Well, all my life you've been exposing a rather minimal B cup, and now suddenly you're a generous C. I would have thought you'd go a lot larger if you were going for implants, but I have to say this is a nice improvement."

I slammed my arms over my breasts. "I don't have implants," I said through clenched teeth. "No one gets implants for a thirty-six C."

If Ian had a sense of humor, I might almost think he was smiling. "Then nature has been extremely generous in the last five years."

It took me a moment to realize what his words meant. He was comparing me to Bella and complimenting me, whether he realized it or not. "Thank you," I said stiffly. "I think."

"Oh, you don't need me falling at your feet like everyone else, Bella-Beast."

What would Bella Do? "No, you've never been susceptible, have you?" I managed Bella's husky drawl.

"Only once," he replied.

And my stomach dropped.

He rose then, scooping up the soiled towels and dumping them in the hallway. When he came back, he had a crumpled paper bag in his hand, and he tossed it on the bed. "These should be a lot more comfortable than your usual designer clothes," he said. "There's blood on the bag, but the dresses inside are fine."

I could have kissed him. And then he ruined everything. "I'll be more than happy to take your pants off for you."

"Go away, Ian," I said wearily. "I can take care of the rest."

"Maybe you'd like me to send Marcus back up. He was never very good at a sickbed, but I'm certain he'd love to strip you down and enjoy those new breasts of yours."

"Don't you dare!" I snapped. For some reason, the very thought of Marcus putting those big hands on me made me feel uncomfortable. That was ridiculous—I'd dreamed about those hands, about the body attached to them, for half my life. "I just want to be left alone."

"'Fraid I can't do that, Bella-Beast. We have orders to check on you hourly. For now you can rest, but I'll be back with food before long and you're going to need to eat something."

I wanted to protest but my stomach suddenly perked up at the thought of food. "Do what you must," I said in resigned tones, and without a backward glance, he headed for the door. I waited until he'd reached it, then my damnable conscience once more reared its ugly head. "And Ian?"

He turned. "What?"

"Thank you for helping me clean up. And for that matter, thank you for saving my life."

He simply stared at me for a long moment. "Will wonders never cease?" he marveled. "Bella being grateful! Amazing."

A moment later he was gone.

THERE IS ABSOLUTELY nothing worse than being ripped from a deep, comforting sleep, hour after hour. First, Marcus did the honors, trying to engage my sleepy brain in conversation, then Maldonado took over, and I counted my blessings. Valerie appeared sometime in the dead of night, all brisk efficiency, and even Mary Alice wafted in, took a cursory glance, and wafted out. They must have tired of it, because I gratefully sank into a deeper sleep around three in the morning, according to my obnoxiously bright bedside clock, and I didn't even dream.

It was still dark when I awoke next, this time of my own volition, with just the faintest tendrils of light spearing into the cavernous bedroom, but I knew I was no longer alone.

"Ian," I said in a sleep-croaked voice, knowing it was him.

"Go back to sleep," he said. "You're doing okay."

I shifted in the bed. "Then why are you here?"

"Someone needed to look after you. Marcus was ready to bed down beside you, but I decided you didn't need the distraction."

My instinctive relief was a surprise, but I said nothing. "I thought someone was supposed to wake me every hour?"

"We all did. Even Mary Alice deigned to take her turn. The rest of the time it's been me making sure you didn't slip into a coma or something equally gruesome."

"I'm surprised you bothered. Given how much you hate me, I'd think you'd prefer if I never woke up."

"Don't go feeling sorry for yourself." His voice was low in the darkness, almost beguiling. "You've got everyone else at your feet."

"You really do hate me?" I sounded forlorn at the thought, and I could have kicked myself. The middle of the night was a dangerous time for me—I was much more vulnerable. It was Bella he hated, not Kitty. And Bella would never sound forlorn.

I could feel his hesitation. "I don't hate the woman I was with today."

Danger, Will Robinson. I should have ignored it, but I couldn't. "What does that mean?"

"It means that you handled the accident with surprising grace, and you haven't been trying any of your manipulative tricks. I can give credit where credit is due."

I would be a fool to push further, having him start wondering why this Bella was different than the others. I changed the subject. "Marcus said you were trained as an EMT."

"Yes."

Not the beginning of a great conversation. "Why?"

"With an operation this size, you need to have someone who can deal with emergencies. It only made sense."

"And you're very sensible." I said. Cold and sensible and disapproving.

"I do my best. Go back to sleep." His voice wasn't nearly as harsh as it had been. "You need it."

I shifted in the bed again, restless and frustrated. I knew what bothered me, as illogical as it was. I wanted Ian to like me. It made no sense at all; Bella had always mocked Ian the Wretch, and like the little toady I'd been, I went right along with it. I had no reason to change my mind.

And yet I was seeing him differently without Bella's influence. He no longer seemed overshadowed by his conventionally handsome brother, and he was surprisingly human once you got past his sarcasm. And there was the kiss. One mustn't forget that. As if there was even the slightest possibility of doing so.

Despite the shock of it, it had been the best kiss of my life, and I still didn't know why he'd done it, why he'd kissed Bella-Beast, the bane of his existence.

"Why did you kiss me?" The words were out before I could stop them.

He laughed in the darkness. "What made you think of that? Were you wanting more? Sorry, I don't think it's a good idea until we're certain your head's okay."

I ignored his attempt at provoking me. "I was curious."

There was a long silence, as the predawn light began to slowly infiltrate my bedroom. "I wanted to see if you tasted the same as the last time I'd kissed you."

Ian had kissed Bella! It was inconceivable—Bella had delighted in teasing him. But what had he said before? Something about not being impervious on one occasion. The very thought was unsettling. For some reason, I felt as if they'd both betrayed me.

"Do you want me to kiss you again?" His voice was very low, enticing.

"No, thank you," I said politely, though it was an effort to keep my voice light. "In fact, you can go away now."

To my shock, he rose, appearing out of the shadows, tall and lean. He was barefoot, dressed in jeans and an unbuttoned chambray shirt, and for what might be the first time, I realized how handsome he was. Not a perfect blond god like Marcus, all rippling muscles and shining teeth and bewitching blue eyes. No, Ian had a more subtle beauty. It was in the way he carried himself, the lines of his face, even the impatience in his dark eyes. It seemed as if he were always impatient with me, and I couldn't blame him. I was just as frustrated.

We were never going to be friends.

He moved over to the bed, and all my senses went into overdrive, while my brain went sailing out the window. Was he going to touch me? Kiss me?

Apparently not. "I'll be driving you into the clinic later today, just to make sure you're completely all right. Don't bother arguing."

I wanted to. Still, where would the harm be? Bella hadn't been around for five years, and it was clear last night that the doctor hadn't known her.

But the real Bella wouldn't want to go off with Ian. "Couldn't Marcus take me?" I demanded, mostly because I wanted to see his reaction.

He didn't give me one. "Suit yourself. I'll give him a heads up."

Rats. I didn't want to drive all the way over to Santa Maria with Marcus, and I wasn't going to worry about wondering why. "Maybe you'd better drive me," I said reluctantly.

He was starting to leave, but he stopped and looked at me. "Don't you need Marcus for your daily infusion of flattery? You can't expect it from me."

"You mean you don't find me attractive?" I managed a lazy drawl. The sun was brightening beyond the windows and I could see him more clearly. This was what Bella would do, taunt him and toy with him. And of course he found me attractive, everyone found Bella attractive, and I was wearing her mask.

He looked me up and down, a considering expression on his narrow, clever face, and I suddenly regretted my question. "Do you want me to?"

His words hung in the air, a taunt, and I could feel my face color. Bella would never blush—I expect she was constitutionally inca- pable of doing so. "Hardly!" My voice was haughty. A sudden thought struck me, and I said it before I could think better of it. "I remember you had a mad crush on me when you were younger. I just wasn't sure you'd outgrown it."

He took a step toward me. "I outgrew it long ago, Bella."

"Then what was the real reason you kissed me?" I demanded, beyond frustrated.

His smile was slow, wicked, reaching his eyes. "You're just going to have to figure that out, aren't you?"

I stared at his retreating figure and I wanted to throw something at him. He just would have laughed, so instead, I slumped back down in the bed, ignoring both my headache and the weird, restless feeling that infused my body. Ian the Wretch was living up to his name, curse him. Even Bella at her grandest hadn't been able to vanquish him, and I was small potatoes compared to her. In a battle of wills, I would never win. The best I could hope for was a draw, and I was determined to wrest that much from our contentious interactions. I'd grown a lot stronger in the last twelve years—I might not win in our battle, but neither would he.

I shouldn't have been able to fall back asleep, given the emotions running through me, but it wasn't even full light. I drifted off, only to be jerked away by Marcus bounding into my bedroom like an athlete about to take the field.

He was gorgeous in the full sunlight, wearing a pale pink polo shirt and white jeans that fit his massive thighs and tight ass. "Bella, my sweet! How are you feeling?" His voice was very loud, and the fading trace of my headache flared for a moment.

"I'm good," I said in a softer voice, trying to contain his puppy-dog enthusiasm. "I just need my coffee."

"Of course you do. And Granda wants us to have it with him, so I thought I'd hurry you along. Do get dressed, that's a good girl, and we'll see what the old man wants."

I didn't like being told to "be a good girl" and I was instinctively wary of anything Granda might want to discuss with us both. "Will Ian be there?"

"Ian? Why would you care where Ian is? You never liked him."

The last time I kissed you. Ian's words stuck in my head, along with the accompanying annoyance. Bella must have liked him well enough at least one time. In fact, it had driven Bella crazy that she could never charm Ian the way she charmed everyone else.

I gave him a cheerful, entirely false smile. "I don't. I was just curious."

Marcus shrugged. He had a swimmer's build—massive shoulders and chest, lean hips and long, muscled legs. He was every woman's fantasy. Why was he no longer mine?

At least that made my life easier. "I'll need a few minutes to get ready," I temporized. "Why don't you go on up?"

"You'll need an hour or more, and I don't want to be the focus of Granda's attention for that long. He always looks as if he's expecting more from me."

Bella never hurried for anyone but herself, but I was too restless to spend an hour primping. "I'll be ready in half that time."

"Then I'll come back and accompany you. Always the gentleman, you know," he said brightly.

I didn't really need another shower but I took one anyway, washing the last of the blood from my bleached and permed pre-Raphaelite curls. It was a lucky thing I wore my own wavy hair in a long braid—Bella without her signature curls would be a lot harder to pull off.

I couldn't get by without changing my contacts and doing a quick version of Bella's elaborate makeup routine. My face was thinner than hers, my cheekbones higher, my mouth wider. Makeup could take care of most of that, and the simple fact that they expected me to be Bella would take care of the rest.

And yet for some reason, I was feeling less confident in my disguise. I needed to finish up and get out of here. My car was now crashed, but I expected I could talk Marcus into finding me some transportation. I needed to get away from Mariposa and the thousands of stolen memories. I needed to get away from Ian's dark, assessing eyes. I needed to get away.

CHAPTER
TEN

By the time Marcus reappeared, I was ready to climb the walls in my need for coffee, and all his flattering smiles didn't do nearly as good as one hit of caffeine would. The halls at Mariposa were wide, and I knew perfectly well where I was going, but Marcus insisted on securely tucking my arm in his, and I didn't want to get into a wrestling match. I gave in and let him drag me up to Granda's suite, ignoring his cheerful banter.

My mood lightened when I saw my grandfather—his color was better, he was sitting up, and if the dishes in front of him weren't empty, it was still clear he'd eaten something.

"It took you long enough," he grumbled as a greeting, but that was typical. "Were you too canoodling in the halls?"

"Canoodling, Granda?" Marcus echoed with his hearty laugh.

"Marcus and I are simply friends, Granda," I said firmly. "Nothing more."

"You're cousins."

"Not technically."

"Close enough," Granda snapped. "Get the girl some coffee, Marcus. Don't you have any manners? And get one yourself."

Marcus jumped to attention, heading to the carafe and filling two delicate cups, when I was desperate for an Americano Grande. I took a sip of the weak stuff, wanting to moan in desperation. "Are you going to have any?" I said, draining the coffee.

"Naaah, I can't stand that caffeine-free crap," he said carelessly.

I almost choked. "Then why are you giving it to me?" I demanded. "I need caffeine, lots of it."

"Ian says you should keep away from caffeine until you've had a full evaluation—it's bad for concussions."

At that moment, I would have done anything I could to give the interfering Ian his own head injury, but I merely gritted a smile. I could make my own coffee, or even chew on beans if I must. I needed my caffeine.

I did my best not to appear caffeine-deprived, taking the seat beside Granda. "How are you feeling today?"

He reached out his hand for me and I took it. It was a frail hand, liver-spotted, when they used to seem huge and strong to me. "The better for seeing you," he said, and there was real love in his eyes, love that I hadn't seen in so long. Love that wasn't meant for me. And then he turned and glanced at Marcus, no longer looking quite so sentimental. "I've been wanting to talk to the two of you for some time, but with both of you gallivanting all over Europe and never coming home, I've had to wait, almost too long."

"We're here now," Marcus said soothingly. I said nothing. I had a bad feeling about this, and I didn't want to encourage him.

Marcus, however, seemed more than happy to listen, moving to Granda's other side and dwarfing the pale thin hand with his own huge one. "We're listening," he continued in a voice that was positively unctuous, "and we'll do whatever you want us to do."

"That's what I wanted to hear." Some of the tension left Granda's frail body, and he squeezed my hand. "You two belong together, you always have. I could leave this life peacefully if I knew you two had gotten over your petty squabbles."

Carefully, I withdrew my hand from his. "I have no argument

with Marcus," I said. "Any trouble we had is long in the past and forgotten."

"Good." Augustin Whitehead settled back against the snowy white pillows, a look of peace on his lined face. "We can have the ceremony as soon as I can arrange it."

"What ceremony?" I demanded, suddenly chilled.

"Your wedding. You know that was always meant to be, you and Marcus, Kitty and Ian."

"Kitty..." I choked, more horrified at that than my sudden assumed nuptials. "Ian hates Kitty and she hates him." Was this a trap? "Besides, they haven't even seen each other in the last twelve years."

"That's neither here nor there. Kitty left, and she couldn't even return when I'm on my deathbed, and there's no excuse of a crazy mother to stop her from coming. And Ian's been working like a dog —he'll be more than adequately recompensed, no matter what an ungrateful young woman has to do with it. It's you two I'm worried about, and the solution is obvious."

"I'm not getting married," I said firmly.

Granda's patrician face looked thunderous. "Then you can leave and never come back."

I released his hand and pushed back from the bed, outraged before I remembered that this was Granda, full of bluster and threats that never came through. Except in my case.

I managed a brittle smile. "You don't want me to go, old man, and I'm not leaving you. You can't bully me into doing what you want, so why bother?"

Granda gave a rusty chuckle. "You always did stand up to me, Bella. It would make things so much easier if you simply married Marcus. You could always divorce him after I'm dead."

"You're too wicked to die," I said, and for once, I was enjoying my Bella masquerade. As a teenager, I'd never dared contradict Granda the way Bella did, and it gave me a blissful sense of freedom.

Marcus had come around my side of the bed, taking my hand in his much larger one. I tried to pull it away, but he squeezed it painfully, in warning. "I'll talk with her, Granda. I'll woo her properly, so she can't resist me."

"You do that, Marcus." He sank back against the pillows, clearly exhausted, but he managed to peer at me suspiciously. "Unless you'd rather have Ian?"

I laughed, trying to cover my start of surprise. "I'd rather marry a rattlesnake."

"And I don't think you'd get Ian to agree with you on that one, Granda," Marcus said jovially. "We'll let you get some rest."

Granda waved a weak hand of dismissal, and a moment later we were out in the hall, the door closed firmly behind us.

"We need to talk," Marcus began, still holding my hand in his tight grip.

This time I yanked it free. "We do not. I hate to tell you this, Marcus, but I'm not marrying you!"

"Why not? It would solve everything, and you know you've always loved me."

Podge had always loved him. Maybe Bella had too. But I'd come back to Mariposa to lay my troubled past to rest, and my passionate crush had died long ago, without a stray spark remaining. He was a very handsome, very charming man. I'd take Ian before him, any day.

I'd take Ian. The thought was so absurd I should laugh. But for some reason, I didn't find it funny. *I'd take Ian.*

"Just hear me out," Marcus said, crowding in on me. I was a good five feet seven but Marcus was over six feet and a whole lot of muscle looming over me, and I didn't like it.

"I don't..."

"I'm not saying we have to get married, though I can't see what harm it would cause. As soon as Granda dies, we can get an annulment. No harm, no foul."

"No!"

"Well, consider this. We could agree to get married, act all lovey-dovey, and start planning a giant wedding here at Mariposa, and

Granda will die a happy man knowing his precious Bella is tied to this place." There was something about his tone of voice that surprised me when he said "this place."

"I thought you loved Mariposa," I protested.

Marcus shrugged. "I'm not like my brother. I don't like to work all the time. I've put everything into this place for the last ten years and I'm sick of it. As soon as Granda dies, I'm out of here."

"Leaving the place to Ian to run by himself?"

He shook his head. "He's leaving this place to the three of us. Ian couldn't buy us out if we want to sell, and that's exactly what I'm planning. And I can't see you spending any more time here than you have to."

I kept my expression blank as my stomach churned in disgust. Granda loved this place with a fierce passion—it would destroy him to know that Marcus planned to split it up.

Then again, the fourth grandchild wasn't one of the heirs—it wasn't up to me to save it. But I wasn't about to help Marcus gut the place.

I pushed away, starting down the hallway. "I don't want to talk about this...."

"Come on, Bella," he said, catching my arm, and a moment later, I was hauled against his big body, his mouth on mine.

For a moment I froze. I had ached for this, with all the lovesick longing in an adolescent girl's heart. But I was a grownup now, and his big hands were kneading my ass, his tongue was slobbering in my mouth, and his groin was pushed against mine.

"This looks cozy," came Ian's drawling voice. "Is the engagement back on?"

Marcus's grip slackened, and I ripped myself away, surreptitiously rubbing my hand across my mouth. "No!" I said, at the same time came Marcus's "yes."

"You make a lovely couple," Ian said in that snarky voice, but there was an odd expression in his dark eyes. If I didn't know better, I would have called it anger.

"We're not a couple and we're not going to be," I said, but no one seemed to be listening to my protests.

"Do I get to be best man?" Ian asked his brother, ignoring me.

Marcus was looking pleased with himself, as if his kiss had sealed the deal. "Hell, no. I can't have a best man who hates my bride."

"Oh, I don't hate her," came Ian's sinuous voice. "In fact, ever since she's returned to Mariposa, I find her quite fascinating."

I *was* going to throw up. What the hell did he mean by that? Did he suspect something?

I needed to get away from them, Without a word, I stalked away, turned the corner, then broke into a run, wanting to get as far from the brothers as I could. This had become a mess of monumental proportions, with Ian distrusting me, Marcus idiotically convinced he was God's gift to women, and my inability to escape. Bella was going to come back to a real mess. It would serve her right.

Funny, we never talked about what would happen when she returned. They were used to my face now, and it passed muster given the lapse of five years and my supposed nip and tuck. What were they going to think when the original showed back up?

That would be her problem. All I needed was to get the hell out of there, and that's exactly what I would do. I had to see the doctor down in Santa Maria de Fe. Surely I could slip away then.

It was a cooler day, a respite from the blazing heat we'd had so far, and while I would have loved to wear one of the new sundresses, I decided I'd better keep it relatively formal if I was going to end the day in Paris. Bella had made me buy a silk tea dress that was the very definition of a "frock", and I grabbed the large leather satchel that was supposed to hold the iPad that had been part of my gear. I shoved my passport, reservations, credit cards, and wads of extra cash Bella had insisted I carry before heading downstairs for my ride to the village. Maybe I'd be in luck and Maldonado would drive me.

Luck seemed to have abandoned me since I arrived back at Mariposa. Ian was waiting for me, in jeans and a chambray shirt, his hair wet from a shower, his expression cynical as he took me in.

"We're going to the clinic, not have lunch with the queen," he grumbled.

"I like to dress well," said the woman who lived in jeans and sweats.

"The people around here will think you're putting on airs."

I didn't show my sudden pang. I summoned my inner Bella. "I don't care what they think. I'm not going back upstairs to change because I intimidate you."

It was a mistake. His gaze narrowed, and he moved closer, and I swear I could feel his body heat through my silk dress. "Intimidate is hardly the word," he said softly.

How could Ian the Wretch feel so seductive? I straightened my back, glaring at him. "Then what is the word? Annoyed? Contemptuous? Suspicious?" Jesus, why had I thrown that word in there? I quickly followed up, "Angry? Jealous?" I was digging myself in deeper.

"Jealous, Bella-Beast? Who would I be jealous of?"

"Your brother," I said flatly. "He's always been taller, better-looking, more charming..."

"More charming? Does that mean you think I have even the slightest amount of charm myself?" There was laughter behind those dark eyes, and I wanted to punch him.

"He has a better smile...."

"With all those big white teeth, the better to eat you, my dear," he crooned. "And he's six two, I'm six three. Granted, I'm not built like a mountain," he added.

I slid my eyes down his lean form with suitable disdain. "You're not," I agreed, trying and failing to sound contemptuous. When I'd been a teenager, I'd been awash with daydreams about broad shoulders and curly blond hair. For some reason, I preferred a leaner frame nowadays.

"But then, you don't seem to be falling at Marcus's feet no matter how hard he tries. Could it be that you're ready to give his little brother a chance?" he purred.

"Over my dead body," I snapped.

All of a sudden his humor vanished, and his dark eyes were flat with warning. "If I were you, I wouldn't toss that option around too carelessly. Accidents can happen—just look at yesterday."

"Is that a threat?" It came out an undignified squeak.

"Let's just say it's a heads up. I'd rather you came to your senses than end up as Marcus's leftovers."

"Marcus loves me!" I shot back, defensive. It wasn't as if I wanted Marcus to love me, but old habit made me defend him. I couldn't believe Marcus had an evil bone in his body, and he truly loved Bella. He always had.

That it shifted so easily to my pale copy wasn't encouraging, but in the end it wouldn't matter. I'd be gone.

"So he does," Ian agreed, an odd expression in his eyes. "You're not in love with anyone else?"

"Of course not!" I said a little too quickly.

"So, give the old boy a break and marry him. You'd always planned to, and he'd be your boy toy for the rest of your life."

"He's three years older than I am," I shot back.

"Two, but who's counting? I love my brother, but he'll always be someone's boy toy. Why not yours?"

Damn, I had to stop forgetting Bella was a year older than I was. "Because I don't want him," I said flatly, firmly. "Did you know he's planning to break up Mariposa? To force a sale?"

"I know. And why would you care? I would think that was what you wanted as well."

Of course Bella would want it. She'd take her money and never look back once Granda had gone.

I said nothing, neither agreeing nor disagreeing. Instead, I glanced up at the clock set in the wall above the recess that held the ovens. "Hadn't we better get going?"

"Your chariot awaits."

The chariot was, in fact, a Mercedes sedan with the Mariposa crest emblazoned on the side panel. Fastening the seatbelt around me, I sighed at the comfort.

"Why didn't you pick me up at the airport in this?" I asked Ian as he slid into the driver's seat.

"The Bella I knew didn't deserve it. You, on the other hand..."

All my muscles froze in sudden panic. "What do you mean by that?"

He glanced at me as he pulled out of the courtyard and his smile was completely innocent. "Just that you've changed, Bella-Beast."

I should let it go, but I couldn't. "For better or worse?"

"Oh, definitely for the better. I could almost like this version of Bella if I didn't know you were a cheat and a liar."

Did he know? It seemed impossible, and yet those words were so pointedly hostile that I wanted to...

Wanted to what? Why would I care what Ian thought of me? He'd always been a pain in the butt, a dark shadow on our sunny, summer days.

Except, I remember, he was the one who first taught me to drive, in a car very much like this one. Bella and Marcus had abandoned me, and I had been sitting in the living room, feeling sorry for myself, when he'd strolled in, the usual scowl on his face.

"Stop feeling sorry for yourself," he'd said back then. "If you smile, I'll teach you to drive the Mercedes."

"Really?" I'd breathed. We'd all been eyeing the new town car lustfully, but only Ian had been allowed to drive it. In fact, up to that time, I'd only driven the old farm truck, and that was exactly twice. I was moving up in the world.

"I figure you deserve some reward for having to put up with Bella and Marcus. Now stop feeling sorry for yourself and get moving."

I'd smiled at him, with all the joy at being offered such a treat could communicate, and yet for a moment Ian had frozen, staring at me in...surprise? Shock?

"What's wrong?" I said uneasily.

The look was gone from his dark eyes. "Nothing," he said flatly. "Come along."

It had been a surprising afternoon—Ian had checked his usual cynicism and unbent enough to be almost...nice. And despite my trepidation, he'd been incredibly patient with me as he let me career around the hilly roads, and if his sneakered foot kept pressing the imaginary passenger side brake, he never said an uncharitable word.

We'd been laughing when we walked back into the house late that afternoon, only to face Bella's accusatory glare, and I remembered my instinctive guilt. Bella despised Ian, and I had just collaborated with the enemy.

And yet all her anger had seemed directed at Ian. "Taking pity on poor Podge, are you, Ian? It won't work."

There were undercurrents that I hadn't understood, but I had no intention of letting them go by. "What won't work?" I demanded, my cheerful mood vanishing.

Bella turned all her attention to me, and her sunny smile wreathed her face. "You'll never learn to drive a Mercedes, Podge. They're too sensitive a piece of machinery. And it's not as if you're ever going to get a chance to again. You'd be better off sticking to the farm truck."

It had been small and mean of her, but then she laughed and the darkness vanished. "Actually, Mercedes are too stodgy for you. If you're really good, I'll let you drive my Alfa."

No one drove her Alfa, and I sincerely doubted I would get that honor, but I knew that was Bella's way of apologizing, and I'd smiled back at her, ignoring her temporary spite.

And now, here I was with Ian once more, though he was the one driving. He probably didn't remember the driving lesson from twelve years ago, when I actually thought I might...like him.

We drove in silence. I leaned back and looked at the view as we wound down to the perfect white village with its spotless houses, the deep blue of the Mediterranean a perfect contrast. I had forgotten how breathlessly beautiful it was, and I could feel my tension begin to fade. How could one feel edgy with all this gorgeousness around?

I turned and sneaked a glance at Ian. If I had to be absolutely honest, I would admit that Ian was part of the gorgeousness. He had more pronounced cheekbones than Marcus, and his dark eyes were oddly compelling. All my life I'd dreamed about Marcus, the perfect man, and now I was reluctantly coming to realize that if I had to choose between one of them, I would go for Ian the Wretch.

Fortunately, both of them were off-limits, even with Marcus's absurd suggestion that we get engaged. He'd been right—we could simply lie about it, wait Granda out, but that was only if I was planning to stay, and I wasn't. I was going to get out of there as soon as possible, hopefully today.

"So when are you and Marcus going to make your happy announcement?" Ian demanded out of the blue, and I jumped, startled out of my daydream. Could he read minds?

"There's no happy announcement. I've told you time and time again that I need to leave, and for some reason you seem determined to keep me here, which is absurd. I'm not going to marry Marcus as a sop to Granda's ambition, and I've been here long enough to say goodbye. If you had any sense, you'd drive me to the airport once we're finished with the doctor."

"If you had any sense, you'd stop fussing about it," he shot back. There was a pause, and he continued in a milder voice. "If you truly have no intention of marrying Marcus, then you should at least come back and explain it to him. To both of them. Granda will sulk, but he'll get over it. He's gotten used to grandchildren who don't do what he tells them to."

"You?" I questioned with real surprise. "Doesn't Granda have final word on everything? He always did."

"He's old. I've been running things for years now, and you know the old man. Sometimes we butt heads."

"I know you," I said.

"Not nearly as well as you think you do, Bella-Beast."

"Don't call me that!"

"What should I call you then?"

I waited, breathless. What if he suddenly said the dreaded "Podge"? Or "Kitty"? For some reason I wanted to hear it in his faintly drawling voice.

"Plain Bella," I said.

"Oh, never 'plain' Bella," he protested. "Not when you've gone to so much trouble to look like this."

My earlier peace had been shattered by his pointed comments. "What do you mean by that?"

"Why, merely the time and effort you take to look so good. Not to mention the surgery."

I was almost stupid enough to ask, "what surgery?" I took a calming breath. "You're right, it requires a certain amount of energy to maintain perfection. After all, I'm twenty-nine years old," I said in triumph, for once remembering that Bella was a year older than I was.

"So you are," he said. "But I wouldn't say you were perfect. There's a trace of the artificial about you that ruins the effect."

He's talking to Bella, I reminded myself, ignoring the odd hurt. He's jabbing at his worst enemy, he's just being Ian the Wretch. I had no reason to feel bad.

"Nature has its way with all of us sooner or later," I said breezily. "Sooner or later, you're going to lose all those brooding good looks and become a podgy old man."

"Brooding good looks? Have you lost your mind, Bella-Beast? I'm your worst enemy."

"Are you?"

His expression gave nothing away. "That's for you to determine. And who are you calling podgy? You do like that word, don't you?"

"What word? Podge?" I was demeaning Bella in his mind now, and I gladly threw myself under the bus. "It's a useful word. It was Podge's own fault that she got all butt-hurt about it."

His eyes narrowed. "Kitty said it never bothered her."

"If you believed that, then you're a fool. No young girl wants to be called fat, even if she knows she isn't!" In fact, the baby fat I'd held on to was merely a few pounds heavier than Bella's naturally willowy frame, and she'd simply been joking, hadn't she? And yet now I could finally admit it had stung.

"Then why did you call her that?" he shot back.

I wasn't sure whether I wanted to laugh or to cry. Ian was defending me, when all those years I thought everyone was oblivious to the cruelty of the name. Obviously, Bella was—I'd let my own feelings cloud my portrayal and I shouldn't have.

"Oh, she and I had a talk about it," I said airily. "All is forgiven." In fact, I had forgiven Bella, over and over and over again.

But I was finding out new things during this masquerade, and I wondered whether I could ever forgive her again.

BY THE TIME I finished at the brand-new clinic in Santa Maria de Fe, I was feeling much more positive about Dr. Madhur. "If it's a concussion, it's a mild one," he pronounced, after checking everything under the sun. "Stay away from alcohol for the next couple of weeks, and be aware of any confusion or odd behavior, but you should be just fine. Call any time if you have concerns."

"What about caffeine?" I demanded, still holding a grudge.

"There's no reason why you can't have caffeine. Just moderation for a while, and you should be fine."

"Tell that to Ian." At least I'd kept Ian at the examination room door when he'd been entirely prepared to follow me inside. I slid off the table with a breezy smile. "I don't suppose you have a back entrance to this place, do you?"

Dr. Madhur raised an eyebrow. "Not for patients," he said stuffily.

"But I could leave that way if you turn your back, couldn't I?" I smiled my best Bella-smile, all charm, and the doctor nodded.

"Why are you avoiding your cousin? Do you feel safe at home?" he asked, focusing on me, and I wanted to laugh. Ian might be a wretch but he would never be physically abusive.

"I have some personal shopping to do, and I don't want him tagging along," I said breezily. "I'll catch up with him in town."

"And what am I supposed to tell him?"

"The truth," I said cheerily. "But give it as long as you can."

He agreed, reluctantly, and five minutes later, I was strolling along the waterfront, the smell of the sea strong in the air, as I tried to figure out my escape.

But for once, luck was on my side. There was a car rental place, so small that no vehicle was immediately available, but it would be within the hour, and I was counting on Ian's bad temper at being abandoned to slow him down. I just needed a little more luck and I would be driving north toward the airport, where I could ditch the rental and get my butt to France, away from the crazy Whitehead family and all their drama.

Except that I was a Whitehead, and I was part of it. I'd been such an idiot to listen to Bella when she showed up at my apartment, but Bella had never had any trouble talking people into doing what she wanted. I'd adored her all my life, in awe of her bewitching charm and silvery laugh, but I was old enough now to know better. Bella could pick up the pieces of the mess she set in motion—I'd be having the time of my life in Paris before I headed home to the mess I'd made.

And if I were fair, I could thank her for this bizarre masquerade. I'd finally, easily, let go of my adolescent passion for Marcus, I'd been able to see Granda one last time, and I'd even made an odd sort of peace with Ian the Wretch. Now if I could just escape, I would count the whole thing a qualified success.

The waiting room at the rental place was small, fly-specked, the shades pulled down against the mid-afternoon heat, and I dug through my bag to make sure I had everything I needed. Credit card, cash, passport, iPad, a change of underwear. I'd left the extra contact lenses behind, which was stupid. Bella's green eyes were legendary, so much more vibrant than my quiet hazel ones, but I doubted that would be enough for them to realize they'd had a cuckoo in the nest. Not exactly a cuckoo—I reminded myself. I belonged there as much as anyone. Granda had even sent Bella to get me, though she'd simply sent me in her place. When I had time, I would be angry about that—for now, I just needed to concentrate on escape.

"Your car is ready, miss," the bored office worker announced, and I rose, my stomach in knots. I wanted this, I reminded myself. I wanted to walk away from Granda and Marcus and most definitely Ian, because there was nothing here for me. Nothing I actually wanted. They would split up Mariposa and sell it, and I had long ago lost any say in the matter.

I headed for the smoked glass door and out onto the portico, to find Ian leaning against the side of the Mercedes, a bored expression on his face.

"You ready?"

I considered my options, which were exactly zero. Glaring at him, I let him open the car door for me as I slid inside. "I can drink caffeine," I snapped as he got in beside me.

"Noted." We drove back to Mariposa without a word.

CHAPTER

ELEVEN

"Bella!" Marcus greeted me with such exuberance that I wanted to wince. I'd gotten used to the low-grade headache that had plagued me after the car accident, but the silent drive back home had shredded my nerves, and all I wanted to do was curl up in a darkened room and not have to pretend to be anyone. "Everything fine at the doctor's?"

"Yes, how are you doing?" Mary Alice was no less strident from her seat on the stiff sofa in the living room. "You look pale."

Before I could answer, Ian stepped in. "The doctor says she's fine. She'll just have a mild headache for a few days."

I was about to object to such a summary dismissal but thought better of it. The more fuss I made, the more closely they would hover, and if I was ever going to get out of there, I would need to convince them that everything was normal.

It was strange, when for so many years I'd wanted nothing more than to return to Mariposa, and now I was desperate to get away. Though in fact, that wasn't strictly true. Mariposa had felt like home from the moment I'd glimpsed it as we came up the drive. It was the two very disparate brothers who were the problem. At this point, I doubted they suspected a thing, but I'd already pushed my luck, and sooner or later I was going to make a major flub. One of them would realize I didn't look quite right, or God, Bella might sashay back, exposing me for the imposter that I was. At this point, I wouldn't put anything past her.

No, I had to get the hell out of here, but as long as Marcus was looming over me with his sunshiny smile and Ian was glowering behind him, I wasn't going anywhere.

"Poor baby," Marcus crooned. "I know just what you need. A quiet dinner *à deux*. I've got it all arranged—we're eating on the terrace overlooking the rose garden. Maldonado has set it up, Selene has gone to a great deal of trouble cooking a glorious meal, and all you need to do is wash and change your clothes and let me ply you with wine and compliments."

"No wine," Ian said sharply. "It might only be a slight concussion, but she needs to stay away from alcohol for the next two weeks. She can drink Diet Coke. With caffeine," he added, snarky as ever.

"I think I'd rather just go to bed," I said weakly, but Marcus overrode me.

"You'll be fine! It'll be very quiet and low-key, just the two of us." Since Marcus's idea of quiet was a muted bellow, I didn't hold out much hope, but Marcus didn't take no for an answer. "I'll even ask Selene to make it an early dinner—I know you prefer to eat at nine o'clock, but Ian's right, you need to not push yourself."

"I don't think I said that," Ian said. "But in fact, it's true. Why don't you give her a raincheck? She's not going anywhere."

Did I imagine the malicious threat beneath that? My irritation flared. Putting Marcus off for even a night was like trying to shove a hippopotamus into a playpen, so I summoned a weak smile. "Dinner tonight sounds lovely."

Marcus beamed, and once more guilt assailed me. He thought I was Bella, the woman he'd loved all his life, when I was nothing more than the plainer, paler doppelganger. "Wonderful! We can talk about old times!"

Shit. "Let's not," I said. "Let's just talk about the future."

"Exactly what I wanted you to say," Marcus said, his smile exposing every single one of his perfect teeth, and I wanted to groan.

"Sounds like it'll be a lovely evening," Ian drawled. "I won't be joining you two, thanks for asking. Young love gives me hives."

"And Valerie and I can look after ourselves, I suppose," Mary Alice said in a long-suffering voice. "We wouldn't want to interfere in your plans." She looked like she wanted to do exactly that.

Marcus startled, looking guilty. "You're welcome to join us if you want, all of you. I was thinking a moonlight dinner would be romantic, but I would never think..."

"Don't worry about it," Ian cut him off. "I made arrangements when I was in town for a romantic dinner myself. I expect to be fully occupied."

And there it was, that slash of pain and something else, something I refused to recognize. I was going to be fending off Marcus's advances while Ian was in bed with that glorious creature I saw the first night I got here. Or maybe someone else—there was no reason to suppose he was in a monogamous relationship, and for some reason that made me feel even worse.

"I'll just go upstairs," I said faintly. "You're right—a shower will do wonders. What time should I be ready?"

"We'll eat at nine. There's time for you to take a short rest before you spruce yourself up. I'll come and get you."

Spruce myself up? Slightly bedraggled Bella was still miles ahead of plain old Podge, and I wanted to kick him, until I saw Ian's smirk. Plastering a charming smile on my face, I nodded. "You'll get the works, Marcus."

"I can't wait."

I really wanted to leave Ian with some parting shot, but everything I could think of gave away too much, so I simply tightened my smile and took off, not relaxing until I was through the door into my room. I slumped down on the floor in relief, leaning my head against the thick, solid door, and let the tension just drain out of me. It wasn't that bad. So Ian knew I wanted to leave—I'd already told him that any number of times, but he was determined to keep me here for Granda's sake. He had no suspicions, no ulterior motives—how could he? I should just relax and enjoy myself in the warm, spring weather. Back in Hanover they'd still be getting frost.

I could see an advantage to all Bella's elaborate potions and preparations. By the time nine o'clock rolled around, I felt unrecognizable beneath the mask of makeup and crimped hair—the real Kitty was deep inside where no one would ever find her, not through the tinted contact lenses or the lipsticked mouth or the arched eyebrows. I was an actress, playing a role, and no one was going to get hurt, except, quite possibly, me. I could handle this.

Marcus's approximation of a gentle knock thundered at my door, and I opened it quickly, determined to get this evening over with, when Marcus looked me up and down with a low, appreciative whistle. "You do clean up well, Bella," he said, holding out his arm. He was wearing a pink linen jacket that accentuated his golden tan, and I knew a million women would be on their knees in gratitude for the promise of a night in his company. It was just too bad I wasn't one of them.

"Could we stop and visit Granda?" I asked, as he led me through the wide hallways and up the tiled staircase.

"He's already asleep," Marcus said, but for some reason the regret in his voice didn't sound quite right. "I told him we were having a romantic dinner and he was very pleased. You know how much he wants us to be together."

I was prepared for this and didn't squirm. "I know."

He drew me out onto the third floor terrace, and the setting was almost laughably romantic—the candlelit table for two, the wine chilling in a silver bucket, the soft sounds of canned music in the background. It was probably called "Music for Seduction" but it was just the sort of gloppy, sentimental mush I hated. Play me a little Marvin Gaye and "Sexual Healing" and I might have even jumped Marcus's bones. If Ian had set up a romantic dinner, the soundtrack would probably include something down and dirty like "Closer" by Nine Inch Nails.

I laughed, when I really shouldn't have, and Marcus pulled me around, a confused expression on his face. "What's so funny?"

"Nothing." I quickly controlled myself. "I was just thinking of something highly unlikely."

Marcus didn't appear particularly pleased with my answer, but a moment later, he plastered his suave smile across his face, the one that used to make me go weak in the knees. "I don't want you thinking about anything but me tonight," he said in a low, seductive voice, and I just managed to hide my knee-jerk reaction. Marcus was a young girl's dream. He was a grown woman's...nightmare would be too harsh, but I couldn't think of any other word. I had plenty of things to think about besides him, things that I'd rather think about.

The evening moved at an excruciating pace, but I played my role perfectly. Marcus's conversation alternated between showing off and showering me with effusive compliments, and I simpered appropriately, letting the words wash over me and paying them no attention. In this case, I was doing exactly what Bella would do—she was so used to being beautiful that she didn't need fulsome praise to shore up a flagging ego. Selene had outdone herself with the food, and I ate quietly as I listened to Marcus's opinions on music, movies, politics, money, marriage.

I heard the last one with increasing edginess. Surely I had made myself perfectly clear, but then Marcus's handsome head was a lot thicker than I remembered. He waited until we were eating *leche frita*, the famous fried milk dessert, to finish off the wonderful meal, and then he went in for the kill.

"I'm not taking no for an answer, Bella," he said with what he must have fancied was a winning smile. "This is too important, for Granda's sake. You don't have to marry me, but I'm hoping you will. We belong together, we both know it, and we've wasted enough time as it is."

What Would Bella Do? Would she want to marry Marcus? They'd certainly been devoted enough when we were young, but Bella had barely mentioned him when she showed up at my apartment with this absurd masquerade in mind. The masquerade I'd said yes to, I reminded myself.

Marcus was charging forward. "But if you'd just agree to an engagement, just to make Granda happy... What harm can it do? The old man needs peace of mind, and you know he always wanted us together, just as he wanted Ian and Podge."

"Well, he failed at that, because Kitty and Ian hate each other." I absolutely refused to call myself "Podge."

"I don't think so." There was a sly expression on Marcus's face. "But then, you never paid them any attention."

No, Bella hadn't. And it would serve her right if she made her triumphant return to Mariposa to find out she was engaged to her ex-boyfriend.

But you said yes to this, I reminded myself. I had no right to be angry with Bella—it was my own damned fault. "I'm not going to marry you," I said firmly.

"But will you at least agree to an engagement? For Granda's sake?"

I opened my mouth to answer when I heard a noise. I turned, and Ian filled the doorway, dressed in khakis and an old tweed jacket that had seen better days. He carried a snifter of brandy, and the smile he gave us reminded me of a crocodile.

"Have you two lovebirds worked out the details of your upcoming nuptials?" he said, strolling out onto the candle-lit terrace.

"Ian, tell Bella that she has to marry me," Marcus whined.

I watched him as he came closer, and my fingers curled into a fist beneath the table. "Marcus says you have to marry him," he said affably, and I wanted to slap him.

I turned my back on him, addressing Marcus. "I told you, time and time again," I said wearily. "I'm not marrying you. Our time is over and you know it." At least I hoped he knew it. "And I'm not going to lie and say I'm engaged just to make Granda happy. He'd see right through it."

"He's half blind," Marcus protested. "I never thought you would be so selfish. Granda's given you everything, and now you can't do this one little thing to make his last days peaceful."

There was absolutely no reason for me to feel guilty. "I never thought Granda was so gothic as to want to build a dynasty."

"Then you don't remember Granda," Ian offered helpfully. "He wants the place tied up—if it's split three ways, there won't be enough money to meet expenses with the groves."

I met his dark, cynical eyes. "Then you'll have to figure something out."

The crocodile smile remained in place. "I already have. Since you won't marry Marcus, you'll simply have to marry me."

"What?" Marcus shrieked, pushing back from the table and knocking over his wine. "What the hell are you talking about?"

Ian the Wretch shrugged. "Granda wants a dynasty. You've already blown your chance—the only one left is me. How about it, Bella-Beast? Will you make me the happiest man on earth?"

"Go to hell," I said sweetly. This was the strangest conversation I'd ever had in my life, and I wanted the both of them at the bottom of the ocean. It was a deliberate insult, in Ian's drawling tones, because worst of all, an idiot might think he actually meant it.

"I'm wounded," Ian said, his dark eyes glittering wickedly.

I'd had more than enough for one day. I flung my brandy glass at his head, but he easily ducked, and the fine Waterford crystal smashed against the stone parapet. "I told you not to drink," he said.

In fact, I hadn't touched the brandy that Marcus had insisted he pour for me, but I wasn't going to tell Ian that. "I've changed my mind," I said abruptly, rising from the table, bringing me far too close to Ian. I looked Ian straight in the eyes as I uttered the fateful words. "I'll get engaged to you, Marcus, but that's all. And only for as long as Granda lives."

"That's perfect!" Marcus cried, but I didn't look at him. Neither did Ian. Instead, we stared into each other's eyes, anger sparking back and forth between us. And then he stepped back with a lazy smile.

"May I be the first to wish you every happiness?" he said in a silken tone, raising his glass in mock salute. A moment later, he spun on his heel and was gone, leaving me alone on the terrace with my unwanted fiancé, feeling curiously bereft.

It took me more than an hour to get away from Marcus. First, he had to toast me and my stupid, pride-filled decision, then he had to try to kiss me, and then there was a solid half hour of compliments meant for the real Bella, all while I was trying to escape. I kept seeing Ian's eyes as Marcus rambled on, and for some reason I wanted to cry.

Of course, Marcus insisted on escorting me down to my bedroom, though by that time he was fairly unsteady from all the brandy he'd been drinking. He clamped my arm against his sweaty body and tried very hard to push his way into my bedroom when we got there, slurring all sorts of stuff about how good it could be, and he'd get me to change my mind about marriage. It was like wrestling with an octopus, but I finally managed to escape, and I locked the door behind me. I knew it was a ridiculous precaution—Marcus might be drunk, but he'd never stoop to rape. It was simply that he couldn't comprehend that a woman didn't want him.

I listened to him stumble away before I went to my window, sucking in deep lungsful of cool night air. What in God's name had I done? I'd let bad temper goad me into making a catastrophic mistake, and now I was stuck with it. Honestly, if I had to do something so stupid, I should have simply told Ian that I'd marry him, not his brother.

A shiver ran across my backbone, and I wanted to cry. I wasn't an idiot, and one could only hide from the truth for so long. For some illogical, self-destructive, totally insane reason, I was attracted to Ian. There, I admitted it. Strongly attracted. And that unfortunate truth had to be hidden at all costs. If he had even the slightest inkling, he would treat me unmercifully, as he had teased Bella and me when we were young. If he knew I was...drawn to him, he'd never let it go.

It was perfectly logical. That kiss in his rooms had been a scorcher, unquestionably the best of my entire life. Maybe I'd just been involved with bad kissers in the past—most men I knew weren't that into seduction. Their idea of foreplay wasn't much better than "brace yourself." Maybe it was the jet lag and the sheer shock that Ian the Wretch would kiss me.

Why had I ever said yes to Bella? It had seemed so simple at the time, a chance to say goodbye to Granda and Mariposa, goodbye to my unresolved childhood and my adolescent crush.

That last part was well over and done with—I couldn't even guess what I had once seen in Marcus apart from his dazzling good looks. If I'd had any taste, I would have had a crush on Ian instead...

And there I went again. Ian and I were enemies—I needed to remember that. If he knew who I really was he'd have me out on my ass so fast...

But he didn't know who I was. To him I was Bella-Beast, an object to tease and torment, but marginally one step better than a liar.

I let my head fall back against the heavy wooden door with a thump that didn't do my ever-present headache any favors.

Would this really make Granda's last days happy and peaceful? If it did, then who was I to deny him? Yes, he'd banished me from Mariposa, but he'd also loved me. I shouldn't feel like I owed him anything, but I did, and for him, I could make this minor effort, as long as Marcus remembered that it was all an act, a lie within a lie.

I rose and stripped off my clothes, washed the makeup from my face and popped out the colored contacts, taking a moment to look at my reflection in the mirror. My hazel eyes looked back at me, the scrubbed face that was only an approximation of Bella's flawless beauty. I was a liar and a cheat, and I'd just dug myself into an even deeper hole out of a fit of pique.

I had to get the hell out of here.

CHAPTER
TWELVE

Granda was already sitting up in his massive bed when I went to see him the next morning, a mountain of pillows behind him.

"I wondered when you were going to find the time to come visit me," he grumbled. "Isn't that ostensibly why you're here in Spain?"

Ignoring his complaint, I kissed his papery cheek. "I thought I'd have my second cup of coffee with you," I said, glancing over at the carafe on a side table.

"Decaffeinated swill," he grumbled.

"I agree, but it's better than nothing." I poured myself a cup and moved to sit by his bed. He eyed me suspiciously.

"What do you want from me, Bella?" he said, and those faded blue eyes were a lot sharper than anyone of his age should have. "Why did you come back to Mariposa?"

"You were sick," I said.

"I'm dying. That's never brought you home before."

"How long have you been dying? Five years? Ten years?"

"Saucy minx. The moment we're born, we start dying, but I'll have you know you're not going to have long to wait for your inheritance. My whole damned body is giving in. I'm ninety-four, damn it. I should live to one hundred, but that's not going to happen. At least I'll live long enough to see you married to my grandson."

"Marcus has already been here," I said, more a statement than a question.

"He has. What made you come to your senses? Afraid I wasn't going to leave you any money if you didn't?"

That was Granda. "I don't want your money," I said, one truth in all the lies I've been telling.

He let out a hoot of laughter that devolved into a coughing fit that wracked his frail body, and I jumped up in alarm, looking for a way to call the nurse who looked after him, but he waved his hand at me while he slowly regained his composure.

"I'm fine," he gasped. "For a dying man, that is. Can't think of a better way to go, dying of laughter. We both know you don't have a pot to piss in, and you have a great fondness for your jet-set lifestyle."

"I have a greater fondness for you, Granda," I said firmly, the truth for once, and I was certain Bella would feel the same way.

"Bullshit," he said. "If you'll pardon my French. But I'm forgetting—you've seen the error of your ways and you're marrying Marcus, as you should. You know—I would have thought you'd choose Ian."

It was my turn for a strangled laugh. "Ian the Wretch? Why would you think that?"

"I've seen the way you look at him. Even worse, I've seen the way he looks at you. How does he feel about your marriage plans?"

"I have absolutely no idea. Happy, I suppose," I stammered. Shit, shit, shit, shit, shit. What was Granda telling me? I didn't need him to be feeding my crackpot fantasies.

"Far be it for me to interfere," said the interfering old man. "Just so long as you marry one of them, then your inheritance is safe."

"I'm not marrying... I didn't get engaged to Marcus because you're blackmailing me into it," I said.

"Hmmph. Women love Marcus. You always did have a stupid crush on him when you were a girl. I thought you might have grown out of that, but I'm glad you haven't."

If anyone had had a crush, it was Marcus, following Bella around like a dazed puppy, but I didn't bother to correct the cantankerous old man. "Are we just going to sit here fighting?" I asked, channeling some of Bella's sass. Quiet little Kitty would never be so brash. "Because I can get a better cup of coffee elsewhere."

"I'll behave," he said unexpectedly. "Just tell me about your travels. You must have broken it off with that gangster you were seeing."

That was a shock, and doubtless more of Granda's hyperbole. "He wasn't a gangster," I said instinctively, wondering what the hell Bella had gotten me into this time.

"He runs half the drugs out of Marseilles and you know it. But you were always blinded by a pretty face. It that over with?"

"Of course." Bella had said nothing about her current involvements, but she'd always had a powerful sense of self-preservation. I couldn't imagine her risking everything for a handsome man. "I'd hardly get engaged to Marcus if I were involved with someone else, would I?"

"You tell me," Granda said. "So, when's the wedding?"

"There's no hurry," I said calmly.

"There's every hurry!" he snapped. "I'm dying. I want to make sure everything's settled before I shuffle off this mortal coil. That's *Hamlet*, you know."

"To be or not to be, yes, I know," I replied, letting some of my own irritation loose. "I'm perfectly familiar with the classics."

"Since when? You went to that girl's school for idiots in Switzerland, and then wasted your time and my money in attempting the Cordon Bleu, dropping it when you grew bored."

"They wanted me to butcher a cow," I said, which seemed reasonable enough for a legendary cooking school. "I declined."

"I don't think you've read a book since you were a teenager, not even a trashy romance."

Considering that among my twelve boxes of books was a goodly selection of romances, I said nothing. "Everyone knows *Hamlet*," I said finally, but Granda didn't look convinced.

"When's the wedding?" he demanded again.

"Marcus and I haven't talked about it yet. Next year, some time."

Granda shook his head. "Your fiancé was here before you. He's agreed to next week."

"No," I said immediately, panicked. "I want a big wedding, with a white dress, and lots of guests and champagne."

"And the glitterati of the world. Yes, I'm sure you do, though I would think the white dress would be a bit of a stretch. That's easy enough—you'll have a legal ceremony next week, followed by a religious ceremony the following year. Plenty of people do that—I have no objections."

I looked at the old man calmly arranging my life. "I do."

"Get over them!" he snapped.

"Are you terrorizing Bella again, Granda?" came Ian's drawling voice from the doorway.

"Nothing can terrorize Bella," Granda grumbled. "Tell her she has to marry Marcus next week."

Ian strolled into the room, looking snarky and bad-tempered, his rough work clothes a far cry from Marcus's pale linen. It was only natural that I liked a man who actually did something, not Eurotrash...

"I won't tell her any such thing. She'll marry my brother when she's ready to—you've bullied her enough already."

Granda looked affronted. "Me, a bully? If anyone's a bully it's Bella, taunting me with my fondest dreams and then holding out."

"Too bad, old man. I'm on Bella's side on this one. I don't think she and Marcus are the perfect match you do. Give them some time to make sure they'll do well together."

"I don't care if they do well together!" Granda's voice was rising in both pitch and volume. "I want my inheritance secured. I didn't work all my life just to lose everything."

"You'll be dead," Ian said heartlessly. "You'll have lost everything already. You can't take it with you, remember?"

"My legacy..."

"I'll be here. The olive groves will continue."

"Then why don't *you* marry Bella? I swear I think you're the better match."

"She turned me down," he said lightly, glancing over at me. "Didn't you, my pet?"

I controlled my instinctive glower. "If you don't leave me alone, I won't marry anyone."

"Not even your gangster boyfriend?"

"What gangster boyfriend?" Ian demanded, amused. "How did I miss this?"

"Because you don't pay any attention to gossip," Granda snapped. "She's been cozying up to Stephano Sierra for the last year."

All amusement dropped from Ian's face. "Sierra is no joke."

"I wasn't kidding. When have you known your little cousin to be sensible? Do you see why I want her tied up with one of you? Better than floating face down in some garbage-ridden canal."

"Good God!" I protested. "I'll have you know I'm smarter in my choices than you think. And that's an awfully precise way to go. Which canal?"

"The same one his last girlfriend was found in," Granda said triumphantly. "Did you break it off or did he?"

"It was mutual," I said, hoping I was right. "He has nothing to do with anything."

"Then marry Marcus next week."

"No!" We were glaring at each other, until I finally noticed that Granda was struggling for breath despite his flashing eyes.

"Calm down, the two of you," Ian said in a bored tone. "I'm taking Bella away from you, Granda, so you can both work on your tempers. I must say, Bella, I don't remember you being so argumentative."

I hadn't been. Neither had Bella, so I was relatively safe at this point. She'd always managed to manipulate to get her own way I managed an edgy smile. "Sorry, Granda."

"We can talk about this later," he said, waving a fragile hand in dismissal, and I bit back my demurral. Not even for Granda would I go through a fake wedding. If I'd had any sense, I would have said yes to Ian, just to watch him squirm.

A moment later, I was ushered out of the sickroom, Ian's hand on my arm. "It's not good to rile the old man up like that," he said evenly.

"It's not good to expect me to get married to suit his whims," I replied.

"You already agreed to it. Why the delay?"

I looked up at him, knowing he had no idea that it was Kitty looking at him through the green-tinted contact lenses. Wondering what he would feel if he knew. Disgust, most likely.

The words came out of my mouth...not Bella's...as I looked deep into his eyes. "Do you want me to marry him?"

The hallway was quiet, the silence almost another person with us, and I saw him hesitate, saw the sudden intensity in his dark eyes. He had loved Bella, long, long ago. Maybe he still had some of that jealousy left behind.

And then the moment passed. "It's up to you, sweetheart. You and my brother are made for each other—you'll make gorgeous children. And I learned long ago not to covet my brother's belongings."

"I don't belong to him." I said quietly, firmly.

"Sure you do, Bella. You belong wherever the grass is greenest, and trust me, so does Marcus. Neither of you will have to face any kind of adversity, everything will go your way. I hope you're very happy together."

It was a perfect exit line and he made full use of it, walking away so quickly I couldn't even come up with a response until he was out of sight.

I spent the rest of the day avoiding Marcus, who seemed determined to get me alone in a corner. Keeping away from him was easy enough—I simply walked in the olive groves, breathing in the deep rich smell of the earth, the sweetness of the trees, the fresh breeze carrying the scent of salt up from the deep blue ocean far below.

In the cities, Spain had moved away from the mandatory siesta, but at Mariposa and the small town of Santa Maria de Fe, the old ways ruled, and I stretched my afternoon nap to a solid four hours, determined to resist if anyone came to roust me out of my comfortable perch. I had a blisteringly sexual historical romance to read, a stack of fashion magazines that Bella insisted I carry and which interested me not one whit. It would have been a perfect time to get some work done, but of course I hadn't dared bring any of Katharine Whitehead's academic work. Settling into my comfortable bed, I dove into the story of Kit and Bryony, only to find their searing kisses were making me uncommonly edgy. Once they got into bed, I had to throw the book across the room. Instead of golden-haired Kit I kept picturing Ian, imaging his hands, his mouth...

No, fashion magazines were a safer choice. The clothes were exquisitely beautiful, the sort of thing Bella would wear, the sort of thing I was wearing. I wanted my worn jeans and T-shirts.

At last I slept, and I awoke with a start, the room pitch-black with only the very faintest glow lighting the inky darkness. Moving to the window, I could see the acres and acres of olive groves covering the hills around Mariposa, and far away, I could see past the white buildings of the small town to the dark blue of the night-time sea. Fumbling for my iPhone, I groaned when I saw the time. It was almost nine o'clock, and dinner would be ready unless Mary Alice had once again ordained that it would be early.

Shoving myself from the bed, I stripped off the rumpled linen sundress and went looking for something more appropriate. I took the fastest shower on record, throwing on one of the simple silk dresses that had cost a fortune. I twisted my hair into a knot at the base of my neck and scrambled downstairs.

There was only one place set in the huge dining room, and I

viewed it with relief and annoyance. At least I wouldn't be fighting off Marcus's advances this evening, and I wouldn't have to think about anyone else. The moment I entered the vast room, Maldonado appeared, ushering me in and holding my chair for me, pouring me a glass of Spanish wine with silent deference before disappearing back into the kitchens. I looked around, down the long expanse of empty table, and a weight settled over me.

I scooped up my plate and headed upstairs, arriving at Granda's room a little breathless and a little annoyed. Neither of those were improved when I pushed open the door and saw Ian seated by Granda's side.

"Bella!" Granda greeted me cheerfully enough. "Come to join us for dinner?"

I glanced at the empty dishes on the tray. "Apparently, I'm too late." I took the seat on the opposite side of the bed, carefully not meeting Ian's dark, cynical eyes. "Where's Marcus?"

Granda looked torn between approval and annoyance. "Where, indeed? He's gone off someplace, I don't know where, and a hell of a time for him to go, right before the wedding."

Before I could protest, Ian slid in smoothly. "I sent him, Granda. The Finacci account is in jeopardy, and you know how good Marcus is at soothing ruffled feathers."

"The Finaccis? They're one of our oldest customers—why would they have ruffled feathers?" He paused for a moment, and annoyance crossed his face. "Stupid question—of course it was you."

"Finacci wanted a ridiculous price. I simply told him no. I was very polite, but I managed to rile him anyway."

"I've seen your attempts at being polite." Granda gave a ghost of a laugh. "What price did he want?"

Ian mentioned a number, though I had no idea whether it was bad or good. Granda frowned. "Serves him right then. What's Marcus going to do?"

"What Marcus does best—flirt and flatter until Finacci is

begging to pay us more. My brother is a consummate charmer—how else would he have won his beautiful bride?"

I was so tempted to drop my plate onto his lap, but I simply nodded. "So true," I murmured.

"Which part—that's he a charmer or that you're beautiful?" Ian said.

"Both. I don't take credit for my looks—it's a fluke of nature, and I just count my blessings," I said airily. In fact, it was Bella's hard work that turned me into a stunner—beneath the designer clothes lurked Cinderella, plain old Podge, minus a few pounds, minus the glasses.

"You know what you should do," Granda said suddenly. "You should take Bella out on the town. It would teach Marcus a lesson not to leave his fiancée alone."

"Hardly. I sent him away—if I turned around and poached his fiancée, he would be rightfully pissed."

"It's because you sent him away that you should take her. You know Bella has an insatiable craving for nightlife. Take her dancing down at the *taberna*. We can't have our Bella growing bored."

Ian gave a long-suffering sigh. "All right," he said. "Unless 'our' Bella has changed her ways and would now prefer a quiet night at home."

That screwed me, and I wondered if he knew. If I claimed I'd rather stay home at night, I'd be adding more fuel to the fire of his suspicions. But if I went out with him...

He was watching me, too closely, and I tossed back my head in a patented Bella gesture. "You're not my idea of a perfect date."

"Neither are you. Take your choice—come down to Max's Taberna for a bit of nightlife or curl up with a fashion magazine."

He knew Bella far too well, even down to her choice of reading material. It was a challenge, one I'd be stupid to accept. But then, I hadn't been making overly bright choices for quite a while.

"Max's Taberna sounds wonderful," I said, flashing Ian a defiant smile. "How soon do you want to leave?"

"How soon can you be ready?" He countered my bluff, but I simply preened.

"Half an hour." I rose and gave Granda a kiss on his paper-soft cheek. "See you in the morning."

"Indeed." But the old man looked pleased. I wasn't quite sure why—as far as he was concerned, I was successfully tied to his older grandson. There was no need to throw me at the younger one who'd always despised the woman I was pretending to be.

"I'll have the car waiting," Ian said.

Bella's wardrobe didn't include anything for dancing at the *taberna*, and the best I could find was a form-fitting dress that clung a little too closely to my curves. It was cut too low in the front, but I yanked it up, hoping my breasts would hold it there, grabbed a sweater and some gold hoop earrings, and made it downstairs in twenty minutes.

Of course, Ian was already waiting. He barely glanced at me, and I told myself his lack of reaction was a relief. After all, I knew what I looked like in the mirror, and it was good enough for me.

He, of course, was looking gorgeous in black pants and a shirt rolled up at the elbows, and I remember Max's Taberna was more working class than high society. I was overdressed, but it was too late to do anything about it.

He flew down the mountain at his usual breakneck speed, and I slid back in my seat, occasionally tugging at my neckline to make sure I was properly demure. He said nothing, which was just fine with me—I had nothing to say to him.

It was a busy night at Max's—cars were parked haphazardly all around the low white building, and music and light poured forth with all the energy and gaiety of the Spanish people I loved so well. I could feel my pulse quicken as I climbed from the car, and I gave my neckline one last tug.

"Enough," Ian said in sudden disgust, and a moment later I found myself pushed against the car. "That fucking dress is not a turtleneck no matter how much you pull at it. You've got glorious boobs, but I think I can restrain myself." He yanked the dress into place, showing a great deal of cleavage, and it took everything I had to keep from quickly covering myself like a nervous virgin. Fuck him. I straightened my back and looked him in the eye.

"You can keep your hands off my glorious boobs, thank you very much."

He gave a long-suffering smile. "Your boobs don't interest me," he said flatly.

"Liar. You wouldn't have called them glorious."

"Well, I figured since you put out so much money on enhancing them that I ought to be properly appreciative. They'd look great on anyone."

I contented myself with a snort of disgust, turning my back on him as I headed toward the crowded entrance.

I'd lost track of the days, and I suddenly realized it was Saturday night, time for everyone to kick up their heels. The bar was jammed with people, the dance floor crowded with gyrating couples, but somehow Ian managed to secure us a table, a beer for him and a bottle of soda for me before turning and talking to seemingly everyone there, everyone except me. It didn't improve my mood to see that he was universally liked and respected. In return, I danced with anyone who asked me, moving on the dance floor with sinuous grace, knowing he was watching me. I never caught his eye, but every time I glanced in his direction, he was looking at me as I moved.

I was feeling beautiful, sexual, powerful, and I was besieged with so many partners I barely paid attention to them. This was what it was like to be Bella—to be the center of attention, to be glorious, to be wanted, wanted by every man in the place except the one man I wanted. I whirled from partner to partner, finally sitting one out at the table.

I reached for his bottle of beer but he moved it out of my way. "No alcohol, remember," he said.

"I'm fine," I said airily. "I haven't had a headache all day."

"I don't want to end up carrying you out of here," he growled.

"That's all right. If you don't want to, I'll find someone who does." *Nailed it*, I thought. *That was exactly what Bella would say.*

Flashing him a brilliant, triumphant smile, I left the table, only to find myself in the arms of a stranger, and I danced into the crowd.

I glanced up at the man. He was very handsome, and I should flaunt him, but there was something about him that made me uneasy. I tried to loosen his hold but got nowhere, and I cast a worried glance toward Ian, who was deep in conversation with a pretty girl. Of course he was.

"You are so beautiful," the man said in my ear. I ignored it, as I'd ignored all the other blandishments. He'd pulled me tight against his body, and he smelled like fish and garlic. "I don't know which I want to fuck more, your pussy or your ass."

I jerked, trying to pull away at his crude words, but his grip was iron-hard, as his voice went on in my ear, telling me the things he was going to do to me. I tried to stop dancing, but he moved me, dragging me over the crowded floor, and no one noticed my struggles, my distress. And then came the *coup de grâce*.

"We've done it all before, Bella, and you've gone down on my prick like a hoover. I'm going to make you do it all again, with me, with my men, before I kill you."

CHAPTER
THIRTEEN

I let out a cry, and without thinking, I rammed my knee upward, anything to break the man's grip. I didn't hit him directly, but it was enough that his hold loosened, and I tore myself out of his arms, only to be immediately enfolded in another pair, pressed against another hard body, and I started to struggle.

"Calm down," Ian said in a rough voice. "It's just me."

I sagged against him in relief as unexpected tears filled my eyes, and his arms were safe around me. I was shaking, I couldn't help it. It wasn't simply the filthy words of the man, it was the cold, implacable evil in his voice, so at odds with his angelically handsome face.

"I want to go home," I whispered against his chest.

"We will," he said, his low voice vibrating in his chest, beneath my ear. "But first, you need to tell me what that man said."

I shivered, and his arms tightened, and I felt some of my panic begin to slip away. "Just ...horrible things. Sexual things."

I waited for him to tell me it was my fault, for throwing myself at everyone, for wearing the wrong clothes, for enjoying myself too much, but he said nothing, just holding me against him as my fear and disgust began to fade.

"Is he still here?" Ian said.

I didn't want to lift my head from the safety of Ian's chest, but after a moment I did so, looking at the dancers surrounding me. I pressed my cheek against him once again. "I don't know. I don't think so."

"I'll take you home." He started to release me, but I held on, not wanting to let go.

"Give me a minute," I said, and if he hadn't dropped his head down, close to mine, he wouldn't have heard me. He smelled wonderful, of warm skin and olive trees and the nearby ocean, and I wanted to drink him in. I no longer cared who I was, who knew it. All I wanted to be was a woman wrapped safely in Ian's arms, safe from unnamable threats.

The man hadn't gone. I couldn't see him anywhere as Ian bundled me out of the *taberna*, but I could feel his eyes on me, cold and merciless. I took a quick look back as we left, and I saw him then, staring at me with cold, implacable hatred in his eyes, and if felt like a body blow.

"What?" Ian said, close enough to feel my reaction. "Do you see him?"

"No." I didn't want Ian to get anywhere near him. Ian was a lot taller, and probably stronger, but the evil was so palpable in that man that even Ian might be contaminated. Besides, I didn't need Ian to fight my battles. I had to remember he wasn't on my side.

Even if I wanted him to be.

The Mercedes looked boxed in by the other cars, but Ian tucked me into the passenger seat with surprisingly tender hands, and then proceeded to drive out of the tiny space without touching any of the nearby cars. The warm spring night spread out in front of us, but I couldn't feel it. I was cold inside the car, and wrapping my arms around my body wasn't doing me any good as I shivered.

I tried to tighten my muscles, to keep from shaking, but I was already stiff from fright and disgust. I needed to get home, get away from everyone, and then I'd be all right. Up until then I simply needed to be calm in front of Ian, act like it didn't matter.

And then I started crying. Fuck! Bella would never cry, Bella would laugh at anyone who tried to frighten her like that. She wouldn't have missed his balls when she kneed him; she would have laughed and had another drink and gone on to the next man.

And I was sitting in the darkness beside Ian, shivering and crying like a baby. I could only thank God that he didn't notice.

We were halfway up the deserted road to Mariposa, and I knew I'd manage as long as he didn't look at me, as long as he didn't express any sympathy. Not that Ian the Wretch ever felt sympathy, at least not for my sorry ass. Bella's sorry ass. I surreptitiously wiped the tears from my face, trying not to sniff.

We'd almost made it home when he suddenly jerked the steering wheel to the right, slamming the car into one of the passing places on the road, shoving it into park and turning to glare at me. "Why are you crying?" he demanded, and for some reason, there was real anger in his voice.

I shrank back against the passenger door. I'd had enough, and I couldn't fight back—Bella had left the building. "I'm not," I said stiffly.

He'd undone his seatbelt, and he reached over and flicked mine open before I realized what he was doing, and then he'd pulled me into his arms.

"Damn you, no!" I sobbed, burrowing against his chest. "I'm f-f-fine!" And then I couldn't say anything at all as I wept. I hated it, I hated the weakness, the vulnerability that was wracking me, I hated the real terror I'd felt in that man's arms, I hated the real comfort I felt in Ian's. In a moment, he would push me away, mock me, tease me, and I thought I would shatter if he did.

He didn't. He kissed me. He kissed my face, wet with tears, his mouth warm and hard against my mine, he kissed my eyelids, my cheekbones, and then my mouth, and this time I kissed him back, my fists tight in his shirt, feeling his strong body beneath my fingers, and I pulled at it, wanting it off.

He pulled back, suddenly. "Don't!" he said.

I felt as though I'd been slapped in the face, and I froze. I needed to get away from him, get away from the lies, the deceptions, the old insecurities, and I fumbled for the door, managing to get it open before he reached over me and hauled me back, closing it once more. "Stop being a baby, Bella-Beast."

It was the last straw. I hit at him, trying to break free, but he was too strong, overpowering me, holding me on his lap, and I could feel how hard he was beneath me, I knew how turned on he was, and it made no sense. But it aroused me. "Stop it," he said again, in a different voice.

Neither of us moved, staring into each other's eyes for a long breathless moment. What would Bella do, I thought dazedly, but my doppelganger was nowhere. And I found my voice.

"Make up your mind, Ian. Do you hate me or want me?" My voice was raw but my words were clear.

"Can't I do both?" Releasing my arm, he slid his hand behind my neck, under the thick fall of hair, and pulled my face to his, my mouth to his, and this time he used his tongue.

I wanted to kiss him back. I wanted to straddle him on the front seat of the Mercedes; I wanted him to fuck the fear, the hurt, the lies out of me.

But he'd said no, and I wasn't going to get hurt again. I pulled away, and he made no effort to stop me this time. "Please take me home," I said. My voice was weaker than I would have liked, but I couldn't summon my righteous anger any more than I could summon Bella. "Please."

Without another word, he put the car into gear, and I realized with shock that the motor had been on all this time. Clearly, he hadn't been that blinded by passion.

We reached the deserted stable yard in less than five minutes, and I was out of the car before he could stop me, putting distance between us. "I can't say it's been lovely." My voice was brittle. "Let's not do this again."

"You're forgetting one thing," he drawled, totally unmoved by my iciness.

"What's that?"

"Someone threatened you tonight. There's no one you annoy anyone more than me, and yet I don't want to hurt you. I want to know who does, and why."

"What a compliment. The man was probably just drunk." But I shivered, remembering the specificity of his words. He knew me, he knew what would terrify me, he knew...

And it wasn't until that moment that I finally realized the patently obvious. He'd been threatening Bella, not me. I almost sagged with relief.

"If you believe that, then you're a bigger idiot that I thought you were," Ian said. "You wouldn't be so freaked out by some random drunk."

"Aren't you going to tell me I was asking for it, dancing with everybody, shaking my ass for the hoi polloi?" I snapped.

He shook his head. "Not likely. Particularly since you were shaking your ass for me, not anyone else."

He'd finally managed to silence me, but only for a moment. "I hate you."

"I know you do. Now go up to your room before things get out of hand."

I was more than ready to get away from him. "Get out of hand?" I was fool enough to question.

"Before I take you to bed and finish what we've started. It's only a matter of time, no matter how much I try to avoid it, but it's been a long day and I don't feel like dealing with you tonight."

Very calmly, I stepped out of my heels, very calmly, I threw them at him, one after the other, one hitting him square in the face, and then I turned and stalked, barefoot, into the house.

CHAPTER

FOURTEEN

I woke up early, took a shower, and applied the bare minimum of Bella-disguise. The only way someone was going to stop me from leaving would be to tie me up, and while I had little doubt Ian would enjoy that, he wasn't about to admit it to either himself or me. Maldonado was nowhere to be seen, but there was coffee in a carafe, and I drank two fortifying cups before he appeared, looking vaguely harassed.

"I thought I might go for a drive today," I said casually. "It's been so long since I've been here that I thought it would be nice to visit some of the old places."

He nodded. "I'll check with Mr. Ian to see if he has the time to spare."

"Oh, I don't need a guide," I said, my voice airy. "I've already taken up too much of his time. I'm happy taking one of the farm trucks if need be. Just something that'll get me around the estate."

"I'll need to check with Mr. Ian," he said stubbornly.

Well, screw that. There were other ways. I gave Maldonado a cheerful smile, then headed back to my bedroom and the brand new iPhone Bella had given me.

Cell service was spotty up at Mariposa, but I'd already found one spot near Granda's room that had an on-again, off-again one bar of a signal, and while any phone call I'd tried to make had immediately dropped, there was a good chance if I went out on one of the upper terraces I might squeak it to two bars and success. I could always call a taxi from the house phone, but I had little doubt that something or someone would get in the way. They couldn't keep me here, damn it.

There had to be someone who'd be willing to drive me to the airport. The Whiteheads might own everything, but I had a wad of cash that would choke a horse, thanks to Bella. Surely I could find a taker somewhere.

I was tiptoeing past Granda's room when I heard him coughing, and I tried to close my ears and my mind to it. But the cough continued, sounding weak, and with a long-suffering sigh I shoved my telephone into my back pocket and opened the door to his bedroom.

There was no sign of his nurse, but then he had a tendency to tell her to go away, and there was just so much abuse a woman could take from a cantankerous, dying old man. He glared at me through his coughing fit, and I pulled the pillows up behind him so he could sit up better, dragging him into a half-upright position.

I was tempted to leave before the coughing stopped, but that would be the coward's way out, and I was proving that although I was phenomenally stupid to fall for Bella's blandishments, and incredibly naïve to think an incognito visit would heal my wounded heart, I was definitely brave to the point of foolhardy.

For a brief moment, the memory of the stranger on the dance floor came back to me, his filthy suggestions and his murderous threats, and all my bravery vanished. I needed to get the hell out of there.

Granda finally wheezed to a stop. "Don't just stand there like a booby, get me some water, girl."

I'd always hated it when he called me "girl." I was surprised to hear that Bella was tarred with the same sobriquet. I immediately brought him a glass of water, then helped him drink it.

"Where have you been all day?" he demanded weakly. "You're supposed to be keeping a deathbed watch, aren't you? At this rate, I'll die and no one will find my body for days."

"It's not even noon yet." I tried for a soothing voice. "Hasn't Ian already been here?"

"He's as bad as you are, leaving me to breathe my very last all on my own. I don't know why you bothered to return if you didn't care whether I lived or died."

"I'm here now, aren't I?"

"I heard you sneaking past my door—don't think I didn't. Though God knows what you expected to find up here."

"A decent cell signal," I replied bluntly. Granda liked to bully, but he didn't have to win, and I wasn't going to let him get away with being awful.

"Ha! There's no decent cell signal in the house—the closest you can get is here in this room, and it's not enough to make a call. If you want to use your cell phone, you'll have to go to Pinnacle Point up past the olive groves. Not that you remember where that is."

"Of course I do. It's the highest point on the estate. We used to climb up there when we were kids."

"*You* didn't," he said maliciously. "You didn't want to ruin your pretty dresses. Ian, Marcus, and Kitty liked it up there, but you made such a fuss about being left behind that the three of them stopped trying."

Not exactly true. Ian and Marcus had stopped, both beguiled by Bella's pouts, but I would still climb up the rocky outcropping when I needed to be alone. And I needed to be alone a lot, always feeling like the odd one out, up to and including the day my mother dragged me away.

I pulled my phone out of my pocket and watched as the dismal, solitary bar alternated with "no signal." "You're right," I said. "I'm surprised you haven't had some kind of booster or antenna installed."

"Ian wanted to, but I told him no. Mariposa has survived more than one hundred years without people being tied to an electronic leash, and it can survive another hundred years." He shifted in the bed, clearly in pain. "And don't you roll your eyes at me, young lady. I know the moment I'm dead Ian will put in the equipment, but I prefer to keep my illusions."

"It would help Marcus and Ian conduct business."

"Marcus has never asked," the old man said defensively.

"And if he had? Would you have agreed?" I don't know why I asked. It made no difference to me if Granda preferred Marcus to Ian —I was going to be long gone. It wasn't as if I had any faith in his ability to judge people—he'd adored Bella and found me dispensable. It only made sense that he'd undervalue Ian.

And why the hell was I feeling protective about that asshole, especially after last night? He'd kissed me as if I were the breath of life, and then shoved me away like I was poison. I wanted to get away from the lies, the deception, the threats. But most of all I wanted to get away from Ian, who threatened everything, not simply my dumbass masquerade but my emotions, for lack of a better, more precise word. I needed Mariposa behind me.

And then I looked down at the querulous old man whom I'd loved with all my heart, whom I still loved, and I knew I couldn't leave him to die alone. It took only one hard look to see that he was barely clinging to life, despite his bravado. It wasn't going to be long.

I was doing a terrible thing by lying to everyone, pretending to be someone I wasn't. The least I could do was endure a few more days of discomfort to give this tired old man a peaceful death.

"I don't really need a cell signal," I said, taking the seat beside his bed and taking one frail hand in mine. "I'm here for as long as you need me."

Granda sniffed dismissively. "Do what you want," he said. But his thin hand tightened on mine.

THE NURSE KICKED me out an hour later, and I wandered downstairs to find something for lunch. Seline and Maldonado were nowhere to be seen, and I was half afraid I would run into the cousins, or even worse, Ian. I had every intention of ignoring him. I was still furious with him about last night, about the way he'd kissed me, held me, the way he felt, the way he tasted, the way he made me feel.

I was still shaken by my nasty encounter last night, though I tried to tell myself it was nothing. Just some drunk, thinking he was being funny—no one could seriously want to harm me. Threats were one thing, but my idea of reality didn't include cold-blooded murder. I climbed onto one of the stools in the kitchen and ate my salad, resisting the urge to look over my shoulder. At least I'd made a final peace with my deception—no more running away. All I had to do was keep Ian at a distance and I'd be fine.

I'd tell Ian and Marcus the truth after Granda died. After all, I neither wanted nor expected anything from the old man, and the two of them would be glad enough to see me gone at that point. I had no idea when Bella would decide to show up, but that would no longer be my problem. They might despise me, but in the end, their opinion didn't matter.

I lifted my head suddenly. I had the strangest feeling that someone was watching me, and I looked around the vast, deserted kitchen. I must have let that man bother me more than I thought. I needed some exercise, some bright Spanish sun to burn away the unpleasantly slimy memory.

Rinsing my plate off in the sink, I started to slide it into the dish-washer when a movement caught my attention, and I stared out the window into the flat, black eyes of a perfect stranger.

A moment later, he had vanished, but this time I'd paid atten-tion. He'd been a big man, with heavy shoulders, a heavy brow, and there'd been something almost eerie about the way he'd been watching me. I didn't think he was the man from last night—that one had been shorter, thinner, with a deceptively handsome face.

I had to talk to Bella, and I couldn't let lack of a cell signal stop me anymore. Pinnacle Point wasn't that far, and I would be perfectly safe. I couldn't allow myself to get spooked, but after my encounter in the *taberna* last night I was feeling jittery. I reminded myself that there was no reason why anyone would want to hurt me. Bella was far more likely to have enemies, and I had to find out exactly what kind of mess she'd gotten me into. She needed to know what was going on here, she needed to get her ass back. I wasn't the one who was wanted here, I was the cuckoo in the nest. If Granda had his beloved Bella by his side, there'd no longer be a need for an interloper like me.

At least there was no sign of Ian anywhere around when I stepped out into the courtyard, and I took a deep breath of the fragrant air, the olive trees, the sun and dirt and the faint whiff of the sea in the background. It smelled like Mariposa—the hot sun baking into the dirt, the flowery scents of roses and bougainvillea playing with my heart. I didn't belong here, but I didn't know if I could bear to let it go.

I was feeling sorry for myself, a habit of my mother's that I'd always particularly disliked. Stiffening my back, I started up the narrow, rutted tractor path, past the neat rows for olive trees with the gnarled branches and silvery leaves, moving steadily upward toward Pinnacle Point.

It had always been a place of refuge when things were bad—when my mother had come to take me away for good, I'd run away and hidden up there, hidden until Ian had found me and talked me into coming back down. He'd been kind then. In fact, he'd been kind on numerous occasions as I was growing up, times I'd forgotten in the ensuing years. Maybe I'd misjudged him in the past, but right now, I'd had enough of his cynical comments and hot and cold behavior.

I was moving farther and farther away from the workers, toward the high rock outcropping that had held so many picnics. Pausing to catch my breath, I looked back over the hillside, and my eyes once again fell on the man who'd been outside the kitchen window.

I stumbled, then righted myself. I was being ridiculous—there was another man off to the left of him, a smaller man, walking parallel to my path. I stared at him, but a moment later he turned away, disappearing down the hillside, leaving only the big man behind.

I hesitated for a moment. A man had threatened my life last night, and now a stranger seemed to be following me. I ought to turn back home and stay there.

But the man wasn't looking at me, thank God. In fact, as far as anyone could tell, he was simply out there to check the olive trees. I wouldn't be here for the harvest, and that was another sorrow. The workers would lay out mesh blankets beneath the trees to gather the fallen fruit, and they'd already started on the lower levels, where the harvest would come due sooner, and everyone would be working and happy. The man was probably just scouting out where they would lay the nets.

And I was being foolish, letting my imagination get the better of me. If I turned back now, I'd run right into him, and while I'd convinced myself he wasn't dangerous, I wasn't eager for a close encounter. Besides, I needed to talk to Bella.

I finally reached the base of Pinnacle Point, the narrow path plunging into the pines that grew at the high levels above Mariposa, out of sight and sound of the workers. I hadn't thought to wear my new sneakers, but the flat sandals provided good enough traction as I scrambled up a path better made for mountain goats. It wasn't as easy as I remembered, but when I came out at the top, I could see all around me, the olive groves in the distance, stretching toward the sea, the beautiful jewel of Mariposa seated in the center.

I sat down cross-legged on the rock and pulled out the cell phone. Sure enough, five bars, and I quickly thumbed through the numbers Bella had programmed in. I immediately pushed my old number, listening to it ring. And ring. And ring.

My automated voice mail prompt didn't come on, just a phone ringing into silence, and for not the first time in my life, I cursed Bella before I hung up. Did she even have my old phone anymore? Somehow, I doubted it—I couldn't see Bella making do with anything but the best. She probably dumped my faithful phone with all the numbers and photos for a shiny new one, damn her. I stared at the one she'd given me in frustration. That was one problem with cell phones—you couldn't slam them down in frustration. Well, you could, but I couldn't see smashing my only form of outside communication on the hard rock beneath me.

I'd tossed and turned last night, more upset about Ian than seemingly minor inconveniences like death threats, and the warm sun beating overhead, the smells that were so familiar and so dear, even the lazy humming of the bees were enough to lure me into a dreamy state. I stretched out, not minding the hard rock beneath my back, and looked up into the bright blue sky, the birds wheeling and calling overhead, and I thought back to when I was fifteen years old and I wanted a beautiful boy to come and find me and kiss me.

He never had, of course. And I didn't want him now, I wanted his stupid brother, and I was every kind of idiot. But I wasn't going to think about that. I was going to close my eyes and just absorb the sounds and the scents and the feeling, just let go. At least for a little while.

"What the hell do you think you're doing?"

My eyes flew open to find Ian looming over me, looking thunderous. I sat up quickly, but I wasn't going to leap to my feet like some guilty trespasser.

"Getting away from everybody," I said succinctly. "Including you."

"Haven't you learned anything in the last twelve years? The world's a dangerous place, and wandering off on your own is asking for trouble."

"On Mariposa? Don't be ridiculous—this is the safest place in the world." Belatedly, I remembered the ominous presence of the big man, but I couldn't very well ask Ian about it after I insisted how safe it was.

"We have over a hundred farmhands on the estate, twice as many seasonal workers, and I can't vet everybody. You need to stay close to the house, not go wandering off alone."

"The only person I know who seems to want to hurt me is you," I said flatly.

His eyes narrowed. "You're forgetting your dance partner. And I don't care enough to want to hurt you," he replied with devastating candor. "I just don't want anything to happen to you on my watch."

"It's not your watch, it's mine," I snapped before I realized how ridiculous I sounded. "Oh, go away, Ian. Just leave me alone."

"Fine. Once you're back at the house, I won't come anywhere near you."

"Good."

"Good."

We were glaring at each other beneath the bright Spanish sun, two combatants waiting for the other to make the first move. I could turn and run, but I didn't move, staring at him. We were so close I could reach out and touch him, so close...

"Do you enjoy driving me crazy?" he said in a low voice.

"Yes," I said with complete honesty.

"We're just going to have to do something about that." Was it a threat? A promise?

"I'd like to see you try," I shot back. Wanting him to try, to put his hands on me, his mouth on me.

But he took a step back with a short laugh, and the heat between us turned cold. "I'm sure you would, Bella-Beast, but I've never been your plaything, and I never will."

"Except for one night," I said, remembering his words.

His eyes darkened, and his mouth curved in an unpleasant smile. "Just one," he agreed. "It was very effective—I'd never seen your manipulative soul so clearly. And I learned my lesson. If you lie down with a snake, prepare to get bitten." He turned away from me. Taking a few steps down the path, he stopped and looked back at me. "Are you coming? It can be dangerous out here."

A chill ran down my back. He was trying to scare me, and he was doing a good job of it. I thought of the big man.

"I'm coming," I said with all the dignity I could muster. "You haven't hired anybody new recently, have you?" *Like someone hired to hurt me,* I thought, then shook myself. I was being ridiculous.

"We're always hiring. Why do you ask?"

"Oh, nothing. Just curious." *I should tell him,* I thought. A man had threatened to kill me last night, and I kept seeing an evil-looking individual dogging my footsteps. It might mean absolutely nothing. Or it might not.

He reached out his hand to help me when we got to the steep crevasse in the stone, but I ignored it, hoping my flimsy sandals would give me enough purchase on the rocks.

They didn't, and I ended up in his arms, breathless, looking up at him, too close, too close. A light flared in his dark eyes and he was going to kiss me again, I knew it.

He didn't. He simply moved me to flat ground and released me, so quickly I might have been the snake he'd been talking about. In fact, in his eyes I *was* the snake.

And I was being an idiot not to say something about the man I kept seeing. "I think a man's been following me," I blurted out, breaking the silence between us as we hiked down the narrow path.

"If you had your way, a thousand men would be following you. What's the problem with that?"

I should have known he'd dismiss it. "He's always showing up when I don't expect him. He was trimming the rose bushes by the kitchen window, and he was watching me as I climbed up here. In fact, half the time when I look, I see him."

"What does this mystery man look like? Is he the one from last night?"

"No. This one is big. Sinister-looking. And he's always around."

"Sorry, but I think you're just looking for attention," he scoffed. "There's no one around here who's out to get you."

"Except you," I shot back.

He halted, and I stopped too. "I don't like liars, I don't like teases, and I most certainly don't like you." The heat in his eyes belied every word, I wanted to throw them back in his teeth. They hurt, because they applied to me just as much as Bella, at least in the liar department.

What Would Bella Do? I summoned my most seductive smile, my sexiest drawl as I gave him Bella's sultry look. "Sure you don't."

I thought he would touch me then, though I wasn't sure if he wanted to kiss me or hit me. Probably both, but Ian would never hit someone smaller than he was, and he towered over me. A moment later, that flash of emotion was gone, and he gave a shaky laugh. "You do like living on the edge, don't you?" he said. "Someday you're going to go too far."

"You'd never hurt me," I shot back, sure of it.

"Darling," he drawled, "I would break your fucking heart."

I froze, mesmerized. I knew it was the truth, not that he could break Bella's ice-encapsulated heart, but Katherine White-head was a different matter. Because I knew the devastating truth. In the midst of this charade, with enemies all around and people threatening to kill me and not an ally in sight, I had fallen in love with the least loveable creature of all. I'd fallen in love with Ian the Wretch, with the heat that burned between us, with the years when he'd been a better friend than a lovelorn Podge recognized. I'd been so besotted with Marcus that I hadn't even noticed that all my good memories involved Ian.

And now he hated me, with good reason. I was lying to him, even though he didn't know it, lying to Granda and Marcus and Maldonado, and it seemed I might have returned to Mariposa with Bella's enemies on my trail.

I wanted to burst into tears. I wanted to tell him the truth, get it all out in the open. He'd really despise me then, but I knew he would help me. Ian was all bark, at least where I was concerned.

Instead, I simply smiled up at him. "You can but try," I said, and walked past him, down to the great house, shoulders straight.

"WHO HAVE YOU BEEN WRESTLING WITH?" Mary Alice greeted me from the kitchen, the last person I wanted to see.

I glanced down at my rumpled self and shrugged. "I climbed to Pinnacle Point."

Mary Alice looked at me oddly. "You've always despised going up there," she said. "It's not like you."

I recovered quickly. "I wanted to see if anything had changed."

"In rock? Not likely." She peered more closely at me. "You're the one who's changed."

Danger, Will Robinson. "Everyone changes, Mary Alice," I said lightly.

"I don't."

Unfortunately, I could agree with that. To my relief, Mary Alice lost interest in my anomalies. "Valerie and I are having dinner with Granda tonight, so you'll have to fend for yourself. You've been hogging him for far too long, and tonight's our turn."

I raised an eyebrow. "He's willing to eat at the ungodly hour of seven-thirty?"

"We'll push it till eight for his sake, though I consider it terrible for the digestion. You can manage to entertain both Ian and Marcus, can't you? If some of the stories I've heard are true, you'd be quite adept at it," she sneered.

"I wouldn't touch Ian with a ten-foot pole."

"No one ever faulted your taste." Mary Alice sniffed.

So, the cousins preferred Marcus to Ian. Another point in Ian's favor, even though I wished him at the bottom of a cliff. There was no need to check Valerie's opinion—she always echoed Mary Alice.

Which meant Ian was on his own in this checkered household, with Granda and Maldonado on his side. At least, I assumed Granda was on his side. With the irascible old man, it was hard to tell.

I could see Ian approaching the kitchen door, and I'd had enough. "I'll eat in my room," I said hastily, heading for the back stairway that led up from the kitchen.

Granda was asleep when I dropped by, and I tiptoed away without bothering him. I could go down and find something for dinner later on, once Mary Alice and Valerie were closeted with Granda. I had no idea if Marcus was returning today, and I didn't particularly care, as long as I didn't have to deal with him or anyone else. I pushed open my windows to the soft summer breeze and curled up with my book, happy to turn the outside world off for at least a brief time.

CHAPTER

FIFTEEN

I slammed into wakefulness, blinking in the darkened room. Something was very wrong. There were noises, footsteps racing along the corridors, and I quickly pulled on the silk robe over my utilitarian boxers and T-shirt, tying it as I pushed open the heavy door. There was no one in sight, but I could hear people talking excitedly, and all my instincts were firing on ten.

I caught Maldonado as he was rushing toward the stairs. "What's wrong? Is Granda all right?"

He barely paused. "Your grandfather has had a stroke," he said abruptly. "The doctor should be here by now." He pulled away, scurrying off without a backward glance, and I didn't hesitate, racing up the broad flight of stairs to Granda's room.

All the lights were blazing, and I remembered how he hadn't liked the bright lights. I saw him lying flat in the bed, struggling for breath, an oxygen cannula doing little to improve his gray color, and his nurse was busy taking his blood pressure, a worried expression on her usually placid face. Mary Alice was nattering on about how he should be in a facility, with Valerie piping up her agreement at regular intervals, all the while Marcus made soothing noises. Only

Ian was silent, standing a little apart from the other grandchildren, a stark expression on his face. For some reason, I wanted to go to him, but I stayed where I was, just inside the door, as the doctor rushed through, followed by Maldonado.

"I need the room cleared," he announced in sharp Spanish.

"I don't see why I should have to!" Mary Alice announced. "He's my grandfather and I want to be with him..."

"He's my grandfather too," Marcus said with just a trace of petulance.

"Mary Alice, dear," Valerie began in a vain effort to soothe things.

"Get out!" Ian said in a tight voice, turning away. "He doesn't need you vultures hanging over him." He appeared to be including his own brother, which surprised me, and Marcus flushed at the reprimand even as Ian headed toward the door, when a muffled sound came from the bed.

"He's trying to say something," Mary Alice pointed out unnecessarily. "We're not leaving until..."

The doctor had bent close to Granda's pale, crackled lips. "Who's Kitty?" he turned to ask.

It gave me no joy that the name seemed to infect the room with temporary paralysis. "Kitty's not here," Marcus said finally. "I need to explain..."

The doctor was leaning down again, and then his gaze fell on me. "He says he wants Bella then."

"Of course he wants Bella," Mary Alice sneered. "I, for one, am not about to sit around while she makes a play for his money..."

"The will has already been notarized," Ian snapped. "It was sent off yesterday morning. He's not likely to change it at this point, though if he wanted to, it's his every right. Now get the hell out of here and leave the old man in peace."

"What about you?" Mary Alice sniped, stress stripping her of her usual *sang-froid*.

"I'm going too. He wants to talk to Bella, and none of us are standing in his way." It was a warning, even a threat, and no one seemed inclined to argue. With a low rumble of complaint, they filed out of the room, leaving me behind, feeling awash with guilt and misery. I wanted to run away too, rather than lie to the old man who still meant so much to me.

But with one cold, final glance at me, Ian shut the door behind them, and I slowly approached the bed.

"Be quick about it," Dr. Madhur said. "We have to try and stabilize him, and he needs calm and peace."

"I can come back..." I said, about to move away, when Granda's pale hand reached out and caught mine in a weak grip. His eyes were open, and he was staring at me, for all the world like he knew who I really was.

"Kitty..." he wheezed, the sound barely audible, and once more I cursed the lies I'd agreed to tell.

"I'm Bella, Granda," I said, hating myself.

He shook his head, whether in negation or as a response to the nurse hooking up a new IV solution. "You must...marry...him..." This time it was a whisper.

Marry him? Was he talking to Bella, or to Kitty? It had to be Bella and the supposed engagement. After all, who was Kitty supposed to marry? "Don't try to speak, Granda," I said soothingly. "Just let the doctor take care of you..."

His grip tightened on my hand. "Kitty," he said again, and my heart sank. "Don't...worry. I did it on purpose." Or at least, that was what it sounded like.

"What did you do, Granda?" I said desperately. "And I'm Bella, not Kitty." More and more lies, hot tears stinging my eyes.

"Kitty," he said with the softest of sighs, and his faded blue eyes closed. Before I could ask another question, they'd snapped an oxygen mask over his mouth, and I was being tugged away from the bedside by the nurse.

"We need to let the doctor work," she said. "He's the only one who can help him now. The doctor and God Himself." She was leading me toward the door, inexorably, and I could hardly put up a fight. I could see as well as anyone that Granda was unconscious, and tonight there'd be no more confused, tumbled words.

And then I was alone in the hallway, the door shut firmly behind me, and I wanted to beat my fists on it in rage and misery. What had he been trying to tell me? But he should know I was Bella! Unless the stroke had managed to confuse him into thinking I was plain old Podge, miraculously transported back...

"What did he say to you?"

I didn't jump. I hadn't seen him, but I'd somehow known he'd be there, waiting for me.

"He thought I was Kitty," I said in a raw voice. For some reason, I didn't want him to see the hot tears that were ready to spill over. He'd already seen me vulnerable, and I couldn't bear his pity, not as I mourned a man I wasn't allowed to claim any longer.

"He's a tough old buzzard." There was no kindness in Ian's voice, but no harshness either. "He'll pull through this. He's made it through worse."

"I don't think so," I said with a muted hiccup. I was not going to cry in front of him.

"Don't look so bereft, Bella-Beast. It's not as if you really cared about him. You're about to come into a hefty bit of money—we all are. No need to be hypocritical about it."

"Go to hell, Ian!" I snapped. "Who the hell are you to tell me who I do and don't care about?"

"Because you don't care about anyone but yourself, not when it comes right down to it. You're a sociopath, a classic one, and crocodile tears aren't going to convince me otherwise." He tilted his head, surveying me. "Of course, you may end up with nothing at all. I don't know if Granda was as enchanted by your little girl act as my brother is. He's old enough to know better."

I closed my eyes, trying to close him out. "Is money all you think about? I really don't care if he's left me anything. If he has, I'll turn it over to you and the farm. I don't want it."

I'd managed to startle him. "Why the hell would you do that? You know you hate this place."

There was no way Bella could hate Mariposa—no way anybody could not love the beautiful old house and the surrounding land, even someone as sophisticated as Bella with her jet-setting ways. But I could hardly protest—Bella hadn't been back here in five years. What would Bella do? Whatever it was, I didn't want to do it.

"Just leave me alone, Ian," I said wearily. "You can believe any damned thing you want, as long as you leave me alone." He was standing between me and the stairs, and there was no way I could get back to my room without passing him, coming too close to him, when that was the last thing I wanted.

He didn't move, and the moment of silence stretched between us. And then he spoke. "Maybe you do care about the old man after all."

"And maybe I don't give a shit what you think. I'm tired and I want to go to bed." There was no reason those words should sound so loaded—he despised me, and right then, I was on my way to a healthy dislike in return.

He started to say something, then bit it back. "Granda's not going anywhere," he said finally. "Get some sleep."

I walked past him, cool and elegant as the doppelganger inside my head, when he reached out and caught my arm. His skin was cool against my heated flesh, and I had a sudden flash of what it would be like, all that cool, beautiful skin pressed against mine. On top of me, pressing me down into the bed.

I froze, staring at him in the murky light of the hallway, and he stared back, neither of us saying a word. I could lean toward him, take a small step in his direction, and I knew where it would end. Where everything with Ian had been leading since I stepped off the plane, where everything had been leading since I was Podge and he was unexpectedly kind to me.

He wasn't kind now. And sleeping with him wouldn't fix anything but scratch an unexpectedly powerful itch. I wasn't going to go there, no matter how much I wanted to, and that need was more powerful than anything I could remember feeling.

"Take your hands off of me," I said in a low voice.

If anything, his grip tightened, and we stared at each other. I don't know who moved first—I had the depressing thought that it was me. I went into his arms, and they closed around me, firm and tight, and all I could feel was his strength, his warmth, the very solidness of his existence as his strength flowed into me.

We stayed that way for a long time, neither of us saying a word. I know I was shaking, but his warmth enveloped me, and I felt like...like I had come home.

"What the fuck is going on?" Marcus's wrathful voice broke through my momentary daze, and I tried to tear myself away. Ian wasn't letting me go. In fact, he turned so that my back faced his brother, and he pressed my face against his shoulder.

"Comfort," he said briefly, but his hold was inexorable, and I didn't really want to break free.

"Find someone else to comfort!" Marcus snarled, and I finally broke free enough to look at him. As far as I could remember, Marcus and Ian had never fought. And now they were fighting over me?

Over Bella, I reminded myself. Always Bella. "Enough," I said sharply. "Don't be an asshole, Marcus."

"I don't want anyone groping my fiancée," he said sulkily, his anger vanishing. "Not even my brother."

"I'm not your fiancée," I said. "It's a sham to make Granda happy. We're not really getting married."

To my amazement, Marcus's dark, sulky expression vanished, as if it had never been there. "Of course not," he said cheerfully enough. "Sorry about that—I just got all caveman all of a sudden."

Ian was watching him with an odd expression on his face, and I was still standing too close to him. I wanted to move closer. The silence between them grew uncomfortable, and I finally broke it with a Bella-like laugh. "All's forgiven," I said lightly.

"Go to bed, Bella," Ian growled, still watching his brother.

Marcus smiled winningly. "Yes, that's a good idea. I know Granda will be right as rain tomorrow morning and..."

"One doesn't recover from a stroke overnight." Ian's voice was low and withering.

Were they still quarreling over Bella? I'd best get my lying ass out of the way so they could work things out. "Good night," I said, and out of the corner of my eye, I saw Ian lift his hand to stop me, then drop it again.

I was out of there a moment later, and my temporarily happy mood vanished as if I'd been slapped in the face. Granda was truly dying, and there was nothing I could do about it, and it gutted me.

I managed to keep calm until I made it safely inside the Queen's Room, when everything erupted. My grief, my guilt, my fears, washed over me as I cried. I had to be the world's biggest idiot. I despised Ian, and yet I'd wanted nothing more than to have him wrap his arms around me and hold me. I was confused, obnoxiously needy, filled with a clawing sense of loss, and my misery served me right. I rubbed at my eyes, trying to push the steady stream of tears away. The salt would bleach my eyelashes, making Bella's makeup even more difficult, and I would have to...

I froze in sudden horror. I was rubbing my eyes. My eyes with no colored contacts in them—I'd taken them out when I'd gone to bed. I'd seen everyone with my hazel eyes, not Bella's vibrant green ones.

Had Ian noticed? No, he couldn't have! The room and the hallway had been dark, shadowed, and our angry conversation hadn't allowed time for him to look soulfully into my borrowed eyes. He had far too much on his mind to notice such a slight anomaly, and besides, there'd been nothing strange in the way he looked at me, not even when he caught me and pulled me into his arms.

I couldn't afford to make mistakes like that. Despite what Granda had said, Kitty wasn't welcome here. She wasn't one of the heirs, she wasn't even a member of the family anymore. All the cousins, from Marcus to quiet Valerie, had more of a right to be here.

At least I'd stopped crying. I hurriedly splashed water into my face, blinking back at my reflection in the mirror. My hazel eyes were almost green—surely no one would have noticed. People didn't really pay attention to eye color, apart from romance novels. I was safe.

Safe from what? I'd been trying to leave Mariposa ever since I got here. If I simply told Ian the truth, I'd be out on my ass in no time, off on my magical week in Paris, and the cousins could deal with it. Bella wouldn't fare too well if our subterfuge got out, but I was past the point of caring. Bella was a far cry from the warm-hearted cousin I'd so foolishly believed in, and she deserved to pick up the pieces of our shattered masquerade.

There was only one problem with my plan. I didn't want to leave Granda. Even in his confused state, he'd known that one of his granddaughters was there, and it would shatter him to know we'd been lying, tricking a dying man. I couldn't walk away from him, even if it was the honorable thing to do. Honor had taken a hike long ago, and all I could hold onto was my hopeless love for the old man. The moment he was gone, I'd be off, with Ian booting my ass out the door.

And what did that mean about Ian? He'd kissed me, and I still couldn't figure out why. Why had he hauled me onto his lap, why had he kissed my panic away, leaving me dazed and longing for something I could never have?

It was all too much. Wiping away the last of my tears, I headed back into the bathroom, turning on the shower and stepping beneath it with no regard for Bella's pre-Raphaelite curls. I stood there beneath the pounding water and let it wash everything away— my grief, my guilt, my confusion, and when I finally had enough, I simply walked over to my bed and lay down, letting the sheets dry my body. The hair would fix itself once it dried—the perm had been worth every cent of the fortune Bella had paid. I would deal with it in the morning. In the meantime, I was going to sleep if it killed me.

At half past five, I was awake, and not going to sleep again. Not with the memory of Granda lying there, so still and gray. Climbing out of bed, I dressed quickly, popping the colored contacts into my still swollen eyes. I had no expectations of seeing anyone at this hour, but I wasn't taking any more chances.

The door was shut to Granda's room, and there was no noise coming from behind it. He was dead, I knew it. I froze with my hand on the doorknob, and then heard the reassuring sound of the ventilator pumping oxygen into him. Pushing open the door, I could see him in a small pool of light, still and silent as the machines breathed for him.

I stepped inside, shutting the door behind me. There was no sign of the nurse or doctor, which meant he had to be relatively stable. Grabbing a large, overstuffed chair, I dragged it to the bedside, the legs screeching against the highly polished wooden floors. I curled up into it, taking Granda's limp hand in mine, and closed my eyes. If he was going to die, I was going to make damned sure he didn't die alone.

Some small sound must have woken me. My eyes shot open, and I could see the early light of dawn begin to peep from behind the curtains. Granda hadn't moved, but if anything, he looked worse, with a gray-blue tinge to his crepey skin, and even though I'd slept, I still held his hand.

Another noise, and I jerked my head around to see Ian at the foot of the bed, lounging in one of the straight-backed chairs, and I braced myself for some snarky comment. He would hardly miss the chance to infuriate me.

But instead, he simply nodded, as if acknowledging our unexpectedly joint vigil, and I leaned back in my chair, trying to ignore the warm feeling that flooded me. Ian and I were enemies, there was no doubt about that. But we were united in our love for this old man, and a grief that we could no longer halt the passage of time. Granda would be gone soon, and there was nothing either of us could do about it.

CHAPTER

SIXTEEN

I would have been grateful the nurse didn't toss us out of the sick room a few hours later if it weren't for the fact that our presence would make no difference. The grief was like a leaden weight inside me, as my own breathing matched his machine-assisted respiration, and I wanted to weep, I wanted to fight; I wanted to do something, anything to keep this from happening.

Instead, I sat, dry-eyed, silent, still holding his limp hand, hoping that he somehow knew I was there.

Ian had disappeared when the nurse returned, and I told myself I preferred it that way. This was between me and Granda, the real me, not the tarted-up parody of Bella. This was Kitty, who'd always adored him, even when he betrayed her and let her go.

What had he said to me earlier? He'd called me Kitty, but that was simply because of his confusion. He knew perfectly well that Kitty wasn't anywhere around, that it was Bella by his side.

And yet the look in his eyes wasn't the look he gave Bella. When he looked at Bella, his gaze was fond and indulgent and just the slightest bit wary...why did I just realize that? When he looked at Kitty, there was nothing but love.

Or had been, until my mother had dragged me away from this place and he'd written me off. I'd hoped to use Bella as a conduit back to him, but she'd explained in the most reluctant of voices that he didn't want to see me. That I'd left and was no longer part of Mariposa.

He was a proud old man, and I'd listened to my mother rather than to him, not that I had any choice. It was perfectly conceivable that he'd hold a grudge.

But there'd been no grudge when he'd asked where Kitty was. And the warmth in his eyes hadn't been for Bella...

Who the hell was I kidding? Of course it had been for Bella—who else would he have thought would be by his side with pre-Raphaelite curls and designer clothes?

I needed to make my peace with him. I needed him to wake up just long enough for me to tell him who I was, to apologize for tricking him, to tell him I loved him.

But Granda, who'd towered over me my entire life, seemed to be shrinking in the big bed, drawing in on himself, and I knew he was going to go without my confession. Probably better for him anyway.

"I love you, Granda," I whispered, holding his hand. "I'm sorry I lied to you."

The slight pressure of his fingers had to be my imagination—there was no change to his face at all. "I just hope you can forgive me." My voice wasn't much more than a whisper, barely heard over the sounds of the machines keeping him alive.

"Forgive you for what?" Ian said from directly behind me, and I jumped, releasing Granda's hand for a moment.

I glared up at him. "For not coming to see him for five years," I said sharply. Score one for Bella.

And then he put a cup of coffee in my hand, and the aroma drifted to my nose. It was black, the way I liked it, not lashed with heavy cream as Bella preferred, and I felt a reluctant warmth fill me. I needed that coffee.

Blinking back unwanted tears, I said a brief "thanks" and took

Granda's hand in mine once more. It was cool to the touch, almost cold, and I glanced worriedly at the windows. They were closed—no stray breeze was going to disturb him.

Ian had brought his own coffee in with him, and he re-took his seat at the end of the bed. We sat there peaceably enough as the nurse bustled around us, checking his vitals, straightening his pillows, and I realized there was nothing she could do, not really. His long life was coming to an end, and even though I wanted to scream and fight and rail against the fates, I was helpless. All I could do was hold his hand and wait.

No one disturbed us until the early afternoon, when Mary Alice strode in, all bustling efficiency, jarring in her bright, almost feral smile. "Enough is enough," she announced. "You've monopolized Granda for too long. I hate to tell you this, Bella, but he's not going to change his will for you at this point—all this show of grief is a waste of time when we all know you'd rather be out cruising around the countryside in your ridiculous car."

I could feel myself shrink at the sound of her strident voice, and I desperately tried to summon my faithful mantra—what would Bella do? I didn't give a flying fuck what Bella would do, I only knew I wanted Mary Alice to go away.

"Her ridiculous car is totaled," Ian said in something close to a growl. "And she's here because she needs to be here."

At another time, I would have been shocked at his defending me, but at this point, I was past caring about anything.

"I have just as much right to be here as she does," Mary Alice said, her voice rising, and I could sense Granda's sudden restlessness. "If she's going to have the chance to play devoted granddaughter then I have the same right..."

"Get out." Ian's voice was low, deadly, and Mary Alice halted her diatribe, staring at him in shock. A moment later, she rallied.

"You can't tell me..." she began.

"Get out!" he thundered, and Mary Alice scrambled to the door, noisily complaining until the nurse shut it behind her. I turned back to Granda, and there seemed like the faintest trace of a smile on his face.

I squeezed his hand gently. I could still hear Mary Alice off in the distance, arguing with someone, but I knew we were safe. She wouldn't come back, not without reinforcements, and even then, Ian would stop her, thank God. I wanted nothing from Granda but his peaceful passing, and I would do anything to keep him quiet and safe. Fortunately, Ian had chosen to be gatekeeper.

She came back, of course, this time with Valerie, but she'd obviously thought better of her deathbed ministry and departed more quickly than I could have hoped. Marcus came, looking everywhere but at Granda, and escaping as soon as he could, but Ian and I remained in silent amity throughout the long hours, as the day lengthened into dusk, and then night.

He slipped away just past midnight, so quietly that I was surprised I knew. Between one labored breath and another, he simply stopped, letting go, and I stared at him in numb disbelief as the nurse rushed in, all efficiency. She tried to detach my hand from his, but I refused to let go, refused to look at her, refused to do anything but watch Granda's face for some sign of life. He was gone, and I could feel the tears drenching my face.

Ian stood abruptly, and I pulled my gaze away from Granda to stare at him. His face was cold, shuttered, as if something had closed inside him. "Don't waste your crocodile tears on me, Bella," he said in a low voice. "I know how much you really care."

Rage sliced through me, hot and furious, wiping everything away. "You know absolutely nothing about me!" I shot back, my voice quiet in the still atmosphere.

"I know you're a cheat and a liar, and that's good enough. Go find Marcus and the two of you can console each other. I have to make arrangements." Without another word, he stalked out of the bedroom, leaving the door open behind him.

Slowly, I released my grip on Granda's cold, limp hand. My stomach had knotted painfully, and a sudden wave of nausea washed over me, so strong that I rose quickly, knocking my chair over as I tried to get out of the way.

"Don't let him upset you," the nurse said in her softly accented English. "Death takes some people that way."

I tried to summon a smile, but my lips were trembling, and I knew anything I came up with would be a travesty. "I have to go," I mumbled, my voice thick with tears.

She nodded. "I'll take care of him. I've been with him for many years, and I can do this for him."

She was a stranger to me, and she'd loved him as I did. I wanted to summon fury at all the years I'd missed, but it would do me no good. I needed to find someplace to hide, someplace where I could mourn undisturbed.

My tears had stopped at Ian's harsh words, and I needed their release. I scrambled through the halls, downstairs to my bedroom and threw myself on the bed, ready to dissolve into uncontrollable weeping. My eyes stayed dry, my heart filled with cold rage. I wanted to kill Ian, whose words had been a verbal slap, stopping my grief cold. I felt dry and empty inside, icy as I tried to force the tears, tried to let go of my iron control. Nothing happened. I had been playing a role for so long that I couldn't break free, couldn't give in to honest emotion.

Ian's contempt for me was a wound I well deserved. I was everything he said, a liar and a cheat, but I loved Granda, and his loss devastated me. Who the hell did Ian think he was, to question the depths of my grief? And why did I care? He was no longer the boy I had instinctively trusted—he was Ian the Wretch, making my life miserable when I was most vulnerable.

I slammed out of my room, not caring whom I woke, but the house was still and silent. Apparently, Ian had decided not to inform the rest of the household that Granda was gone—apparently he thought he had the right to make such decisions. He could do any damned thing he wanted—if I stayed locked up in my room for a moment longer, I would suffocate.

I was outside, barefoot when the rain started, just a light sprinkle at first, then growing stronger, the punch of thunder shaking the hills around Mariposa. I didn't care. It was pitch-black, but I knew where I was going. Straight across the courtyard to the stables, to Ian's apartments, to tell him...to tell him...

A hand clamped down on my shoulder, whirling me around, and I screamed, terrified, my emotions at fever pitch. Recognizing Ian in the brief flash of lightning did the opposite of calming me down.

"Bastard!" I screamed at him over the wind, and slapped him across the face so hard my hand went numb, but it gave me no satisfaction. "You cold-hearted monster, how dare you...how dare you ..." I didn't know what I thought he dared, because the tears came then, as I was beating at his chest with my fists, furious, shattered. His arms came around me, stopping my useless blows, pulling me tight against his body in the pouring rain, and I only fought for a moment longer before I gave in to the tears that had finally returned.

He held me. He pulled me close, pressed my face against his shoulder and simply held me as I wept, noisy, ugly tears.

"Shhh," he said softly in my ear as he cupped my head against him. "It's all right."

"It isn't!" I sobbed. "Granda's dead, and I loved him, and I hate you, you miserable bastard, I hate you!" My words were garbled but clear enough, but Ian kept stroking rain-soaked hair.

"Of course you do," he murmured inconsequentially, sounding unbelievably gentle. "Just cry it out..."

"I don't want to cry it out!" I screamed at him. "He's dead!" But I had grown weaker, no longer able to fight him, and I was shaking with grief and despair.

He scooped me up in his arms, and I made no effort to push him away, simply letting him carry me in out of the rain, through the stable and up the steep, shadowy stairs. A moment later, he'd kicked the door open to his apartment, carrying me into the inky darkness. Another flash of lightning illuminated it for a moment, and then everything went black again.

"Shit," he muttered. "Power's out."

I finally realized where I was, and I started to struggle. "Put me down!" I said furiously, the effect ruined by my tear-thickened voice.

He paid no attention to me—when had he ever—and carried me across the room in the darkness, dumping me on what had to be a sofa. I immediately struggled to get up, but he simply shoved me down again.

"You need a drink," he said. "And I need to get out of these wet clothes. What the hell did you think you were doing, running around in a thunderstorm? Aren't things bad enough without you getting yourself killed in the bargain?"

I barely reacted to the lack of logic in that statement—no one was going to kill me, for God's sake. "I don't want a drink. I just want to go home."

"Mariposa is the only home you've known," he said flatly. "You're already here."

"I'm not wanted here!" I said wildly. "This is no home to me..." I darted up, trying to avoid his shadowy outline as he loomed over me, only to smash my shins against a table. I cried out in pain, and immediately his arms came around me again, and before I realized what was happening, we were both on the sofa, I was sitting on his lap as he held me.

"Just cry it out," he said in a low voice. "You're right, I'm a heartless bastard, but I'm here for you. I know you loved him. Just cry."

And I did. I cried for Granda, and all the years lost, I cried for my idiocy in agreeing to this stupid charade, I cried for Ian and Marcus and loving the wrong man, and then I didn't know what I was crying for.

His long fingers wiped the tears from my face, his body was warm and solid beneath mine, and he cupped my chin, looking at me for a long unreadable moment as I snuffled and cried. And then he kissed me.

This wasn't like the other kisses—there was no anger in it, no threat. His lips were soft, a sweet solace against the rage of my grief, and I let him kiss me, savoring it, my tears dissolving into stray hiccups as I slowly, tentatively kissed him back.

They were innocent kisses, safe kisses, comforting kisses, and when he deepened it, there was such a naturalness about it that I followed him into a world of sensation that flowed through my body, warming me in the cool night air.

He was so big, so strong, and that strength felt like safety, not a threat, as I leaned back onto the sofa cushions, beneath him as he followed me down. He was hard, and I recognized that with a kind of triumph, sliding my arms around his neck and pulling him to me, moving my hips beneath his, pressing. His hands slid down from my shoulders and cupped my hips as he thrust against me, and I made a sound of uncontrollable pleasure. This was what I wanted, this was what I needed, all the pain and lies and uncertainty wiped away in an act of blinding passion.

And then he pulled away, abruptly, pushing up. "No," he said, his voice raw and breathless.

It was a slap in the face, a shocking blow that made me freeze in my erotic daze. "No?" I echoed in a shocked whisper. He was right, of course. This was the worst thing we could do.

He was looking down at me. It was so dark, I couldn't be sure if he could see me, but his shoulders were tense, and emotion vibrated through him.

"Yes," he said then, his voice sure in the darkness.

"Yes," I said, reaching for him. "Yes."

There was danger in the darkness, there was safety. His hands on my body were deft, stripping the clothes away from me so quickly I barely had a chance to reach for my buttons. He was in a hurry, and I thought I knew why—he didn't want enough time to pass that he thought better of what we were doing. I heard the rasp of his zipper, and then I felt him, hard and heavy against me.

There was no question as to whether I was ready or not—I was wanting him so badly that all common sense had vanished, and I only knew that this was Ian, and he was mine.

He braced himself over me, pushing inside me, and I gasped in surprise. He was bigger than what I was used to, and in the past few months, I hadn't been used to anything at all, and my body protested his steady invasion as I clutched at the smooth warm skin of his shoulders, biting my lips to keep from crying out.

Reaching down, he pulled my legs up around his hips as he drove home, and I made contradictory sounds of pleasure and pain, tightening my hold on his body.

"Am I hurting you?" His voice was little more than a rasp.

"Don't...stop," I choked out, and he moved, his first thrust so powerful it shoved me deeper into the cushions. And then again, and again, as his rhythm grew fluid and I arched up to meet him, my natural instincts taking over. I knew how to do this, and yet somehow everything felt new and different, with the darkness all around us and only Ian alone with me, claiming me, owning me in ways I'd never thought I wanted. It no longer mattered what lay between us— he was elemental, eternal, and rational thought had deserted me.

I could barely see him in the darkness, so I reached up and cupped his face with my hands, needing to touch him everywhere. He kissed me with hot, devouring kisses, and the tension inside me rose, until I was so close to exploding.

He fucked me in cool, determined silence, and I wanted to scream with pleasure and despair, as he moved faster, harder inside me, and I was about to lose it completely when he moved his hand between our surging bodies and touched me, so deftly, so purposefully, and for the first time in my life, I screamed as I came, as I felt him grow and expand inside of me and I realized he hadn't worn a condom.

And I was stupidly glad. I was his, he'd claimed me, and I'd wanted nothing between us.

I slowly drifted back to a breathless reality, calling myself all sorts of a fool, calling him all sorts of a villain. He pulled out of me, and I felt bereft, but a moment later, I was in his arms and he was carrying me through the inky black apartment to the wide expanse of a bed. I thought he was going to leave me alone, but a moment later, he was back a damp towel to wash me off. He finished stripping off the last of his clothes, all without saying a word, and then lay down beside me, pulling me into his arms, tucking me against him.

When he spoke it was depressingly prosaic. "I didn't wear a condom."

"I know. Don't worry about it—I take care of myself."

"I've never forgotten before," he said, his voice unreadable in the stillness. Was it self-disgust, surprise, or something else?

"You're safe from me," I said dryly, knowing I should pull away. So, we were having the awkward morning-after talk and it wasn't even morning.

"I wish," he muttered. "You're the most dangerous woman I know."

I wasn't. Bella was, and I'd just had sex with Ian while pretending I was someone else. I wanted to curl up in shame. I certainly hadn't deserved the best orgasm of my life.

Guilt erupted in me. "I need to tell you..." I began, determined, but he stopped my mouth with his.

"Don't tell me anything," he growled when he lifted his head. "Just feel."

He was growing hard again, to my amazement, and I was growing aroused. In fact, despite the power of my release, I'd stayed minutely attuned to his body and his touch, the way he made me feel.

He was right—this was no place for confession. I'd tell him

tomorrow when we were both fully clothed and he could yell at me all he wanted.

I would take tonight, what little there was left of it, I would take everything I could from Ian, and give him everything in return. Tomorrow, when I told him the truth, he could throw it back in my face, but I would still have the memory, the pain and pleasure of it. It would have to do.

CHAPTER
SEVENTEEN

I woke up in my own bed with the oddest sensation suffusing my body. Something was devastatingly wrong, and something was so very right. I lay still, and let the memories wash over me. Granda was dead. And I had had sex with Ian the Wretch.

Guilt washed over me. He'd thought I was Bella, cool, manipulative Bella, who hadn't a vulnerable bone in her body. Instead, it was soft-hearted Podge, blindly seeking comfort from the one person she trusted. And it was true—I trusted Ian, even if he despised me, or was it Bella he despised? It was both of us, two liars who'd played him for a fool. When I told him the truth, he would never forgive me.

But did I need to tell him the truth? What kind of difference would it make in the long run? I'd be gone and it would be up to Bella to explain what we'd done. I'd gone past the point of berating myself for my stupidity—now I was having to learn to live with the incredible mess I'd made.

I barely remembered Ian carrying me back here. I'd been so tired, so awash in emotions that I hadn't paid attention as he tucked me into bed. As a lover he was...formidable.

After last night, all I could think of was his long, muscled body, the smell of his skin, the texture of the hair on his legs, the taste of him in my mouth, the marks he'd left on my body. Even Bella's million-dollar makeup couldn't cover up all traces of our night together.

The first thing I did was take a shower to try to wash away the haze that still clung to me. Today would be a tough day, even if I hadn't made the abysmal mistake of going to bed with my vaunted enemy. Granda was gone, and I had spent the night in ecstasy. Ian had been right about everything he'd said about me—I was a liar and a cheat.

I flopped back down the bed, wrapped only in a towel. I had no right to mourn the man I'd been lying to, and I lay there, silent and dry-eyed, staring into the shadows. At last, I could leave. Ian would be hating me after last night's weakness—he would probably prefer it if I weren't around for the funeral, and what would Bella do? Probably skip it to go shopping.

Paris awaited me, and I was now free of any obligation. I'd done what I'd promised Bella, I'd had my time with Granda. Even if my tears had finally dried up, they would emerge again, once I was safely back in the States and trying to resurrect my old life.

Why had I ever listened to Bella? She'd caught me at a vulnerable time, missing my family, but I'd been a fool to say yes. It had been so long since I'd seen Granda—my grief would have been sincere but not so intense if he'd simply stayed a memory. Now everything I'd loved and hated about him had come back, and I couldn't view his passing with anything close to equanimity. It didn't matter that he'd live a long life and was ready to go. I hadn't been ready to lose him.

And I hadn't needed to realize how I felt about Ian the Wretch. Except it hadn't been his wretchedness that had called to me, it was his rare, undeniable sweetness. But that sweetness was for someone else, not the real Bella, not the lying Podge. We were miles apart, and always would be.

190

I needed to go home and lick my wounds—even the idea of Paris couldn't cheer me. All I wanted to do was curl up into a ball and cry, and the night in Ian's bed had denied me that option. The best I could do was run.

IT DIDN'T TAKE me long to pack. I left the accoutrements of Bella's life in the closet—silk jumpsuits and cocktail dresses, tailored suits and thousand-dollar jeans. Instead, I made do with the sundresses and sandals I'd purchased in town. I applied the makeup carefully, making my last be the best, and I went downstairs in one of Bella's less garish day dresses, the only one in a relatively sober shade of blue.

Mary Alice and Valerie were sitting in the women's salon, Mary Alice stretched out on my chaise with a pale hand held to her forehead, the remains of a hearty lunch on the coffee table beside her. When she heard me come in, she lowered her hand to look at me balefully.

"Had a long enough beauty sleep?" she inquired peevishly, while Valerie made a soft noise of protest.

"I'm leaving," I said abruptly, in no mood to justify my grief. "We don't need to fight over him anymore."

"You aren't going anywhere. Ian's gone to get the lawyer for the reading of the will, and Marcus isn't back yet."

"I don't need to hear the will—I doubt I'll be mentioned."

"Don't be coy, Bella," Mary Alice shot back. "I saw the way you sucked up to him, turning him against the rest of us. I wouldn't be surprised if he left you the whole kit and kaboodle."

"I doubt it," I drawled as best I could. It was a horrifying thought. I'd have no choice but to explain who I was, and I could just imagine the cool contempt in Ian's eyes. "Where's Marcus?"

"Apparently, he left early last night, before Granda passed,"

Valerie answered, earning a censorious look from her older sister. "He said he wanted to get you a present to cheer you up."

Was Marcus really that dense that he thought a present would be suitable recompense for the loss of my grandfather? I was afraid he was.

"I'm not in the mood for presents, nor for reading the will. Someone can let me know if I come out a pauper or an heiress. In the meantime, I need to see if Maldonado can drive me to the airport."

"Maldonado went with Ian to make arrangements for the funeral and reception. There's no one here to drive you," Mary Alice said.

"Don't you want to get rid of me?" I asked, desperate. "You could drive..."

"They took the Mercedes. The only thing left are farm vehicles and I'm hardly likely to drive one of those. We'll just have to get along until Ian gets back and gets rid of you."

"Who's getting rid of Bella?" Marcus's voice boomed into the room. He had a huge smile on his face, and his bright blue eyes were unshadowed.

"No one," I answered.

"Why all the long faces? Granda will recover—he always does, and the meantime I brought you the most fabulous present to celebrate our engagement..."

"We're not engaged," I said. "And Granda died last night."

Marcus blinked in disbelief. "No," he said flatly.

"Yes," Mary Alice broke in, blowing her nose vigorously and wiping away her nonexistent tears. "And your fiancée wants to get away as soon as she can. I told her that was impossible but..."

"Will you drive me to the airport?" I interrupted as I looked at Marcus. "There's no need for me to be here anymore, and I need to get back to..." I was about to say New Hampshire before I thought better of it.

"But your present?" Marcus protested, not looking particularly distraught at Granda's death.

"For heaven's sake, what is it?" Mary Alice demanded.

"A new Alfa," he said, preening a bit. "Ian said your old one was totaled, and I know how much you loved that car."

"You bought me a new Alfa?" I demanded in stunned disbelief. "Are you out of your mind?"

"I love you," Marcus said as explanation, and I wanted to shake him. "And we're all about to come into quite a bit of money—this'll be a drop in the bucket."

"I'll drive that to the airport and you can arrange for someone to pick it up," I said tightly, ignoring the fact that I couldn't drive stick. I could figure it out. "I don't need a new car."

"Where's Ian?"

"Making arrangements," Mary Alice and Valerie spoke in unison.

"Well, you certainly can't leave before we bury the old man. How would that look?" Marcus was now looking suitably chagrined, and I wanted to tell him I didn't give a damn, I didn't belong here, I wasn't wanted here, I just needed to be home, wherever that might be.

"Don't worry, Marcus," Mary Alice said. "She's not going anywhere. Not until Ian says she can."

"Ian can go..." I didn't finish the sentence when I heard the door open and the sound of male voices reached us. "He must be back."

He came into the room wearing a sober black suit, an older man with a briefcase beside him. I'd never seen Ian in anything but jeans, and the sight of him was formidable. I immediately focused my gaze on his left shoulder—there was no way I could meet his eyes.

I could feel the damned color flood my skin. I shouldn't even be thinking of last night, but something subconscious sprang to life, and there was no part of him I could look at without remembering. His mouth, everywhere. His clever, wicked hands.

"This is Mr. Fergell, Granda's lawyer," Ian announced to the room in general, and I knew he was avoiding looking at me as well. "We'll be gathering for the reading of the will after lunch in the library. The service and reception will be in three days—that was the soonest we could manage. Any of you could always leave and come back. Or not," he added, and I knew he meant me. For some reason, I wasn't going to be allowed to escape, no matter how hard I tried.

Mary Alice immediately began to complain, but I tuned her out as I took a tentative glance at Ian when I was certain he wasn't looking.

He was. Our eyes met, and his cool gaze was like a punch in the stomach. What had I expected—the tender lover he'd showed me last night? "We need to talk," he said grimly. "I'll get Mr. Fergell settled and you can meet me in the estate office."

"Oh, don't let us disturb you." Mary Alice's voice was thick with irony.

Even she quailed slightly beneath his withering glance. I ignored him. If he thought I was going to present myself to be yelled at, he was sadly mistaken. "I have things to do," I said coolly.

"Show up," he said. "Don't make me come and find you."

There was no missing the threat in his voice. I watched him go, considering my choices. I turned to Marcus, who had been watching all this in silence. "Will you drive me to the airport?" I demanded abruptly.

"Ian wants to see you," he said uneasily.

"I don't want to see him. I want to get out of here."

"No one's stopping you," Mary Alice snapped.

"Everyone's stopping me. Will you take me, Marcus?"

He shook his head. "Talk to Ian first, then we'll see. I don't think you really want to leave before we bury Granda."

"He's gone," I said flatly. "It won't make any difference whether I'm here or not."

"Talk to Ian."

That was the last thing I wanted to do. My earlier determination to tell him the truth had vanished in front of his cold glance. Clearly, he thought the most important night of my life was a big mistake, and I didn't want to hear it. I didn't want to hear the will either— Granda was a fair man. He would leave enough for everyone, and when Bella showed up, she could claim her share and make her explanations. I didn't want to see any of them again.

I was heading upstairs when he caught me, grabbing me by the wrist and stopping my forward flight. "I said we needed to talk."

I yanked, but he held tight, and I considered kicking him in the shins. Instead, I waited for him to remember that touching me was the last thing he wanted to be doing, which didn't take long.

"What about?" I said, resisting the impulse to run up the stairs. He'd probably come after me, and I didn't want him to have an excuse to put his hands on me again. Not when a wicked part of me wanted it.

"About last night," he snapped. "It was a mistake."

I let out a long-suffering sigh. "I didn't see you putting up a fight."

"It meant nothing. Just a normal biological reaction to stress."

"You pompous asshole," I shot back. My wrist hurt from where he'd grabbed me, but his words were far more painful. "It was comfort."

"It was lust," he said flatly. "There's no need to make a big deal out of it. It's not as if we haven't done it before."

That was enough to shock me. Bella had slept with Ian, the man she insisted she hated? Bella had shared what I had last night? I wanted to throw up.

"Do you have to bring that up?" I said in my best Bella drawl, hoping my face didn't show how stricken I was. "It's ancient history."

"I just wanted to make sure you know it didn't mean anything."

"Of course it didn't. In fact, I don't see any point in me staying here any longer. Surely there's someone here who can drive me to the airport. I'm going to Paris."

He let out a snort of disgust. "Not now, you're not. We've got a grandfather to bury, and we need to present a united front."

"No!" I cried, near the breaking point. "I stayed for Granda's sake. I'm not staying for yours."

"You can always walk," he said. "We're reading the will in less than an hour now. Maybe Granda left you enough to buy you a new car."

"Marcus already did."

"He did what?"

"He bought me a new Alfa."

"Then drive that to the airport," he snapped.

I could hardly confess that I couldn't drive stick, not with my history with the Alfa. "I hate you," I said.

"So you've told me. I'm not too fond of you either. It's a shame we're so good in bed together. Be in the library by one or I'll come to get you, and I don't think you'd like that."

"I don't like bullies."

"I don't like liars," he shot back, and left me.

I SHOWED up in the library at the dot of one, only to find the entire family and staff had gathered. Mr. Fergell sat at Granda's huge desk, papers in front of him as he fiddled with his glasses. There was only one seat left, directly in the front, next to Ian, and for a moment, I considered whether I could just lurk in the back of the room. I would have tried it, except all eyes turned to me, and Mr. Fergell looked up.

"Come in, young lady. There's a seat for you up front."

What Would Bella Do? I tossed my hair over my shoulder and sauntered into the room, taking my seat next to Ian. Come hell or high water, I was leaving this afternoon. Somehow, I would wrangle that overpowered death trap into sedate behavior and abandon it at the airport. It was up to Bella to deal with it.

Plastering a suitably demure expression on my face, I sat there, acutely aware of Ian so close beside me that I could feel his body heat, as Mr. Fergell droned on in Spanish and English, through all the formalities. My Spanish was good, but not up to antiquated legalese, and I was so busy ignoring Ian and everyone else that I paid little attention to what was read. The amount Bella inherited had nothing to do with me, though I suppose I should plan to act gratified or outraged, depending on the bequest, but at the moment, I really didn't care. Granda was fair, and besides, it was his money. He could do with it what he wanted. As long as he left Ian enough money to run Mariposa, then he could lavish the rest of the money on whomever he chose—maybe a home for aging dogs. No, scratch that —Granda had hated dogs.

More droning by Mr. Fergell, and I allowed myself a brief glance down. I could see Ian's hand on the arm of the chair, and a sudden heat filled me. He had beautiful hands—long, deft fingers that...

The sound of my own name brought me out of my distraction and I jerked my head up in surprise. My name, not Bella's. Katherine Mirabel Whitehead.

The sudden silence in the room was deafening, and I wondered what in God's name had been said. It didn't take long to find out.

The room erupted into screeches, shouts of protest, with Marcus charging up to the lawyer and practically yanking him out of his seat. Fergell stood up, trying not to cower in the face of Marcus's raging bulk, and Mary Alice was next to him, an unintelligible string of protests shooting from her mouth. Beside me, Ian hadn't moved.

Pandemonium reigned for the next few moments, and then Ian rose. "Enough," he thundered, and everyone froze.

"But Ian..." Marcus began with just the trace of a whine.

"I won't stand for this!" Mary Alice said, her voice strident. "He's not cutting us out of our inheritance—we're more family than you are, Ian, and I'm not about to sit back and—"

"Be quiet!" he snapped, doing the impossible and silencing Mary Alice. "Everyone just calm down."

"You, of course, have the right to contest the will," Mr. Fergell said calmly. "But Doctor Madhur was one of the witnesses, and he assured me your grandfather was of sound mind when he made this extraordinary decision."

What extraordinary decision? I'd been so busy mooning over

Ian's hands that I hadn't been paying attention. And what did it have to do with me?

"Bella, don't just sit there!" Marcus said. "Say something!"

"She's in shock, and no wonder," Mary Alice said shortly.

"Yes, Bella." Was it my imagination or did Ian's voice caress the name with cynical emphasis? "What do you think of the terms of Granda's will? If affects you more than anyone."

"That's bullshit!" Marcus thundered. "We're all left high and dry by the whim of a senile old man."

"He wasn't senile," Ian corrected him, but I could feel his eyes on me. "And Bella needs money more than the rest of you—she goes through it like water. What do you think?"

"What do I think?" I echoed, stalling for time.

"About the fact that Granda left every single penny to our long-lost cousin Kitty."

A proper heroine would have fainted. But I was afraid that I was the villain of the piece, and I didn't have that option. "That's ridiculous!" I said faintly. "He hasn't seen Kitty since she was sixteen."

"Is there any kind of explanation, Mr. Fergell?" Mary Alice demanded. "Some rationalization for such a crazy decision?"

"As I said before, your grandfather was of sound mind. It was not my place to ask him why he made the decision he did. However, he did leave a letter for one of you."

I immediately looked at Ian. Surely, he must have given him some explanation. He met my gaze, and I recoiled at the cold disgust in his eyes.

"It's for Bella Whitehead," Fergell broke in, reaching out with a sealed envelope. I made no move to take it, and with a muttered curse, Marcus snatched it and shoved it at me.

"What does it say, Bella?" Mary Alice demanded. "Surely he'll give you a good reason for disinheriting his little darling." Her voice was like acid.

"Yes, what does he say?" Marcus added impatiently.

I folded the letter in half and shoved it in my pocket. "I'll read it later."

"Aren't you curious?" Valerie asked, the first time she'd spoken since all hell had broken loose.

"Not particularly," I said lightly. "If he tells me anything I think you all need to know, I'll be sure to pass it on."

"Bitch," Mary Alice said under her breath.

I gave her Bella's most charming smile, the one that left men besotted and had women sharpening their nails, but I didn't say a word.

"He must have been very angry with all of us, to leave everything to Podge," Valerie mused.

"Everything? Including Mariposa?" I couldn't quite fathom it.

"The house, the lands, the olive groves, the vineyards," Ian said in an icy voice. "Everything."

Guilt swamped me, but I had no reason for it. "Don't blame me. I lose out like the rest of you." I looked at Ian. "He really left you nothing?"

"Mr. Whitehead will be adequately compensated for his years of work on the estate," Mr. Fergell intoned.

"Like a goddamned servant," Marcus fumed. "I don't mind so much for me, but for Ian to lose everything..."

Ian made a dismissive gesture. "I don't know about the rest of you, but I've got work to do. The rest of you can fume and fuss all you want—I've got plans to make."

I wanted to go with him. Of course, Bella would be the last person he'd want near him. No, he'd be even less welcoming to Kitty, who'd somehow managed to take everything away from him that he'd worked so hard for.

And what in God's name was I going to do? Tell them who I was? Slink away and refuse the bequest? That made a certain kind of sense, more sense than Granda leaving everything to the child he'd banished. I touched the letter in my pocket. Maybe that would explain things, but I wasn't about to open it. I would leave it behind for Bella whenever she planned to return. Though if there was nothing in it for her, then she might not bother.

It wasn't until that moment that I realized how thoroughly disillusioned I was about my glamorous cousin. I'd let her use me, as she used everyone, and now I was in so deep I didn't know how to crawl out.

"I'm going out," I announced as Ian strode from the room without looking back. "I've got a lot to think about."

"It won't do you any good to chase after Ian—he's in as dire circumstances as the rest of us," Mary Alice said.

"When have I ever chased after Ian?" I said in an icy voice.

There was a sudden, damning silence in the library, and it took all my self-control not to blush. Had I been that obvious? Obvious that even Ian noticed? Of course he'd noticed—I'd spent the night in his bed without a single objection.

And I did want to chase after him. To make him admit that last night was more than simple lust, that it meant something. It would be a waste of time. The man had just been effectively disinherited—he wasn't going to be worried about a night of hot sex.

It was warm and sunny in the courtyard, and there was no sign of Ian. I looked out over the fields and saw they were full of workers. I would be perfectly safe. Wouldn't I?

The man in the *taberna* had terrified me. The huge dark man at Mariposa had sealed my paranoia, and the last thing I wanted to do was be caught alone with him. He could break my neck with a twist of his massive hands, and no one would ever know.

There was only place I felt safe, and this time I was wearing better shoes. Dangerous or not, I was heading back to Pinnacle Point to think about this bizarre turn. Shoving my mane of curls behind my ears, I took off.

It took me longer than I expected to reach the cleft in the rock that delineated the secret path. I'd seen Ian's tall, lean form in the distance, so I knew he wouldn't disturb me, and I thought I recognized the bulk of the man who'd been watching me, far enough away that he'd be no danger to me. There was absolutely no one to disturb me as I followed the winding path through the scattered stones to reach the clearing at the top. No one to ask me pointed questions. I was safe...

"What took you so damn long?" a strident voice demanded when I reached the top of the outcropping. "I've been waiting here forever."

Bella.

CHAPTER

EIGHTEEN

I froze in disbelief. She looked magnificent, of course. White silk pants and jacket, a brilliant flash of color for a top. There was a smudge of dirt along her arm, and a disgruntled expression on her beautiful face, but I still couldn't imagine how I'd managed to fool anyone into thinking I was this dazzling creature.

"What are you doing here?" I demanded.

She ignored the question. "Tell me about the will—I know they were reading it this morning. How did I make out?"

I didn't bother to ask how she knew. "Penniless," I said briefly.

She stared at me in shock, and she no longer looked so stunning. "Don't be ridiculous—Granda adored me. He never would have cut me out of his will!"

"He cut everyone out. He left Mariposa and everything else to Katherine Whitehead."

I'd seen Bella look sunny and charming, I'd seen her frustrated and angry, but I never once suspected that I'd see her looking murderous. "You bitch!" she spat.

The change in her was unnerving, and I shook myself. "I had nothing to do with it. He thought I was you. Believe it or not, I've managed to fool everyone." And then I suddenly realized what her reappearance meant. "What are you going to tell everyone?"

She was still looking at me with hatred in her eyes. "I'm not going to tell anyone anything. Do you think I can just waltz back in after you've been passing yourself off as me? The resemblance is surface—side by side, anyone would know the difference. And it looks like I have no reason to come back, now does it? You're engaged to my boyfriend, you've taken all the money..."

"I'm not engaged to anyone!" I shot back. "I agreed to a fake engagement to make Granda happy, that's all. And as far as Granda knew, he was leaving his money to someone he hadn't seen in over twelve years."

"I'd like to believe you, Podge, but I'm not as gullible as everyone else." She ran her eyes up and down my rumpled appearance. "I don't know that you fooled anyone. You don't really look that much like me."

Facing her, I had to agree. Even in one of her rages, she looked angelic, and she was right, I was just poor old Podge, a little thinner, a little older, but always a pale copy.

"What I want to know," she said in a biting tone, "is what you intend to do about this debacle. You'll refuse the money, of course."

"Of course." There had never been any question of it. I wasn't going to take Mariposa from Ian, and I certainly wasn't going to take a fortune based on a lie. I'd long ago given up the idea that Granda was going to leave me anything—I wouldn't be any worse off than I had been when I'd started this mess.

"And just how are you going to do that?" Bella's tone was icy.

I looked at her, at beautiful, charming Bella who was eying me like a skunk, and something finally snapped. "I'll manage," I said in an equally cold voice. "In the meantime, you'd better make up your mind. Someone's going to see you and then you'll have no choice but to explain yourself. You're right—side by side we're not that much alike. But no one's going to believe I came up with such a ridiculous idea in the first place."

"I don't think you'd want me coming clean, Podge. After all, that would out you as the heiress, and then no one would have your back. I believe you when you say you didn't manipulate Granda, but the others might not be so kind."

"Then go away," I said wearily. "I'll figure out a way to get us out of this mess." This mess she had instigated, but I wasn't going to deny my responsibility. I'd been fool enough to say yes.

It was odd how such perfect features could look almost ugly. Her eyes were narrowed, her full mouth twisted in distrust. "You should go back home."

"I've been trying to, ever since I've arrived!"

"Try harder," she said coldly.

I'd never been the object of Bella's rage and scorn before, and it was deeply unnerving. I'd been an even bigger idiot than I'd realized, letting myself be manipulated by her sugary sweetness. The sense of betrayal overruled everything, and I wanted to scream at her. Instead, I bit my lip.

"Granda left a letter for you," I said, abruptly remembering. "You're the only one he did." I dug in my pocket and handed it to her, and she snatched it, ripping it open.

It was long, two pages worth in Granda's spidery script, and she glanced through it before folding it back up and pushing it into the white Hermès handbag she'd brought with her. For some reason, the sight of that priceless accessory was the final straw, the last veil falling from my eyes as I looked at my selfish, venal cousin.

"What did he say?" I asked, knowing full well she wasn't going to tell me.

"Just a pile of excuses," she said briefly. "But that's not going to matter, is it, Podge? You're going to do the right thing, aren't you?" Just like that, her cold anger vanished, and she smiled at me, that sweet, wheedling smile that used to feel like sunshine on an icy day.

But I was still frozen. "Yes," I said. "Ian's wanting me to stay for the funeral, but I'm trying to leave sooner."

"Stay for the service," she said suddenly. "It's only two days away, and it would look odd if you just disappeared. It'll be easy enough to deal with things once you get back to the States." She shoved her perfect mane of curls back away from her face. "Everything will be just fine, Podge," she said. "It'll be easy enough to fix. In fact, I'll come and help you. Of course there'd be no way you'd want to keep all that money—you've always been the fairest of us."

I gave her a tight-lipped smile in return, saying nothing, but Bella was oblivious. "You're right, I'd better get out of here before someone sees us and all our hard work is in vain." At that moment, I couldn't think of her particular share of the hard work of the masquerade, but I didn't point that out. I was feeling wretched and guilty enough.

She started past me, smelling of some fresh and innocent perfume, and then halted. "Tell me, how has Ian been? Has he given you any trouble?"

Nothing but, I thought as I shook my head. "I haven't seen much of him." A straight-out lie, to go with her lies.

"I suppose I should have told you, but he and I had a bit of a fling a while past. You know he's always been in love with me, and he's been desperately jealous of Marcus. I hope that didn't make things uncomfortable. It was long enough ago that he wouldn't be any more likely to notice the difference between us."

Another piece of information I could have happily done without. "He's been busy—if he was in love with you, I'd guess he's finally over it."

An ugly look crossed her face for just a moment, and then she had her sunny smile once more. "Let's hope so. It was tremendously tiresome." Before I could realize what she was doing, she pulled me into her scented embrace. "You've been a better friend than I deserve, Podge," she murmured in my ear. "I won't forget it." A moment later she was gone.

I looked down and saw that my hands were shaking. My sense of betrayal was overwhelming—I'd loved and admired Bella my entire life, holding her up as a vision of what a Whitehead ought to be. When idols fall, they fall hard, but oddly enough, my anger wasn't for her, it was for me, for being so goddamned vulnerable, for believing in those years of sugared sweetness. She was the one who'd given me that hated nickname that still made me feel fat and clumsy.

I shoved my hair away from my face, Bella's hair, and realized my face was wet with tears. Of course, it was. All I seemed to do was cry nowadays, over Granda, over Bella, over Ian.

No, not over Ian. Never over Ian. He hadn't made love to me, he'd made love to the ghost of Bella, and even that he'd regretted. I was the outsider, the one who didn't belong. I couldn't even begin to fathom why Granda had changed his will—maybe his letter to Bella had explained his decision, but she hadn't bothered to share any of it.

I stiffened my spine. Enough was enough. I'd been kept prisoner here for the last few days, despite my half-hearted efforts to escape. No more. Leaving everything to me was just one more of Granda's manipulations, and while I loved him, missed him already, I wasn't going to jump to his tune any longer. I was going home, refusing the inheritance, and getting on with my life.

But first, I was going to tell Ian exactly who I was.

My walk back to the house was uneventful, the only uncomfortable moment when I saw my watcher once more, loitering near the cleft in the rock that led to Pinnacle Point. He wasn't close enough to speak to, and I was half tempted to march over to him and demand to know why he was following me, but there was no one else in sight on this perversely sunny day, and I wasn't a complete idiot, even if I'd been acting like one. I gave him a friendly nod and started down across the fields. He didn't nod back.

By the time I returned to the house, everyone was at lunch—I could hear Mary Alice's strident voice and Marcus's deep one from the dining room. I almost headed straight upstairs until I remembered I had vowed to talk to Ian. Once he knew the truth, I would be out of there so fast my head would spin.

All conversation stopped as I walked in the room, but Ian wasn't there, just the cousins and Marcus. Marcus had traded in his pale pink jacket for something more somber, and the sisters were both in over-the-top funereal black. Clearly, they'd arrived here ready for mourning.

"Where have you been?" Mary Alice demanded.

"Walking," I said briefly.

"Well, you can't expect us to hold lunch for you if you go wandering off. And really, it's most inconsiderate of you. There are things that have to be decided, plans to be made..."

"I thought Ian was taking care of all that," I said. "Where is he, by the way?"

"God knows," Marcus said. "Probably doing what we've been doing. Trying to track down Podge."

God, I hated that name! "And did you?" I asked innocently.

"You're the only one who's been in touch with her over the last few years. Apparently, she'd been living in New Hampshire but she's disappeared without a trace. You must have her phone number somewhere."

Bella had my phone—it would serve her right if I gave them that number. I shook my head. "I haven't talked to her in ages."

"Someone has to tell her Granda died," Marcus said.

"And that she's managed to end up with everything," Mary Alice added in an acid voice.

I could have told them all the truth—after all, Ian would have that opportunity, but for some reason, it was important to me to tell him first. "Does Mr. Fergell have contact information?"

"He has nothing," Mary Alice snapped. "Clearly, we need a new lawyer—he's been completely inadequate. In fact, I wouldn't be surprised if he was working with Podge and splitting the money."

"Don't be ridiculous," I said wearily. "Kitty hasn't been here in over twelve years—Granda banished her. The idea that she could manipulate him into leaving her money is absurd."

"Did you see your car?" Marcus said eagerly, changing the subject.

The new Alfa had been sitting in the courtyard, a gleaming red. I'd barely glanced at it. "It looks very nice," I said lamely.

"No one cares about the goddamned car," Mary Alice snapped. "We've got more important things to worry about."

"I'll go upstairs and see if I have any information on getting in touch with Kitty," I said, unable to bear their company a moment longer. "Would you tell Ian I need to talk to him?"

"What about?" Marcus demanded suspiciously.

"About my leaving," I said truthfully.

"You can't go until after the service," Valerie spoke up.

"Watch me."

At least no one tried to follow and reason with me.

Mary Alice's voice trailed after me. "Typical. She was only here for the money and now that she's lost that, she has no time for anyone."

"Except Ian," Marcus voice followed, and there was an odd note in it.

Fuck. Them. All. Particularly Ian.

It wasn't until I reached my room that I remembered Bella's conversation. She knew about the fake engagement, she knew the will was being read. How? Was someone in on our ridiculous charade? Who could have possibly told her—these things weren't public knowledge.

Someone in this house, or anywhere on Mariposa, was a spy, and my bet was on the mysterious man who seemed to follow me wherever I went. But why would Bella do it? She'd always treated the workers as beneath her notice, including Maldonado. The idea of her setting up an informant was both unlikely and extremely creepy.

The truth of the matter was that my disenchantment with Bella ran deep, and I didn't trust a word she said. Whatever had been in that letter might have explained a great deal, and she'd done nothing but shove it in her handbag.

I was steeling myself to face Ian—at some point, I expected I was going to have to confront Bella herself. That, or maybe I could just fade away. Bella had always had a habit of showing up when she wanted something, and once I got rid of the bequest, I wouldn't have anything she needed. She'd take care of the ghosting.

I picked up the state-of-the-art iPhone Bella had given me, with its ridiculous numbers of cameras and its facial recognition, and resisted the impulse to hurl it against the wall. There was still no signal down here, but there must be internet access somewhere. There'd be no way for Ian to do business without it, and Mary Alice had said they'd been searching for any trace of me—where else but on the internet?

On top of that, there had to be goddamned telephones in the office and the kitchen, and I'd never even thought of that. Escape had always been closer at hand than I'd imagined, and I'd been a total idiot.

No, I hadn't. For all my complaints, I hadn't really wanted to leave. I hadn't wanted to leave Granda, I hadn't wanted to leave Mariposa, the only constant home in my life. And damn it, I hadn't wanted to leave Ian.

I was more than ready to go now. The mess was so bad that the only way I could make sense of it was with an ocean's distance between us. I had no intention of taking Bella's money and heading to Paris—I wanted someplace to curl up and lick my wounds. I had no idea where that was, but New England was a start.

There was no sign of anyone when I went down to the kitchen—even Maldonado had disappeared. The telephone hung on the wall, but there was nothing useful like a telephone book. I tried my luck with information and my decent Spanish, but got nowhere in my search for a car, and I ended up slamming down the phone in frustration.

I wasn't happy with the idea of broaching Ian's office, but if I was looking for internet, that was where I'd find it. I knew he'd taken over Granda's old library, but I'd kept strictly away, not wanting to run into him and the way he looked at me. Not anymore.

The graceful room was a travesty of what it had once been. The rows of leather-bound books were gone, replaced by file boxes and electronic equipment. His desk was littered with papers—odd, I would have thought he would be almost compulsively neat. Most control freaks were, and there was no question that Ian had been trying to control my presence here since I first arrived. The desktop computer was turned on, but of course it had password protection up the wazoo, and God knew I couldn't begin to guess what he would use. The phone by his desk had three lines, none of which were lit up, and I opened the top drawer of the desk, hoping to find an internet password conveniently stuck there.

Instead, I found a gun. I stared at it in numb disbelief, then slammed the drawer shut again. I shouldn't be surprised—rabbits were both a constant problem and a national delicacy, and hunting them was an expected part of farm life. But who would hunt them with a handgun? I didn't want to think about it.

I looked around me nervously. At any moment, I expected Ian to appear, cold and contemptuous as he had been the last time I'd seen him. He had no reason to direct all that anger at me—as far as he knew, I had nothing to do with the contents of the will. In truth, I hadn't. For some reason, Granda had dispossessed all his relatives for a virtual stranger, and I had no idea why. All I could figure was that rather than a gift to me, it was more about the slap to everyone else. I couldn't even take hope from a long-lost gesture in my favor.

I was half-tempted to take the gun with me. The man who lurked in the shadows unnerved me, the memory of the man on the dance floor still upset me. I didn't feel safe, but I knew I was being ridiculous. The man at the *taberna* had been a crude drunk, the man who followed me was simply one of the many workers. And I had no idea how to shoot a gun, if by any chance I felt I needed to. No, Ian the Wretch could keep it safe to take potshots at rabbits nibbling on the grapevines.

The first person I ran into when I left the office was the last person I wanted to see. Marcus was there, and I wondered if he'd been lying in wait for me.

"Bella, darling!" he crooned from behind me as I closed the office door. "I've been looking for you everywhere!"

"Why?" I said briefly, in no particular mood to deal with him.

"We need to talk. You know we do."

"Why?" I said again, keeping my voice clipped.

"Our engagement..."

"We're not engaged," I said wearily. "We never were—you know it was just a charade to make Granda happy. Now that he's gone, there's no need for any more pretense."

"It wasn't just pretense on my part. I love you," he said earnestly. "I still want to marry you."

I just looked at him for a long moment, wondering what I had ever seen in him. He was very handsome—there was no doubt on that score. But there was something...empty about him, all that surface charm and nothing beneath it.

Whereas his brother was his complete opposite. No charm at all, but emotion and torment and anger seething beneath him, and all that anger was directed at me.

"You don't," I said. How could he look at a stranger and think it was the woman he loved? Because he never looked beneath the surface. Anyone who looked like Bella would do.

But Marcus wasn't easily cowed. "Come for a drive with me. You haven't even tested your new car. We could drive along the cliffs, watch the birds."

"I don't want the car." My, I was being selfless nowadays, considering I was basically penniless. Not only was I giving up a fortune, I was tossing aside a car worth...God, I didn't even know what an Alfa cost, but it was certainly more than an aging Subaru.

"Just come for a drive with me," he insisted. "We can talk..."

"No. I'm going for a walk. Alone." I decided it on the spur of the moment.

"I'll come with you."

"Alone," I repeated. A walk in the wood would do me good, away from bickering relatives and Ian, who'd simply disappeared.

He looked crestfallen, like a child deprived of a treat. "At least tell me where you're going. Someone needs to keep track of you, so we can find you if you don't come back."

"Why wouldn't I come back?" I demanded uneasily.

He shrugged his massive shoulders in the perfectly-tailored dark gray jacket. "You could get lost. Twist your ankle in one of the rabbit holes that litter the place. Remember when you fell in the cave?"

I remembered all too well. I remembered who had abandoned me and who had rescued me. "I'm not going anywhere near the caves."

There was a sudden odd expression on his face. "Keep away from Pinnacle Point. No one would see you or hear you if you got into trouble. It's too wild out there. Promise me."

"I'm just going for a walk," I said wearily. "I need time to think."

"Ian wouldn't want you to go off on your own."

He couldn't have said anything more likely to get me going. "I don't give a rat's ass what Ian does or does not want." I was losing what little calm I had. I needed to go somewhere and cry, somewhere no one would find me.

"Bella," he said with long-suffering patience, and I wanted to scream at him. *I'm not Bella, I'm Kitty!*

"Just leave me alone!" Without another word, I stomped away from him, down the hallway and through the deserted kitchen to head straight back toward Pinnacle Point. I was going to cry again, and I was damned if I was going to let anyone see me.

The olive groves were empty—no workers in sight. I glanced around to see whether my watcher was anywhere around, but I didn't see him, and I breathed a sigh of relief. At least I could have an afternoon of peace, away from everyone, to figure out what I was going to do next.

I reached the narrow trail that led up to the point, moving into the deeper forest as I tossed solutions around in my brain. Maybe I should just go to the lawyer and explain the situation. The ugliness of that conversation made me cringe, but there was no way getting around it. I was going to have to come clean to everyone, and I dreaded it.

Unless I could simply disappear and send word through lawyers that I was relinquishing the bequest, turn myself back into Kitty. Back into Podge.

I no longer knew who I was. Was I vain, beautiful Bella with the charm and trustworthiness of a snake, was I plump and awkward Podge, or was I a failed academic hopelessly in love with her wretched cousin-by-marriage? Or some miserable combination of all three?

I needed to step out from the trap I'd willingly walked into, I needed to find myself first, before I began to deal with losing Ian.

Not that I'd ever had him. Heightened emotions and sorrow had thrown us into bed, and that wasn't going to happen again. We were all learning to deal with the loss of Granda, each in our own way, and we'd be very careful to avoid such mistakes.

And then I heard it. The snap of a branch, the shuffle of leaves. I wasn't alone in the woods.

I froze, looking around me, but the trees and shrubbery were so dense I couldn't see anyone. Nevertheless, I knew. Someone was watching me. Someone who meant me harm.

I shook myself. I was getting paranoid in my old age—no one was out to get me. I was perfectly fine...

Something sped past me, so fast I couldn't see it, and there was a solid thwack into the tree trunk up ahead. I was staring at it stupidly when I heard the crashing sound of something large moving through the woods, fast, coming straight at me.

I turned to run, blind panic slicing through me, but it was too late. The man who'd been watching me burst through the woods and flung himself at me, hitting me with the full force of his huge body and taking me down to the ground.

I fought him like a wild woman, scratching and hitting at him. I opened my mouth to scream for help when his large hand clamped down on it, muffling any sound.

"*Colar!*" he said in a low, tight voice. "*Collarse la boca.*" Shut up. Shut your mouth.

I wasn't about to do any such thing, and I sank my teeth into his hand as hard as I could, hoping to draw blood, but he didn't even flinch. "They have a gun," he whispered urgently in my ear. "Do not move."

It took a moment for his words to sink in, and I stopped moving, holding very still. And then I heard it, the sound of someone else moving through the woods, stealthy, like a hunter stalking his prey. And I was the prey.

I don't know how long we lay there, silent, barely breathing. He was heavy, but he made no move to get off me, and I shifted uncomfortably, a rock digging into my back. "Stay still," he whispered sharply, and I did so.

I have no idea how much time passed—it seemed endless—until the man finally rolled off me. "I think they are gone," he said in heavily accented English.

I answered him in Spanish. "Who? Who's gone, who are you, what the hell is happening?" My voice was rising in incipient hysteria.

"I am Salvador. I've been watching out for you."

I stared at him in amazement. "But why?"

"Because he thought you might be in danger."

"Who did?" I demanded, but I knew the answer.

"Señor Ian. He told me to keep you in sight at all times. I thought maybe he was crazy—men get that way over a woman." He shrugged. "I was supposed to keep out of the way, but then someone took a shot at you and I could not hide any longer."

"Someone took a shot at me?" I repeated stupidly.

"*Idiota,*" he muttered under his breath. "What did you think that was back there—a bumblebee?"

I shivered in the hot afternoon sun. "But who would want to kill me? I haven't done anything to anyone." Not strictly true, but hardly worth killing for.

"I do not know, I only know what Señor Ian asked me to do." The huge man scrambled to his feet, looking around him, and then held out a hand to me.

I rose, brushing myself off. I felt like I was in some sort of alternate reality, one where people wanted to kill me and nothing was as it seemed. "We should tell the police," I said.

"That is up to Señor Ian," Salvador said darkly. "I will bring you back to him."

"No." My reaction was immediate, and I wasn't quite sure why. Part of me wanted to throw myself into Ian's arms and weep. He was strength, he was safety.

He was also someone with a gun. He had no reason to take a potshot at me—if he wanted to get rid of me, he could have made that happen at any time, instead of consistently foiling my attempts to escape. Nor would he have set up a bodyguard. Whoever was a threat to me, it couldn't be Ian.

Salvador grabbed my arm ungently. "We will tell Señor Ian," he said again, his voice brooking no objections, and I went along with him, down the rocky trail, all the time feeling that I had a target on my back.

I felt a little better by the time we reached the olive groves, and Salvador released his death grip on my arm. He must have sensed my acquiescence, and he strode down the rutted road to Mariposa, standing majestic in the bright Spanish sun.

But Ian was nowhere to be found. It was the hour of the siesta and I assumed the rest of my so-called family were resting. I doubted if Ian bothered with it.

Any of them could have been in the woods leading to Pinnacle Point. It was absurd—no one had a reason to want to harm me, but they were the only ones here.

Unless they knew who I really was. If any of them had an inkling that I was Granda's unexpected heiress, they had many millions of reasons for wanting me dead. But so far, everyone had taken me at face value, a far cry from the days when I was a plainer, paler version of Bella.

"Stay here," Salvador ordered me once we stepped into the empty kitchen, and he started off into the rest of the house. Not being the obedient sort, I followed right after him, straight to Ian's office. It was still empty.

Salvador made a sound of annoyance. "I will find him. In the meantime, you should go to your room and stay in there. Don't let anybody in."

I just stared at him. "You think someone here wanted to hurt me?"

"Someone here *did* try to hurt you," he said oppressively. "They had to come from somewhere. Do as I say."

Ah, Spanish men and their lordly ways! Though his bossiness was reasonable, given the situation. "Tell Ian to come talk to me when you find him," I said in answer. "If he doesn't, I'll come looking for him."

Salvador looked disapproving but he said nothing, and for a moment, it was a stand-off in the hallway by the stairs, as he waited for me to obey his orders. With a low, decidedly American curse under my breath, I climbed the stairs, still with that uncanny feeling of a target on my back.

Dutifully, I locked the door to my bedroom, then kicked off my shoes and lay down on the bed. Siestas had never been my thing, and after the events of the day I was even less likely to sleep, but I'd misjudged just how exhausting a near-death experience could be. I was asleep within minutes.

The pounding on my door woke me up in the early dusk, and I stumbled out of bed, woozy and disoriented. At least Ian and I would finally talk, but without thinking, I opened the door. It was Marcus standing there, filling the frame, an unsuitably cheerful expression on his face. "There you are, sleepy-head. The cousins and I are going out to the Constanzas for dinner, and I knew you'd want to come."

"Is Ian coming?" I temporized.

"Ian?" he echoed. "I doubt it. No one's seen him all day, and besides, he hates the Constanzas."

If he hated them, it was good enough for me. "I think I'll skip it." I hesitated, considering it, before I said, "I had a bit of an adventure today."

His placidly cheerful face didn't change. "You did?"

"Someone took a shot at me as I was climbing toward Pinnacle Point," I said flatly.

He frowned. "You must have imagined it. Why would anyone want to shoot you? Everybody loves you!"

Now that was a complete lie, but Marcus might be blinded by whatever it was he called love. "The bullet went into a tree, but it was definitely a close call."

"If it happened, and I'm saying if, then it must have been an accident. People shoot rabbits all over that area—you must have run afoul of a poacher. Did you call out? Warn people you were there?"

I wasn't about to tell him about Salvador or Ian's concern. Concern that didn't help much if the damned man was going to disappear for days on end, I added to myself.

"I didn't," I answered him. "I was too shaken."

"Well, there you go! You got in the way of a hunter, and you're just lucky you weren't hurt. You've got to pay better attention, Bella. We don't want anything to happen to you!" He sounded so sincere.

"Maybe," I said. "Do you know where Ian is?"

"You don't want to bother him with this," Marcus said. "He's got enough on his plate right now, trying to find Podge."

"I need to talk to him."

"Why?" Was Marcus being particularly dense, or was he somehow jealous? He had no reason to be, as Ian had made abundantly clear.

"I just do." I replied stubbornly. "Where is he?"

Marcus shrugged his massive shoulders. "Beats me. I haven't seen him all day."

So it wasn't just me he was ghosting. What in God's name was he doing?

"I think you should come with us tonight. You know the Constanzas would love to see you."

"No." My voice grated a bit, and I managed to summon a faint smile. "But give them my best."

Marcus beamed. "That's my girl. Let me know if you change your mind."

That wasn't happening. I wasn't going anywhere until I saw Ian and confessed my sins. He needed to know that Mariposa, the olive groves, and the vineyards were still his. I didn't want them.

But why did he think I was in danger, enough that he had someone watch over me? I hadn't told him the details of my encounter on the dance floor, that the man had threatened to kill me. Was he the one who had shot at me? He'd frightened me, but I hadn't for one moment thought he was serious. Unless...hadn't Granda mentioned Bella's drug-dealing ex-lover? Surely she wouldn't have set me up as a patsy if a criminal was after her. Would she?

I shook myself, mentally and physically, but it did no good. I was seriously afraid. Too much had happened in the last few days for me to just shrug it off. If someone truly was trying to hurt the person they thought was Bella, then I needed to get out of here. Telling Ian the truth would finally make him let me go.

CHAPTER

NINETEEN

When I woke, it was in darkness, and I scooted over on the
bed to turn on the meager bedside lamp. I hadn't meant to
fall asleep, but exhaustion must have overtaken me, and I'd slept
through the afternoon and into the evening. Dragging myself out of
bed, I shoved a hand through my unruly tangle of hair and blinked.
Depending on the hour, the house was probably empty, and for the
first time, I was regretting my refusal to join the others.

I shook myself. I was being silly—Maldonado would be here, and
I would finally be able to track down Ian and settle things. There was
nothing to be nervous about.

The light beside my bed flickered, and then went out, plunging
me back into the darkness, and I had to swallow a little squeak of
dismay. The electricity at Mariposa was notoriously unstable—the
power had gone out on at least three occasions in the few days I'd
been there. Maldonado would fix it.

Maldonado did not fix it. There was a bright, three-quarter moon
overhead, streaming a fitful light through my open window,
complete with the soft scent of bougainvillea, and I took a deep,
encouraging breath. I knew where the electric panel was; I could

219

throw a breaker as well as anyone. I had an iPhone with a flashlight app on it—I'd be perfectly fine.

The inky darkness of the hallway wasn't particularly reassuring, but I held my phone on high, illuminating the pathway. The cousins were at the opposite end of the house, and I had no idea where Marcus slept. There would be no one close by, assuming they were even in the house.

They weren't, I knew that, and I didn't like it. I was entirely alone in the old house I'd always loved, but I told myself there was nothing to be nervous about. That gunshot this afternoon had to be a random hunter—there was no reason anyone would want to hurt me.

I was near the top of the stairs when I realized I'd forgotten to put on shoes, making my progress unnervingly silent. I was about to start down the stairs when I heard it—the soft scuffle of a shoe, the almost imperceptible sound of someone breathing.

"Is anyone here?" I called out, steeling myself.

There was no answer, just the quiet squeak of the old wood as someone stepped on it. "Hello?" I tried again. Silence.

I wasn't going to panic—there was nothing to be afraid of. I could simply turn and shine the flashlight to the top of the stairs and see who was there. Stalking me.

I took another step down, holding on tightly to the banister. Again, an answering creak from above, and all my brave self-talk began to vanish. I descended the staircase a little faster, as my heart began to race and my breath caught. *There's no one there, it's just the sound of the old house, there's no one there*, I told myself, over and over again as I edged my way down into the darkness. *Everyone's gone out, no one wants to hurt me, I'm perfectly safe...*

I reached the first floor and my fragile bravado failed me. I began to run, racing barefoot across the tile floors to the massive stone staircase that was the centerpiece of the house. My heart was beating so loudly, I couldn't hear if anyone was coming after me, but it didn't matter. Panic had taken hold of me, and I knew I had to get away from there. I scrambled down the last flight, almost tripping in my haste to get away, and I reached the bottom with a gasp of relief.

Peering back up the stairs, I could see no one, not even with the help of the flashlight, but I was sure I hadn't imagined those quiet footsteps. Someone had wanted to frighten me. The same with the gunshot earlier today—it had been a warning, and I had better start paying attention.

But why would someone want to hurt me? I hadn't done anything to anybody, I was just...

I was just Bella. Bella, with the gangster boyfriend and the devious ways, Bella who cared for no one but herself. I realized that truth now without an ounce of surprise—I had always believed in Bella's vision of herself: charming, kind, glamorous. She was charming and glamorous, all right, but that kindness had been nothing but a front, and clearly she'd made more enemies than she or I realized.

No, cancel that. She probably realized all too well how many enemies she had. I'd been the perfect patsy—anyone who wanted to hurt Bella would come after her doppelganger. That sudden, sharp knowledge was like a stab to the heart.

I felt cold, so cold, even on this warm spring night, and I didn't know whether I was shaking from the chill or fright. How could they have left me at the mercy of whatever dreadful thing wanted to hurt me? How could Ian have simply vanished...?

He hadn't vanished after all. There was a light under the library door, and I froze. Had he finally returned? Or was it one of my enemies, lying in wait for me again, determined to finish me off?

Suddenly my panic dissolved into anger. How dare he abandon me like that, how dare he disappear, leaving me to the mercy of God knew what? Ignoring my chill, I strode across the hallway, reached the door to the library, and slammed it open in a fine fury.

He was standing over the desk, and he looked up at me in the moonlight, clearly not glad to see me. Fuck him.

"Where the hell have you been?" I demanded.

He just stared at me. "None of your goddamned business. What's wrong?"

I looked at him, taking him in for the first time in days. He looked exhausted, those piercing blue eyes shadowed in the moonlight, his hair rumpled, unshaven, beautiful. And I couldn't allow myself to be vulnerable.

"Why did you tell Salvador to follow me?" I demanded abruptly.

"Someone threatened you at the *taberna*."

"Yes. But I saw Salvador before that happened."

"Let's just say I wasn't sure you were safe, especially after the Alfa crashed—I'd just had it serviced. The brakes shouldn't have failed. You've made a lot of mistakes over the years, Bella-Beast. Your latest boyfriend's a murderer and you've done something to piss him off, which wasn't wise on your part. There have been people in town asking after you, strangers showing up at Mariposa. If you're going to get yourself killed, it's not going to be on my watch."

"I'm touched," I said sweetly. "Then why don't you let me go?"

"You're still my responsibility."

"I am not!" I shot back. "I can take care of myself."

"You haven't been doing a very good job of it—you've probably amassed any number of enemies over the years. I was just making sure you were safe."

"You weren't doing a very good job of it. Someone shot at me today," I said, and his cold cynicism dropped for a minute.

"You were shot at? When? Where?"

"Ask your stooge. He scared the hunter away, said he was someone going after rabbits, but I don't believe him any more than I believe you. Someone wants me dead, and it's probably you!"

A thunderous look crossed his face, and he took a step toward me, then stopped himself. "It's tempting."

All the calm that I'd managed to drag around me short-circuited, and if he'd been near enough, I would have slapped him. The best I could do was say "fuck you" as I slammed the library door behind me, heading back up into the darkness and the shadowy nemesis that may or may not be there.

I heard the library door slam open again, and I ran, determined to lock myself in my bedroom away from everybody. My fury had overtaken my earlier panic, and if I weren't such a coward, I would have gone straight out to the brand-new Alfa and ground its gears all the way down into town.

He was right behind me, and I knew he was no mysterious threat. He was Ian, and he was enraged, even more so when I tried to shove my bedroom door closed.

He was much stronger than I was, and the door bounced against the wall as he shoved it open. He reached for me, and I fought him, struggling as he held me tight against his body, kicking at him.

"Stop it!" he ordered, and his words only made me madder. His hand was in reach, and I bit it, hard.

"You little cat," he said, releasing me. "Calm the fuck down."

"Get out of my room." I seethed with fury.

He slammed the door shut behind him, closing us into the darkness. My breath was coming in harsh, tearful gasps, and I wanted... I wanted...

I wanted him, God help me. "What do you think you are doing?" I demanded.

He didn't say a word. He simply moved and pulled me into his arms, his mouth hard on mine.

All I had to do was say no, and he'd leave me. I knew it, knew that it would be forever. There was no future for me with this man I was obsessed with, no happy ever after. But I could have it tonight, one last time.

I was wearing a light sundress, and he tore the buttons down the front. I should have struggled, should have pushed him away, but the feel of him, so big, so strong, so warm, short-circuited my common sense. It didn't matter that I was furious with him—I reached up and caught his face with my hands, pulling him down to my mouth.

It wasn't a gentle kiss, a worshipful kiss—it was raw and carnal, and I couldn't get enough of him, of his arms around me, clamping me tight to his body, of his hungry mouth, of everything I wanted in this life and couldn't have.

He was hard, and I was wet, and more turned on than I'd ever been in my entire life, as he yanked the flimsy panties off me and then hoisted me up in the air, his body pinning me against the door. Putting my arms around his neck, I held on.

The scrape of his zipper was my only warning, and then he was inside me, thrusting sure and hard and deep as my body welcomed him, my soul needed him, my heart loved him.

Sinking my head against his shoulder, I held on, needing this, needing him. Needing him inside me, filling me, pushing, thrusting.

The unfamiliar position added to the power of his possession, and without thought, I sank my teeth into his shoulder, hard, and this was no gentle coupling. His thrusts were rougher, faster, as I clung to him, the uncertainty of balance an added arousal.

I came, hard, burying my shriek against his shoulder, and he froze in my arms. And then he moved, never breaking our connection, and carried me through the darkened room to my bed, the two of us sinking down onto the mattress.

The sexual frenzy that had controlled us had shifted, changed. Bracing himself on his arms, he looked down at me as he moved, slow, deliberate thrusts that made me shiver in a carnal response. I wouldn't have thought I could still feel so much after such a bone-shaking orgasm, but everything had changed, the hurry gone, and his kiss was slow, drugging, tender.

I could feel the desire building inside me again, and I knew I was shaking, I couldn't stop.

His hands were on my breasts, deft, arousing, and I knew that this time, I wouldn't survive.

I gasped, calling out his name. "I can't..." I said in a choked voice. "It's too much."

"You can," he growled in my ear, and he slid his hands beneath my butt, pulling me up so that my clit rubbed against his hard length, and this time, there was no burying the sound of my shocked scream.

It was so powerful I felt suspended in time and space, a convulsing entity that had no purpose except to react to the things he was doing to me.

The fierce grip of the orgasm began to loosen just as he sped up, and I held him, so lost in delight that I didn't know where I ended and he began.

He came, hard, sinking against me, and a last shimmer of response rippled through my body as I cradled him. I had promised myself I wouldn't cry again, but my face was wet with tears. I loved him, and I'd betrayed him, over and over again.

I don't know how long we lay like that, his big body covering me, warming me, but I knew the lie had gone on too long. He would hate me, he would walk away from me, but I had to tell him.

He pushed up, still inside me, and the soft look in his eyes broke my heart. "Did I hurt you?"

Wordlessly, I shook my head, but that didn't reassure him. "I was too rough," he said.

My eyes met his, and I signed my death warrant. "I'm not Bella," I said before I could stop myself. "I'm Kitty." And I steeled myself for his disgust.

But his eyes didn't harden, his luscious mouth didn't curl in contempt.

"I know," he said.

CHAPTER
TWENTY

I froze in his arms. And then I shoved him, and he rolled off me, on to his side, perfectly at ease with the bombshell he'd just dropped on me. "For how long?" My voice was accusatory.

"Since you got off the airplane. I tend to remember the women I sleep with, and you weren't Bella. I just couldn't figure out why."

"But why did you treat me like I was Bella?" I couldn't help but ask.

"I don't like liars."

It was hardly promising, and I felt the familiar shame wash over me. "I just wanted to see Granda before he died," I said quietly. "It was my fault—I never should have listened to her."

"You're right. She's a treacherous bitch. But why didn't you come all those other years when Granda asked for you?"

"He never did," I said miserably. "He told me he never wanted to see me again."

"He asked Bella to bring you back for the last ten years, and you've always refused."

"I never..." I let my voice trail off.

"She never told you, did she? I'm surprised Granda trusted her, but then, the old man always had a soft spot for the two of you."

This was making no sense. Everything I'd believed in, known to be true, was shattering around me, and I struggled to sit up in the bed, my sundress down around my waist. I quickly started to yank it up when his hands stopped me. "Where do you think you're going?" he asked lazily.

"I don't know. I need time to think..."

"You can think in bed," he said as he deftly did away with the rest of the tiny buttons that held the skimpy dress together. "You're staying here."

"And if I don't want to?" I shot back. He wasn't the enemy, I was. So why was I being so hostile?

He smiled at me, a lazy smile that made my stomach knot in longing, and then he leaned over and kissed me, slowly, thoroughly, scattering my desperate attempt to make sense of all this. "You don't want to go anywhere, do you?" he whispered, nipping at my lower lip.

"No," I said in a very small voice.

He knew. He'd always known. I felt foolish, raw, exposed, but he took my hands and placed them on his strong shoulders. "We can talk about this later."

"You should leave," I said instead.

"You should stay," he said, mimicking my tone of voice. "We've barely begun."

"I finished," I said flatly. "And so did you."

He shook his head, that lazy smile of his totally demoralizing me. "We're far from finished, Kitty. I don't know if we ever will be."

It had been so long since I'd heard that name in his rich, gorgeous voice. It wasn't a declaration of love, but it was something, and he was tugging me back into his arms, and I was going, unable to resist him, and there were no more words.

WHEN I AWOKE, I was alone, a small mercy. I felt...so many things. Exhausted, confused, angry. And though he hadn't said the words, loved.

He had touched me in ways I'd never been touched, coaxed me into doing things I'd never considered, and every time I was ready for sleep, he would touch me and I roared to life again. The ugly truth was inescapable. My childhood passion for Marcus's big muscles and dashing smile was exactly that, the passion of a child. Ian's drugging, deeply erotic actions of the night before had stripped me down to nothingness, externally and internally, and all I could think of was him.

In the daylight, the other side of my bed was empty—and I realized with shock it was after eleven. I didn't ask myself how I'd managed to sleep for so long. Given the things he had done to me, the things we had done together, it was amazing I was thinking clearly at all. I grabbed the sundress I'd left on the bathroom door and pulled it over my head, and despite the fact that we'd taken a long, depraved shower together, I still needed another one. But before I planned to do anything else, I had to find Ian. I intended to sneak down the back stairs and confront him. He'd never said a word to me last night, apart from slow coaxing, and I needed to know what he was going to do. Tell everyone? Profess his dying love, or hatred for that matter? No, he didn't hate me. I would be an idiot to think so. I just needed him to set my mind at ease, and then I'd disappear back into my bedroom. Where I might just strip down and roll in my rumpled sheets, remembering.

I was practically tiptoeing down the massive stone staircase when I heard Marcus's voice and swore beneath my breath,, whirling around to try to escape.

Too late. "Bella!" he called out, appearing in the doorway, his handsome face wreathed in smiles. "We've had the best surprise ever!"

I wasn't keen on the idea of surprises, but I plastered an interested smile on my face. I swung around, hoping it looked as if I were just heading upstairs. "Oh, really? You can tell me about it when I come back down. I need a shower and..."

"Where have you been?" he demanded, his eyes narrowing, and I prayed to God I didn't look guilty. Not that there was anything to feel guilty about.

"I got up early and went for a walk," I lied.

"Next time, wear shoes," he said, and came toward me. "Come and see her."

"Her?" I echoed as he pulled me into the blue salon where the family was gathered. "Who...?"

"It's Podge!" he announced cheerfully. "Just in time for Granda's service."

She was standing there, a sweet smile on her face, something very close to a smirk in her eyes. "Hi, Bella," she drawled in my American accent. "It's been too long."

I didn't move as she came forward and hugged me, her small hands hard and painful as she clutched me to her. "Get your shit together," she hissed in my ear, and then took a step back, beaming at me. "You look wonderful, as always."

It was more than I could say for her. She'd braided her long hair and tucked it into a bun, she wore no makeup, a pair of horn-rimmed glasses that I'd never wear, and she'd either been eating nonstop in the time we'd been apart or she was wearing padding around her middle. This was her vision of Podge: plump, plain, bespectacled.

I was too numb to do anything more but smile faintly. "It's good to see you, Kitty," I said. "When did you get here?"

"Oh, hours ago! I shocked the hell out of Ian, but he recovered quickly enough. You didn't tell me how handsome he is, Bella."

Ian was nowhere in the room—just Marcus and the cousins and Maldonado. "I suppose so," I said carefully. "Where is he?"

"Oh, he had to go out to deal with some paperwork, he said," Marcus volunteered. "Probably dealing with that fool Fergell."

"Fergell? Oh, the lawyer," I said.

"Keep up with things," Mary Alice snapped from her position on the lounge. "We've got a will to fix."

I cast an immediate look at Bella, but she was smiling happily, like a nitwit. "Don't worry, Mary Alice," she said sweetly, and I suddenly remembered her name for her. Ian was Ian the Wretch, I was Podge, and Mary Alice was Malice. Valerie wasn't enough of an entity for her to bother with a nickname. "I'm sure we'll be able to clear everything up once I get back to the States."

"Why wait till then?" Mary Alice snapped.

Bella turned to her, all dewy innocence. "My lawyer is there. Surely you don't think I should do this without my lawyer."

"Do what?" I demanded.

Bella smiled sweetly at me. "Make Granda's will right. I have no idea why he left it all to me, but I'm sure we'll figure it out."

The letter I gave her should have explained at least part of it, I thought, but she was still looking at everybody like a halfwit, eager to please. Was that really how she saw me?

"As long as it's fair," Mary Alice said, and Valerie made agreeable sounds.

"Of course," Bella said, and maybe it was only me who noticed that she hadn't said she was giving up the money.

Why the hell had she decided to show up? How was she possibly going to convince everyone of her real identity when she returned, and what did she expect me to do?

"I'm tired," I announced abruptly. "Kitty, why don't you come upstairs with me so we can talk? We have a lot to catch up on."

"Oh, Bella, I'd love to!" Her eyes were shining with delight, and it turned my stomach. Had I really been that needy? "But I really need a nap myself. Jet lag, you know. Can we talk later?"

I could hardly insist. "Whatever you need. I'm in the Queen's Room when you're up to visiting."

Bella's eyes narrowed. "Of course you are." She let out a heartfelt sigh. "I always loved that room."

"You should give it up to her," Mary Alice said. "After all, for the time being, she owns the house and everything here."

"Nonsense," Bella said. "I couldn't ask Bella to give up her bedroom."

I gave her a tight smile. "Of course you couldn't," I said, deliberately not offering. The old Kitty, Podge, would have immediately offered to move out. I had no intention of doing so.

A strained silence filled the room, and then Bella shrugged. "Which room am I staying in?"

"Selene is making up the blue room on the third floor." Maldonado spoke for the first time. "It should be ready by now."

"Bring up my bags, will you?" she said carelessly, too much like the old Bella, but Maldonado's face was inscrutable.

"I will!" Marcus said. "I want to get reacquainted with my long-lost cousin."

He'd never had time for me before, and I wondered at his sudden friendliness. Not that I wanted to think badly of him, but the woman he thought of as Podge now controlled everything, at least for a while, and Marcus was a sensible man.

I headed upstairs after them, just as Mary Alice was launching into a diatribe about who should sleep in the Queen's Room, but they were out of sight by the time I reached my hallway. For some reason I locked the door behind me.

An hour later, I was cleaned up, neatened up, made up, though I was sorely tempted to give up the Bella mask I'd been wearing. Now that she was here, the truth had to come out, and the sooner the better.

But clearly Ian hadn't spilled the beans. I didn't know whether that was a blessing or a curse.

The timid knock on the door didn't fool me. Scrambling off the bed, I went to unlock it, to face my doppelganger. "Let's go for a walk, shall we?" Bella said innocently. "I've been cooped up for too long."

I didn't want to. I wanted her to tell me exactly what the hell was going on, but for some reason, I didn't want her in my coveted room.

"Okay," I nodded. "Let me get some shoes." I slipped on a pair of sandals. They were stylish and comfortable, but a disaster if I needed to run. What an odd thought! Why would I need to run?

We kept up a stream of meaningless chatter on the way downstairs. As far as I could tell, she'd left New England the same day I flew out of Logan, but I had no idea where she'd been. She waited until we were outside in the bright, sunny courtyard to berate me.

"What the hell were you doing, wandering in looking like you'd spent the night with a squadron of Russian soldiers?" she hissed. "I've got my reputation to consider."

Considering that her reputation was better suited to Russian soldiers than mine was, I said nothing. "I went for a walk," I said stubbornly, knowing there was no way to prove otherwise.

"Then why did you have that 'thoroughly fucked' look about you?" she demanded, her servile sweetness vanishing.

I had been. Quite thoroughly, quite gorgeously. Even if I didn't know quite where I stood. "Your imagination," I said briefly. "How did you get here?"

"Easy enough. I called the house and Marcus came down to fetch me in the town car." She'd walked over to the Alfa that had sheltered me last night. "He should have brought this." She turned to me, her face alight with enthusiasm. "Let's go for a drive!"

"I can't drive the thing. I don't know how to drive stick." For some reason, I didn't want to get into that car with her.

"I can."

"Bella never let anyone drive her car," I pointed out. "Make Marcus take you out."

"But I want to talk to you." She opened the driver side door and looked in, a satisfied expression on her face. "Come on!"

"What are you trying to do, Bella?" I demanded, staying a good distance away. "Why did you show up? You've put this entire insane masquerade in danger."

"Don't be such a wimp. We'll carry it off, as long as you don't lose your nerve." She looked at me, and even beneath her unflattering disguise, I could see the real Bella, the hard Bella. "So why don't you tell me what's between you and Ian?"

That was the last thing I wanted to discuss with her, when I had no idea where I stood. I did know he'd pretended to accept her as Podge, and I wasn't about to set her straight. If Ian wanted to keep our secret, he must have some reason, and I wasn't about to say anything until I talked with him.

"Nothing," I said. "We fight all the time."

"Well, at least that's nothing new. And he seemed normal enough when he greeted me. He was very sweet. You know, I used to wonder if he had a thing for you, Podge. After all, he couldn't have me, and there'd always been a protective air about him where you were concerned."

I ignored that. "And he didn't doubt who you were?"

"Not at all," she said smugly. "He gave me a kiss on the cheek and even called me 'Podge.'"

What the hell was going on? Ian would have known who she was —why hadn't he confronted her? "You must have been doing your job well," Bella continued. "I never thought you could carry this off."

"You sent me off thinking they were going to recognize me?" I demanded, horrified.

Bella shrugged, that insouciant gesture I'd worked so hard to replicate. What Would Bella Do? "It was worth the chance."

Not for me, it hadn't been. But then, I had learned the hard way that Bella didn't think about anyone but herself.

"Come on, Podge, get in the car," she wheedled, that pretty smile on her face. "You can drive us down to the first turn and I'll get behind the wheel after that. I've missed my car!"

"This isn't your car. It's an exact duplicate. Yours was in an accident."

Her fine eyes narrowed. "Who was driving it?"

"Ian. The brakes failed and we plowed into a tree." In the ensuing days, I'd almost forgotten about my concussion, but right now my head was pounding.

"So where did this come from?" She was sounding very displeased.

"Marcus bought me a new one."

"Don't you mean Marcus bought *me* a new one?" she said in a silken voice.

"Whatever. It's definitely yours, not mine."

"I want to drive it. Get in."

I shook my head. "I don't want to."

"Don't be such a stick in the mud. Obviously, I can't take it out myself, and it's been too damned long. Besides, we need to talk where we can't be overheard."

She made sense. I was being irrational and stupid about the car —just because I'd had an accident in one didn't mean the replacement was a death trap. I reached out for the passenger side door when I saw something out of the corner of my eye, over by the stables.

It was Salvador, and he was shaking his head "no." I practically jumped back from the car as if it were electrified. "Come up to my room—we can talk there. I want to know why you decided to show up out of the blue..."

"They were looking for me. For you. Sooner or later, they would have found out too much—it only made sense to show up. After all, it's not every day that you're bequeathed hundreds of millions of dollars."

"You weren't bequeathed it. It was a mistake, something Granda should have fixed. The moment I get back to the States, I'm going to take steps to relinquish it."

"I wouldn't be too hasty about that."

I froze, dumbfounded. "You wouldn't?"

"It's a lot of money. You and I could split it, and there's nothing anyone can do about it. And you needn't worry about your precious Ian—I'd give him enough to keep the farm going."

"You're not serious!"

"Aren't I?" Bella asked. "Get in the damned car, Podge, and we'll talk about it."

I couldn't help it, I looked at Salvador again, and Bella followed my gaze, her own eyes narrowing. "Who's he? Your guardian angel?"

"You might say so. Come up to my room when you're ready to talk." Without another word, I turned and walk away, knowing, just knowing, the fury with which she watched me.

TWENTY-ONE

She didn't come to my room, and I didn't leave it. They all had luncheon on the terrace by the pool, but I remained in my room, eating there, waiting for her, waiting for Ian, waiting for something as I paced the floor. I couldn't imagine what Bella thought she'd gain by showing up here, but since she didn't appear to be in a confiding mood, I was left to guess, and none of it was good.

When I finally couldn't stand my self-imposed exile any longer, I went downstairs, only to find that Marcus and Bella had gone out, while Mary Alice was crushing Valerie in some card game so arcane I suspected Mary Alice had made up the rules simply to trounce her younger sister. Valerie went along meekly enough, sparing a smile for me when I reclaimed the disputed lounge, while Mary Alice shot daggers at me.

"I never would have thought Marcus would see anything in Podge," she said casually. "Aren't you two engaged? If I were you, I wouldn't like anyone stealing my thunder, particularly Podge."

That was one thing unlikely to happen, I thought. "Marcus and I weren't truly engaged—we agreed to it for Granda's sake. He wanted to see his dynasty continue." I sat down in one of the overstuffed chairs, tucking my legs underneath me. I would have preferred a fast exit, but I couldn't think of an excuse.

"How did he think that would happen when he left all his money to Podge? Trust Marcus to know which side the bread is buttered on. I suppose Granda's so-called dynasty could continue just as well with him and Podge. Though I can't really see the two of them together—he's always been drawn to style and flash. Podge grew up just I expected her to—fat and plain and boring."

I considered throwing something at her but there was nothing close at hand, so I reached for one of the glossy fashion magazines that littered the tile-topped coffee table. I was mortally tired of anorexic child-women posing in impractical clothes, but for the time being, I was still Bella, and I would play the part till the end.

An endless hour passed, followed by a second one, and I was ready to climb the walls when Maldonado made his appearance with the tea tray, thankfully supplied with coffee. "Mister Marcus has called, and regrets that he and Miss Whitehead will be eating dinner out."

"Did Ian call?" I asked a little too eagerly, then could have bitten my tongue. The last thing I wanted to be was obvious. Where the hell had he gone, and did the real Bella's sudden appearance have anything to do with it? Most likely, but I just wished I knew what was going on.

"No, Miss Bella."

"That's fine," Mary Alice said in her best grande dame manner. "We'll have dinner early, then, Maldonado. With the funeral and reception, we'll have a long day tomorrow."

"Tomorrow?" I echoed with horror. "Why so soon?"

"Ian arranged it. I don't know why he's acting like he's in charge —he's out on his ass like the rest of us."

"I still don't see why we don't have the reception here," Valerie was bold enough to volunteer in her soft voice.

"We do what Ian says was," her sister said, disgruntled. "Apparently, he doesn't want hundreds of strangers crawling all over the place and disrupting his precious farm. Not his for much longer unless Podge does something about it."

"We can't have it tomorrow—it's too soon," I said. "I'm not ready." Not ready to say goodbye to the difficult old man I'd loved with all my heart.

"Well, get ready," Malice snapped. "If you didn't spend all your time primping in your room, you'd be more on top of things. I certainly hope you have something black to wear."

"I'm afraid the closest I can come is dark blue," I admitted.

Mary Alice sniffed. "It will have to do. I want the family to present a united front, dignified in our grief. And we must make certain no one has any idea of the contents of the will until it is settled."

"No one would be rude enough to ask, Mary Alice," Valerie said softly.

"I would," her sister said.

Yes, you would, I thought unkindly. "And what has Kitty said about the will?" I asked instead. "She's going to break it, isn't she?"

There was an uncomfortable moment of silence. "Of course she will," Mary Alice said finally. "She's already alluded to it."

Alluded to it? I knew Bella better than anyone else, better now than ever. Why wouldn't she come right out and say she was giving up the money that wasn't even hers in the first place? It was the only way she was going to end up with anything from Granda, and she should have been the first to contest it.

Unless she had some other plan. Paranoia swept over me and I shook off the sudden flash of fear. Bella had some plan, all right, but I couldn't believe it would involve hurting anyone. I had that much faith in her. She could always expose me as an imposter, but there was no reason that would invalidate the will, and I couldn't even begin to imagine what was going on with her.

Would Marcus recognize her beneath her disguise? I doubted it —he hadn't been able to tell the difference between me and the woman he'd spent his life devoted to. I'd never been fool enough to think Marcus was a man of great depth, and he must simply rely on appearances. Though something must have drawn him to Bella beneath her frumpy disguise.

I needed Bella back here, to talk to me, to tell me what was going on in her Byzantine mind. I needed Ian back, to take me in his arms, to tell me everything was going to be all right. Instead, I was stuck with the cousins and their interminable card game and no hint of what was going on.

"You're awfully quiet today." Mary Alice fixed her cold blue gaze on me over her prescribed early dinner. "Is something wrong?"

I met her eyes. "I just lost my grandfather," I said quietly.

"Oh, spare me!" Mary Alice said dramatically. "If you'd cared about him at all, you would have spent more time here. I know as well as anyone that you haven't been home to Mariposa in five years, and if a fortune wasn't on the line, then you probably wouldn't have come now."

"Well, I'm shit out of luck with the fortune, aren't I?" I snapped, finally having had enough of Malice.

"Don't be vulgar. We'll overturn Granda's absurd will and we'll get what's fair. Even if we can't, Podge has always been the best of us —she wouldn't let such an injustice pass."

No, I wouldn't. I wasn't so sure about Bella, however. How long did she mean to continue this crazy masquerade? Was it up to me to put it to rest?

"I wonder where Ian is." Valerie spoke up suddenly, a rare case of her initiating a conversation. "He took off just after Kitty arrived and we haven't seen him since."

"It must have something to do with the will," Mary Alice said reprovingly. "But if he thinks I'm going to sit around waiting for him to fix this, he'll be greatly surprised."

"Nothing you do can surprise me, Mary Alice." Ian's smooth voice came from behind me, and I felt my stomach drop.

I turned to look at him, but his eyes were focused on Mary Alice, and I felt the first inkling of anxiety. He hadn't promised anything, said anything last night. He looked tired, a stubble of beard on his thin face, work clothes on his long, lean body. He didn't even glance in my direction.

"Don't be unpleasant, Ian," Mary Alice said. "Did you discover anything useful today? I presume you went to see Mr. Fergell?"

"I did." He took a casual step toward her, his back toward me.

"Well?"

"We've got the funeral tomorrow, Mary Alice. Can't you wait till that's taken care of?" he drawled.

"No, I can't. This entire thing is absurd, Bella and I were just discussing it, and I think it needs to be set straight immediately. Now that Podge is here, it should be easily settled."

"Where is she?" He still didn't look at me.

"She's gone off someplace with Marcus, and we haven't the faintest idea when they're getting back. Do they even know we're having such a rushed funeral service?"

"They know. For the time being, there's nothing we can do. We'll wait till after the funeral to fight over his remains."

"You always had an unpleasant tongue on you," Mary Alice said with a shudder. "You could at least tell us whether you've found out any good news."

"I could. Good news for one person can be bad news for another." For the briefest of moments, his eyes glanced at me, then shifted away, and I wanted to shiver from the coldness in his gaze. It was as if last night had never happened.

And then he dismissed me. "I'm going back to my rooms. I have work to do, and I need some time alone."

He was gone before I could say anything. Not that there was much I could say. He'd made it very clear that he wanted nothing to do with me, and I wondered what the lawyer had come up with to turn him off so completely. Was I going to jail for what I'd done?

"Are you two fighting?" Valerie spoke up.

"Don't be ridiculous, Valerie, they're always fighting," Mary Alice said. "They hate each other—you can see it in their eyes."

Not in my eyes. He needed time alone, did he? I was tempted to storm across the courtyard, up the stairs to his apartment and...and...

And leave him alone. He hadn't made any promises last night—his body had spoken, telling me what I wanted to hear. Maybe there was nothing between us but insane sexual chemistry, and he was already regretting giving in to it.

"We're not fighting," I said wearily. "And we don't hate each other. We simply don't have anything in common."

"Apart from Granda, and Mariposa, and your childhood," Mary Alice pointed out.

I pushed back from the table, my food barely touched. "I'm going to bed," I announced.

"You're running after Ian," Mary Alice said. "Any fool can see that. Make up your mind which one you want—you can't have both, even if you're used to getting everything you want."

"I don't want either of them. I want my bed," I said coldly.

Some futile part of me had hoped he'd be waiting for me when I left the dining room. I even went down to the kitchen where Maldonado was sitting with a cup of coffee. "Have you seen Ian?" I asked, trying to sound casual.

"He's gone to his apartment," Maldonado said repressively. "He said to make sure no one bothered him tonight."

That was the second warning, and I wasn't about to ignore it. He'd effectively rejected me after the best night of my life. So be it. I could pull up my big-girl panties and get on with it. One thing was certain—I was not going to cry. Not over him, not over any damned man.

Oddly enough, I slept heavily that long night. Well, maybe not so odd considering how little sleep I'd had the night before. I only woke up once, when Marcus and Bella returned, laughing, tipsy, and I wondered if Marcus had subconsciously recognized his real love. I pulled my pillow over my head and went back to sleep.

***I've always hated funerals. The ritual, the formality of them, the oh-so-polite mourners in their dark clothes and crumpled tissues. Death wasn't polite, it wasn't formal, it was a screaming pain that ripped into you, and the last thing I wanted to do was stand around and chat with Granda's old friends, particularly in my Bella disguise.

But I wasn't going to cry over Granda either. That would come later, when I was back home, wherever that was. I would grieve him then, as I grieved Ian, and I would have no witnesses.

I rode with Valerie and Mary Alice down the hill in one of the big black town cars, and I assumed Bella went with the brothers. I breathed a sigh of relief. The last person I wanted to be closeted with was Ian. This was going to be hard enough—my best chance of making it through the day in one piece was to shut him completely out of my mind and heart.

I could still feel him, the imprint of his body on mine, the smell of his skin, the aching emptiness inside me. I longed for him, desperately. But he wouldn't even meet my gaze.

And I didn't want to be anywhere near Bella if I could help it. I had not the slightest idea what was going on in her brain, but I knew she wasn't about to tell me until she was good and ready. At this point, I didn't give a royal goddamn what she had planned, because I would be long gone.

I was past ready for this masquerade to end, no matter how explosive that ending might be. I was everything Ian had called me, a liar and a cheat, and I had no excuses. That I was turning over the estate and all the money to the others was the only mitigating factor. Maybe he wouldn't still hate me.

The procession down to the small country church was endless, with the farm workers in their Sunday best following the family to the parking lot that was studded with Bentleys and Rolls and the occasional Ferrari. All of Granda's friends had made the trek to the village church, and it was going to be jammed. Maybe jammed enough that I could slip out when no one was looking, without ever having to see Ian again. I hadn't bothered to pack, and I'd left most of the money that Bella had given me, taking only enough to see me safely back in New Hampshire. I would figure things out from there.

I looked up toward the front of the church, the candles glowing in the warm morning light, the casket in a place of honor, and I wanted to run. I'd already said goodbye to Granda—I didn't need this artificial fuss to make my peace with his death.

It was past time to make my goodbyes to Ian, not that he'd ever realize it. I had absolutely no idea what he really felt about me, only that he wanted me in his bed. Or he had. Now, once again, I seemed to be persona non grata, and I couldn't really blame him. The one thing I could do for him was leave, and this time, he wouldn't try to stop me. It was my own fault that it hurt so damn much. I'd fallen in love with him, whether it made any sense or not. In fact, I think I'd been a little in love with him when I was young and he'd rescued me from that cave, but I'd been too dazzled by Marcus's megawatt smile.

I couldn't avoid our formal trip to the front row with the rest of the family, but I did manage to get put at the very end of the row. Ian and Marcus were at the other end, Mary Alice and Valerie in the middle, and right next to me was Bella, in her Podge persona, her muddy hazel eyes blinking behind the heavy glasses.

I'd like to think I managed quite well, even when Ian looked down the row of family with a stony expression that was close to hatred before staring straight ahead and pretending once more that I didn't exist. It went on forever—by the time we got to the final hymn, I was past ready to bolt. I started to move, and Bella's hand clamped down over my wrist painfully.

"Where do you think you're going?" she whispered harshly.

"I need some fresh air," I said as everyone sang around us.

"Suck it up," she hissed.

I had had enough. Of her, of Ian, of everything. I twisted my wrist painfully, breaking her hold, and slid out of the pew, moving swiftly down the aisle to the back of the crowded church. The only shoes that matched the somber navy blue dress were high heels, not made for moving quickly, and underneath the voices I heard the sharp *tap tap* of my heels on the old stone floors.

The sun was shining brightly overhead when I finally stumbled out of the darkened interior of the old Protestant church, and I held up my hand to shade my eyes, looking for one of the town cars. I was getting out of here, not wandering around making polite conversation while I was playing a role. The funeral and reception could continue without me. I was going home.

No, not to Mariposa, though it felt like home to me and always had. I was going to have the town car take me to the airport and I was getting the hell out of Dodge. If Ian had anything to say to me, then he would have to find me. Otherwise, I'd simply sign the papers and have done with it, with Mariposa, with all of them. With Ian.

The driver was leaning on the town car, smoking a cigarette which he quickly extinguished as I approached him. "I need you to take me to the airport," I said in Spanish. "Now."

For a moment, he looked confused. "I was hired to take the family from the villa to the church and back again."

People were just beginning to exit the church and I needed to escape before I was drawn into any polite conversations. "I need to go to the airport, not the villa. Will you take me?"

"Sennñorita, I'm not supposed to..."

"Pay no attention to her." Bella came up beside me, grabbing my arm once more. She must have been close on my heels. "She'll go back to the house with me."

I tried to yank free. "I don't want to go back..." I began, but she twisted my arm painfully.

"Don't be a baby," she shot back. "We'll return to Mariposa and get your things and then I will drive you to the airport in my car."

"And how are you going to explain your ability to drive the Alfa?" I demanded.

She shrugged in the ill-fitting black polyester dress. "I'll tell them the truth. It's about time, don't you think?"

Past time. I should offer to stay, to face the music along with her, but I kept remembering the cold, distant expression on Ian's face as he glanced down the row at me, and my courage failed me. The truth wasn't going to come as any surprise to him—Bella didn't need my moral support to face his contempt.

"All right," I said. "If you promise to take me. I want to be gone before the family comes back."

"Absolutely." Bella's grip loosened, and she flashed me her sunny smile. "Don't make such a fuss about it, Podge. I'll clear everything up, and you don't even have to be there to see how much they all despise you."

She gave me a little push, and I climbed into the back of the car, moving over as she followed me in. The driver no longer seemed to have any compunctions, and he put the car in gear, sailing slowly out of the crowded parking lot as the mourners poured out into the sunshine. At the last minute, I looked back at the crowd, only to see Salvador at one of the entrances, trying frantically to signal me. I turned my face away from him.

We drove in complete silence, back up the long, twisting road to Mariposa, and I fought back the guilt, the second thoughts. I was running away, like a coward, rather than facing Ian. The look on his face as he stared at me during the funeral had chilled me to the bone, and I couldn't bring myself to fight for what I wanted anymore. I would take the escape that was offered.

Mariposa was deserted, as I'd known it would be, when the town car pulled into the courtyard and Bella hustled me out of it. I stood, watching, as he drove back down the road to the church, and in the distance I could hear the bells. The funeral was over and everyone would be adjourning to the hotel for the elegant reception Maldonado had overseen. No one would return to the house for hours. Ian wouldn't return for hours, and I'd be gone like the coward that I was.

"Get in the car, Podge," Bella said agreeably enough, as I stared down into the distant village.

"I need to get my suitcase," I murmured, my thoughts on Ian. I felt betrayed by his distance, his coldness. But was I betraying him in return, without giving him a chance to explain?

"You won't need it. They're hardly your type of clothes. Be a good girl and get in the car," she said in that charming wheedle that she'd used so well over the long years.

I turned to glance at her. "Maybe I should wait for Ian," I began to say, and then my voice froze. "What are you doing?"

It was a large gun in her small hand, but it was absolutely steady as it was aimed at my head.

Again, that lovely smile. "I'm afraid I need you to do what I tell you, and so far, you've been annoyingly reluctant to follow my lead. I've given you everything—the best clothes, a last chance to see the grandfather who never cared for you, to top it all off with a fortune which you foolishly think you'll give away. Not as long as I'm around. And, miraculously enough, I was already you when I inherited Granda's estate. I'm Podge, and no one's going to ask any unfortunate questions."

I was staring at her in shock. "Why do you have a gun?" It was a simple question, but I dreaded her answer.

Bella's smile was so warm and charming in the bright sunlight that I felt like I was losing my mind. "To make certain you do what I want."

"You wouldn't shoot me," I scoffed in disbelief.

"Of course I would. I'm not sentimental when it comes to getting what I want. My former boyfriend has been trying to find me and kill me for the last three months. When they find your body, they'll assume Sierra did it. Everything will be nicely tied up."

I didn't move, frozen to the spot. My high heels were treacherous on the cobblestones, and I would have no chance if I tried to run for it. "You had me pretend to be you, knowing someone was trying to kill you?"

"Don't be obtuse, Podge. Of course, I did. You know I'm always practical. I assumed Sierra would get rid of you and I'd be free to live out my life as you. Granda's fortune was just an added benefit. Clearly, fate is on my side."

"It isn't supposed to be my money," I snapped. "He had some reason..."

"If you'd had the sense to read his letter you'd have known. You were hardly the great success you hoped to be—Granda recognized you. He left the letter for the person he knew was Podge."

"Kitty," I corrected stupidly. I couldn't stand to hear that hateful nickname from her smiling lips. "What did it say?"

"Oh, some garbage about dividing it equally after giving Ian half to keep up the farm. It doesn't matter—the place will be sold, farm and all."

"And what's going to happen to me?" I demanded, wondering if I could slip out of the heels and make a run for it.

"I'm afraid, dear Kitty, that you'll be dead. I didn't want to have to do it—I'm very fond of you, after all. But I really have no other choice—Sierra will keep coming after me until I'm dead, and once more, you're just going to have to take my place." She took a step closer, signaling with the gun, and her calm smile dropped. "Now get in the fucking car."

"Someone's coming," I said, hearing the distant noise of a fast car on the road up to Mariposa. "You can't very well kill me with witnesses."

"There will be no witnesses. Don't you think I've got this all carefully planned? I don't make mistakes." She tossed her head back, that patented Bella move that I'd copied so successfully, and I wanted to throw up.

"Why did you leave your gangster boyfriend in the first place if he was so dangerous?" I said, anything to keep her talking until the car crested the hill and she no longer dared hold a gun on me.

"I grew tired of him. I grow tired of everyone eventually,

everyone but Marcus. He's not too bright, but he adores me, and he'd do anything for me. Wouldn't you, darling?"

To my absolute horror, Marcus stepped out of the house, still in his somber clothes, an unhappy expression on his face. When I'd last seen him, he'd been sitting beside Ian in the church—he must have come up the back way from the village. "Bella," he said in a pleading voice. "I don't think we should do this."

She didn't even look at him, her gun and her attention fully on me. "Don't be ridiculous. You sabotaged the brakes on the Alfa for me—you were ready enough back then."

"And I nearly killed Ian!" he protested. "Why do we need to hurt Podge?"

"You were in on this?" I demanded in shock, ignoring the woman with the gun.

"Of course he was," Bella said irritably. "He was supposed to take care of you with the car crash before anyone guessed you weren't me. He fucked that up, of course, and apparently, you weren't quite good enough—Granda recognized you anyway."

"So did Ian," I said desperately. "He'll know that some random gangster didn't shoot me!" The car was getting closer, and I knew, I just knew it was Ian coming after me, coming to save me.

"I'm not going to shoot you unless I have to. You're going to take a tumble down the cliffs on the west side of the land. It will be over fast and less painful than being shot."

"Kind of you," I said bitterly. "And you're going to let her do this?" I turned to Marcus, who was looking helpless.

"Bella, please stop," he said, stirred to action. "It's gone too far..." They could hear the car now, racing up the road, and Marcus swore. He grabbed Bella by the arm, jerking the direction of the gun away from me. "Come on!" he said urgently.

I ran. Or I tried to run, but the thin heels of the shoes caught in the cobblestones, sending me sprawling just as a gun fired, the bullet smashing into the stone beside me. I tried to scramble to my feet, kicking off the treacherous shoes, when I saw Marcus wrestling with

Bella. She was fighting him like a wild woman, clawing at his imprisoning arms, but he was massive against her small frame, and she was helpless as he grabbed the gun and threw it across the cobblestones.

"We've got to get out of here!" Marcus shouted, and there was no missing the desperation in his voice as he half-dragged Bella to the Alfa, shoving her into the passenger side before leaping into the driver's seat. She fought him, desperate to get back to me, to kill me, and I watched in horror, frozen to the spot where I stood. The engine roared to life, and then they were spinning on the cobblestones before they headed down the hill, almost clipping Ian's car as they drove by.

He came to a screeching halt too near me, and Ian leapt out. "Are you all right?" he demanded. "What the hell did you think you were doing, going out alone with Bella? Don't you have any sense at all?"

I found I was shaking. "I couldn't believe she wanted to hurt me," I said faintly.

"Believe it. She'd stab her own mother in the back if she had one. Where did she go?"

"She and Marcus took off."

"Marcus?" Shock brought him up short. "Marcus knew?"

I couldn't tell him the awful truth, that Marcus had almost killed both of us. "He took the gun away from her," I said instead. "He didn't want her to hurt me."

"Jesus Christ!" Ian said. "I don't believe it."

"I'm not lying," I said.

"I know you're not. I just can't believe that Marcus..."

"Mr. Ian!" Ian hadn't come back to Mariposa alone—Salvador had accompanied him. "You need to stop your brother."

"Let him go," Ian said bitterly, staring after the speeding Alfa as it raced down the twisting road..

"No, you do not understand. I saw someone near the car, someone I did not know. I'm afraid it might have been tampered with. I was going to tell you, but there was no time."

I had never seen someone's face whiten the way Ian's did. Without a word, he turned back to the car he'd driven up in, and I was a few paces behind him, jumping into the passenger seat as he was already starting the engine.

"Get out!" he snapped.

"No. I'm going with you!"

He swore beneath his breath. "I don't have time for this shit." He shoved at me, but I held on, and I barely had time to close the door before the car leapt forward.

He roared down the twisting roads, driving like a maniac as he chased after the bright red Alfa. He was muttering under his breath, half prayer, half cursing, and I held on for dear life. In truth, we were in greater danger than the car up ahead as we drifted around a corner, then sped up again, and I wanted to tug at his arm, beg him to slow down, when the explosion rocked the sky.

I couldn't see the Alfa, I could only see the ball of fire that shot up, straight into the sky, the pieces of metal raining down on the conflagration. Ian slammed the car into park and jumped out—we were on the narrow edge of the road, overlooking the explosion, and I scrambled after him. The force of the blast had picked up the car and tossed it in the air, coming down on its side, and all I could see was the steel framework being engulfed in flames. Marcus and Bella were gone without a trace, lost in the powerful inferno, and I sank to my knees beside the road, staring at the conflagration in wordless horror.

I was barely aware that Ian had climbed back in the car and continued his breakneck journey down the twisty roads. I simply stayed where I was, shock and grief threatening to overwhelm me. I could feel the waves of heat from the burning wreckage, and I watched, numbly, as I saw Ian's car reach the wreck. I backed away from the cliff, unable to watch as he searched for his brother. I knew there would be nothing left.

Salvador reached me first in one of the old farm trucks. Taking one look at my face, he bundled me inside, fastened the seat belt around me, and started back up the hill, passing several emergency vehicles as we went. I was barely aware of them. Marcus and Bella were dead, and I'd come far too close to meeting the same fate. I was too numb to feel relief—my insides were a great, yawning hole of grief and anger. This didn't need to happen. Bella's desperate need for money and control had set this in motion, and now she and Marcus lay dead, presumably at the hands of her gangster boyfriend. I felt a strange pull of grief in my heart. For better or worse, they had been my family, and now they were gone in the conflagration.

But the one who would be hurting the most was Ian, who'd lost his brother. I couldn't see how he could be other than broken.

The house was empty when Salvador dropped me off—Mary Alice and Valerie must have been manning the reception as his grandchildren died in flames. There would be questions, there would be police, there would be the ungodly mess of identifying which granddaughter had actually died in the flames, and it was too much for me to even consider. I wanted to run away, to never think about this appalling tragedy that I had been instrumental in bringing about.

Ian would never forgive me, which was all right since I would never forgive myself. If only I hadn't listened to Bella's blandishments. If only I'd seen through her surface charm to the real danger beneath it. If only...

CHAPTER

TWENTY-TWO

The next few days passed in a blur. The truth came out, as it was bound to, but no one had any particular interest in talking to me after my initial interview with the police.

Ian was encased in ice. He showed no grief, no distress about the horrendous scandal that spilled over us despite Mary Alice's best efforts to stop the gossip, and he did his best to keep from looking at me, talking to me. I didn't blame him—this was all my fault.

And then he was gone, disappearing from the villa without a word to anyone, and I realized there was finally no one to stop me. I could go now, and that was what Ian would want, to see the last of my deceitful, lying ass.

I left in the farm truck, leaving all of Bella's clothes behind. Mary Alice agreed she would see them donated to the proper charity, and I finally left Mariposa for the last time, without green contact lenses or perfectly curled hair or heavy makeup. I was just me, Kitty, without all the artifice. I would never be Bella again.

My first stop was Mr. Fergell's office on the way to the airport. He spent the entire time viewing me with strong disapproval until I explained to him what I wanted to do with the money.

"Half to Ian and Mariposa, the other half to be divided between Mary Alice and Valerie," he'd repeated in something close to a harrumph. "What about you?"

"I don't want anything."

"You'll change your mind," he warned.

"No, I won't." I didn't want Granda's money, I didn't want any more ties to Mariposa. I didn't deserve it. I was letting go in the fairest possible way. Ian would have the house, the farms and groves and vineyards, and enough money to keep it in good heart for decades to come. Somehow, I'd figure out what was best for me.

I was wearing a sundress and sandals—clothes I'd purchased for myself—and could only hope New Hampshire was at least a little warmer than usual, though why I was going there was a question. The funding for my research project had run out, I had no place to live, and God only knew what Bella had done with my aging Subaru and all the detritus of my life. I didn't know and I didn't care. I only knew that I couldn't spend another day waiting for Ian to come back to me when I knew he never would.

I was in love with him, and there was nothing I could do about it. I'd lied, even though he'd always known it was a lie. I'd cheated, and he'd lost the most important person in his life. If I just hadn't been blinded by Bella's blandishments, Marcus would still be alive, and Ian knew it. It was no wonder Ian couldn't bring himself to look at me. I felt like a whipped dog, and all I could do was run home and hide.

I just managed to get the second to last spot on the small commuter plane that would take me to Madrid and transatlantic flights, and I settled into my seat, looking out over the bleached white villages that dotted the hills. I would never come here again, and a quiet pang filled my heart to join with the gut-wrenching pain of losing Ian. Not that I'd ever really had him. This was the home of my heart and always had been, but that time had passed. Ian was my heart, but he was gone as well.

Of course, with my current run of bad luck, the plane had

mechanical trouble, leaving us sitting on the runway in the blinding sun for an hour and a half until they finally cancelled the flight. The next one would leave in four hours—four hours to doubt my choices, four hours to change my mind, four hours to sit in a corner and silently weep. I'd survived worse.

This time when I walked down the hallway in the terminal, there were no men salivating at the sight of me, no women casting jealous glances my way. In my sundress and sandals and long braided hair, I was just another tourist, not the princess of Mariposa. It would have felt good if I wasn't so absolutely gutted.

I went back through security, heading toward the gate, when I saw him, leaning against the wall, still in work clothes, the chambray shirt rolled up to reveal strong forearms, his dark hair tumbled over his forehead as he watched me approach, no expression to give me a hint of what he was thinking.

I wanted to turn and run, I wanted to run into his arms.

I didn't have a choice. He straightened up, crossed the area separating us and simply tossed me over his shoulder before he strode to the entrance of the tiny airport.

"Put me down!" I demanded, beating at his back. My small carry-on was abandoned, but I managed to hold on to my purse even as I banged away at him, kicking and struggling.

A sharp, stinging slap on my rear did nothing to quiet my outrage. What the hell did he think he was doing? People were watching us with amusement and a scattering of applause, and I pounded at his back.

The sun was brilliant overhead as we came out of the airport, but he made no effort to set me down, just kept carrying me over to the same damned farm truck he'd picked me up in. Sliding me off his shoulder, he pushed me back against it, glowering at me.

"Where did you think you were going?" he demanded.

"Getting out of here!" I shot back. "I don't belong here, nobody wants me here, and I..."

"Bullshit! You're running away."

I didn't answer that—it was obvious that I was. "Why are you here?"

"Why do you think? I came after you. I thought I was going to have to fly to Madrid to catch up with you."

"Why?"

He made an impatient sound. "Don't play games with me. You know why."

"I don't know any such thing," I said, furious, but the heavy weight inside me was beginning to lift. "I would have thought you'd be ready to see the last of me."

"I should be," he said. "But there's a lot of unfinished business between us, and you know it."

"I already took care of it with Mr. Fergell. You don't have to come after me at all."

"Fuck Mr. Fergell. That's not what I'm talking about," he said, his voice tight.

"Then what...?"

"I love you." He said it as if he were confessing to an axe murder.

The words hit me like a blow. "You love me?"

Again with the impatience. "Don't sound so incredulous. You already know that."

I stared at him in shock. "I don't."

"Well, then, you're not as observant as I am. I know perfectly well you're in love with me."

"But the things I did," I stammered. "It was my fault..."

"It was Bella's fault and you know it. Bella's fault that Marcus is dead. Bella's, and Marcus's. He never learned not to listen to her."

"But I..."

"It would be nice if you paid closer attention. I told you I love you, and I'm not in the habit of saying that. So, stop asking me stupid questions and kiss me." There was a challenge in his dark blue eyes, and the knot in my stomach untangled and blossomed into pure heat.

"Are you sure?"

"Last stupid question." And he was the one who kissed me, pulling me into his arms, against his hard, lean body. His mouth was hot, wet, overwhelming, and it was everything I wanted, everything I needed.

And then it turned sweet, his lips brushing against mine with breathtaking sweetness, and he kissed my forehead, my eyelids, my cheeks, and my mouth again.

"Oh, for God's sake, don't cry!" he said when he tasted my tears.

"I'm happy," I said, sniffling. "I do love you. I think I always have."

"Bullshit. You were gaga over Marcus when you were young." A shadow crossed his eyes at the mention of his brother's name, but he managed a small sigh. "You don't know how jealous I was."

"You were a wretch," I said shakily.

"You were never a podge," he replied, kissing me again, a little harder this time. "I'm a cranky bastard. Do you think you can stand me for the long haul?"

"Now who's asking stupid questions?"

ABOUT THE AUTHOR

Anne Stuart has been writing since the Dawn of Time. She's been published by every major publisher, and made the *NYT, USA Today,* and *Publisher's Weekly* Bestseller lists. She's won numerous awards, including four RITAs, as well as RWA's Lifetime Achievement Award, and she's known for her dark heroes, black humor and hot sex.

Follow her on her website at Anne-Stuart.com social media at:

 facebook.com/author.annestuart

 x.com/TheAnneStuart

instagram.com/Annestuartwriter

Also by Anne Stuart

THE FIRE SERIES

Consumed by Fire

Driven by Fire

Wildfire

THE ICE SERIES

Black Ice

Cold as Ice

Ice Blue

Ice Storm

Fire and Ice

On Thin Ice

THE HOUSE OF ROHAN

The Wicked House of Rohan

Ruthless

Reckless

Breathless

Shameless

Heartless

TROUBLE AT THE HOUSE OF RUSSELL

Never Kiss a Rake

Never Trust a Pirate

Never Marry a Viscount

DON'T LOOK BACK—THE MAGGIE BENNETT BOOKS

Escape Out of Darkness

Darkness before Dawn

At the Edge of the Sun

HISTORICAL ROMANCES

The Devil's Waltz

Hidden Honor

Lady Fortune

Prince of Magic

Lord of Danger

Prince of Swords

To Love a Dark Lord

Shadow Dance

A Rose at Midnight

The Houseparty

The Demon Count Novels

The Spinster and the Rake

Lord Satan's Bride

Angels Wings

Demonwood

Cameron's Landing

Barrett's Hill

WOMEN'S FICTION

When the Stars Fall Down

ROMANTIC SUSPENSE

Into the Fire

The Widow

Silver Falls

Still Lake

Shadows at Sunset

Shadow Lover

Ritual Sins

Moonrise

Nightfall

Now You See Him

Special Gifts

Break the Night

The Fall of Maggie Brown

Winter's Edge

Hand in Glove

Tangled Lies

The Catspaw Collection

Against the Wind

Return to Mariposa

SUSPENSE

Seen and Not Heard

ANNE STUART'S GREATEST HITS

Cinderman

The Soldier, the Nun and the Baby

One More Valentine

Blue Sage

Night of the Phantom

Falling Angel

CONTEMPORARY ROMANCE

The Right Man

A Dark and Stormy Night

Wild Thing

Rafe's Revenge

Heat Lightning

Chasing Trouble -

Lazarus Rising

Rancho Diablo

Crazy Like a Fox

Glass Houses

Cry for the Moon

Partners in Crime

Bewitching Hour

Rocky Road

Museum Piece

Heart's Ease

Chain of Love

Against the Wind

Return to Christmas

COLLABORATIONS

Dogs & Goddesses – with Jennifer Crusie and Lani Diane Rich

The Unfortunate Miss Fortunes with Jennifer Crusie and Lani Diane Rich

SHORT READS

Blind Date from Hell